For my wife, Karen, with love

PART ONE

NEW YEAR'S EVE

2042

ONE

Do I dare disturb the universe?

—T. S. Eliot

New Orleans

The noise from the street was deafening. Excited shouting and singing blended with the occasional burst of raucous laughter, which in turn combined with the happy squeals of drunken women.

The whoop-whoop of a police cruiser's siren fought to make itself heard over the combined voices of thousands of inebriated revelers. Instead, it became a counterpoint to the incongruous melody of raucous yells and singing rising from the mass of dancing bodies as the squad car slowly pushed its way through their midst.

Jim Baston, his eyes red and tired, tried to concentrate on the paragraph he was writing, but the blare of the rowdy crowd below his window was just too distracting.

He exhaled a long sigh. "Save tonight's work and forward a copy to the house inbox, please," he said eventually, before exasperation could get the better of him.

"Yes, Jim." The female voice of the computer's AI was soft and comforting. *"I've done as you requested, Jim,"* the AI said a second later. *"Is there anything else you would like?"*

"No, thank you. You can shut down. I won't need you for the rest of the night."

"Very well. Oh! And Jim . . ."

"Yes?"

"Happy New Year."

"You too," he whispered, and looked around at the sparsely decorated room.

For the past ten years he had been coming to this same hotel. Same room every time. He was on first name terms with the owners—John and Caroline, a pleasant couple from North Carolina—so he didn't even have to tell them who he was when he called a few weeks ahead to confirm his arrival. His reservation for the following year was already penciled in each time he ended his stay.

This was usually the quiet part of the city, but for some reason the crowds had chosen to congregate under his window. He could only imagine what it would be like in the more popular areas.

The sense of frustration he had felt at the disturbance of his work still burned in his chest. He felt like throwing open the window and screaming at them to *shut the hell up*! Couldn't they see he was trying to work? Didn't they know how important this book was to him?

Of course, who could blame them? It was after all New Year's Eve, and if he had even half a life and twenty fewer years on his clock, he would be out there too, welcoming in the New Year in as much of a drunken stupor as the rest of the city.

Instead, he stood, stretched his aching arms—careful to avoid the ceiling fan twirling almost noiselessly above his head—walked stiffly to the window, pulled up the blinds, pushed open the French doors, and stepped out onto his balcony.

The noise that had been a grumbling rumble now became a cacophony, bolstered by the hundreds of jazz and salsa bands scattered throughout the city. The sound swelled up like a wave over the balcony, rushing over him. From his third-story vantage point, Jim looked out over a significant part of New Orleans, the city's incandescent glow helping the full moon fight back the surrounding darkness. Far off to the south a thick roll of thunderheads, black and roiling, threatened a damp end to the year.

Jim didn't think a sudden soaking was going to do anything to squelch the spirits of the tens of thousands of revelers walking the streets this night.

Resting a shoulder against the doorjamb, he pulled an already-open soft pack of Marlboros from his shirt pocket and tapped the pack against his thumb. Jim lit the cigarette with an antique Zippo, with a cupped hand sheltering the fragile flame from the light breeze gusting over the rooftops.

He took a long drag and held the smoke in his lungs for a few moments before exhaling it into the cool evening air in one long, slow breath. He was trying to give the things up, weaning himself off them slowly by using the promise of the nicotine rush as a reward. Each time he completed five pages of the book, he got to have a smoke.

Of course, he had been using the exact same excuse for the past ten years. So it didn't look like his technique was working too well. And at twenty dollars a pack, it was amazing anyone could still afford to smoke the damn things. Countries and presidents, ideologies and industry—they all came and went, but cigarettes outlived the lot of them. Jim wasn't sure whether that was a testament to the resilience of people's freedom of choice, or just to the obscene amount of money tobacco companies still threw into their marketing and advertising campaigns.

He hadn't completed his five-page quota today; it wasn't for lack of trying on his part, and he'd be damned if he was going to take a ride on the guilt trip express just because he fell down this once.

It's New Year's Eve, for God's sake, he reminded himself.

Jim glanced at his wristwatch. It was almost 10:00 p.m. There was still an hour left until the ball dropped in Times Square.

If he was quick, he could change into some fresh clothes and head to one of the bars littering Bourbon Street. Jim didn't want to see in the coming year stuck in a room on his own. He would take a wander down Bourbon Street and see the sights, have a few drinks, and maybe even treat himself to a cigar.

That's what he loved about this city: you could amble through the streets drinking a glass of wine and smoking a big, fat stogie if you wanted, and no one would look at you sideways. If he tried doing that in LA, he would have half a dozen unemployed actors—"Between jobs," they would be quick to correct—yelling in his face about how much harm he was doing to himself, how he was depleting the ozone, blah blah blah. He'd heard the same arguments for God knows how long. *Even good sense can start to stink if your nose gets rubbed in it for long enough*, he thought.

Jim laughed at himself, a quiet, half-mocking snort. A cigarette, the promise of booze *and* a cigar? Damn, he was living dangerously these days.

What the hell! Why should he care? He was sixty years old, after all. A couple of smokes and a few drinks weren't going to shorten his life by more than a couple of minutes. He deserved a break. He had thrown himself into the latest book with more gusto than usual. It had consumed him for the past four months, but it had also taken a toll on him, both physically and mentally. A few hours away from it would do him good, give him a chance to clear his mind and reset his imagination.

Jim Baston had never once encountered writer's block during his career as a writer. He'd published twelve books, all of them in the top ten of all the right bestseller lists. The books had flowed from him. He had written them on the fly, straight from his imagination to the computer. The completed novel invariably needed little in the way of editing, such was the clarity with which he was usually able to visualize the story and its characters.

But this one was different. It was his first work of nonfiction, an autobiography of sorts.

Facing his past was difficult, painful even. So many mistakes were locked away, hidden in the darkness of his earlier life. And as he released the memories from their mental holding cells, carefully removing the psychic padlocks that kept them safely sealed away, he was forced to confront them in all their horrible glory.

As he watched the thunderheads moving closer to the city, Jim realized just how weary he truly was.

Exhausted, he thought. Tired of getting up in the morning alone, of drowning himself in his work, of the only calls he ever received being from his editor. He was tired of life, exhausted by the weight of his past. One night of relaxation would be a good thing. He could rejoin the human race for a little while. Just a little while.

Flicking the cigarette butt onto the concrete of the balcony, he extinguished it with his foot, turned, and walked back into the room. A shiver ran through him; it was cool out there.

Jim grabbed his overcoat from the hanger behind the door, threw it on, picked up his wallet and keys from the side table, and headed out the door that would take him to the streets of New Orleans.

TWO

Byron Portia slipped his silver-gray Peterbilt Hydro-Con into gear, rumbled out from the truck stop off I-15, and headed toward the interstate on-ramp.

In his late fifties, Byron was a man who just seemed to slip past the view of most people. If he had walked into a restaurant and blown away a couple of the patrons, the survivors would have been hard pressed to remember any distinguishing feature. "Nondescript" was the word most people would use to describe him, if they remembered him at all.

Of course, they would be completely wrong.

His unremarkable appearance was carefully cultivated. He did not *want* people to remember him. The mop of graying hair, usually hidden beneath a Mets baseball cap, changed color at a whim with the use of an off-the-shelf hair dye. He didn't favor wigs—too much chance they could fall off in a struggle. The paunch jutting out over his belted Levi's was sufficient to suggest a lazy, relaxed lifestyle of nights in front of the TV and a diet of Coors and fast food. His naturally frost-blue eyes would occasionally become green, hazel, or brown, altered with the use of disposable tinted contact lenses, and he was always quick to cultivate a beard or mustache, interchanging them as he saw fit. Underneath the baggy, blue flannelled shirt and paunch, he was a tightly muscled man. He worked out regularly using the dumbbells he kept in the back of his big rig, putting in three hours most afternoons.

Strong as an ox, as his dear departed mom had often said.

He was meticulous about one other thing: maintaining his mask.

It did not matter how careful he was with all of his physical disguises; he knew that if you didn't take into account your mask, then you were screwed. He had learned that little lesson early on in his career. No matter how well he manipulated his appearance to be nonthreatening, however shy or coy he acted, how big brotherly or fatherly he appeared, if he could not control the unconscious thoughts behind his mask he would betray himself.

The bitch in Las Vegas had proved that to him.

The big rig thundered up the on-ramp. The ramp metering light showed green, so he slipped the gear stick up a notch and gently eased his foot down on the accelerator, pushing the speedometer toward sixty. He did this on instinct, his subconscious running through the routine of controlling the rig. His conscious mind . . . elsewhere.

Byron could have activated the rig's artificial intelligence system and had it drive the vehicle, but he was a man who liked to remain in control of every situation. In all the years he owned the truck, not once had he even thought about turning the AI on. Instead, he allowed his mind to drift, running through memories almost a quarter century old.

Vegas, baby! *What happens in Vegas stays in Vegas.* That's what the old ads had said. That whore of a city, built by the Mob and run for years by a mayor who had represented more killers and triggermen than he could probably remember. It was in this godforsaken place his calling had almost ended before it had even begun.

He had picked her up not far off the Strip. There were plenty of out-of-the-way saloons and cantinas scattered throughout Vegas catering to the lonely trucker back then. Besides, it was always safer to pick them up in a bar rather than straight off the street; much less chance of them being an undercover vice cop.

While he was sitting at the bar nursing a rapidly warming Bud—he didn't enjoy beer, so he only occasionally took a sip from the long-neck—she sauntered up to him, taking the vacant bar stool next to his.

She was all tits and makeup. She wore a short sequined dress that shimmered and glittered when she moved, cut just low enough to show off her implants. It rustled like a windblown tree when she sat down. Peroxide-blond hair framed a face pretty enough for her age . . . and her profession.

"Hi," she had said, her voice husky from too many cigarettes. "In town long?"

He had shaken his head and smiled at her, then taken a swig from the beer and turned his focus back to the football game playing on the flat-screen TV above the rack of liqueurs.

She pulled a cigarette from her clutch bag. He picked up a book of matches sitting on the bar, tore out a match, struck it, then lit her cigarette with it. She made sure she leaned low into him so he could see the goods, in all their glory. *Why do they always smoke?* he wondered.

"My name's Jenna," she said between puffs, extending her hand. He took it and shook it gently, returning her smile. Her skin was warm and dry to the touch. It sent a thrill of revulsion through him.

"Anthony," said Byron. "Tony to my friends." He was careful always to use an assumed name.

"Well, Tony"—another goddamn smile—"do you need a date?"

And that was when he made his mistake. For a second he saw what he was going to do to her, its exquisiteness playing through his mind like a scene from a movie. First, the shock of her realization when he showed her the blade—"the tool of the trade," as he preferred to call it; the skittering look of confused terror on her face as she felt the steel slip between her ribs and pierce her heart; the muted gush of blood that would be accompanied by his own gush of liquid as he ended her dreadful, sinful life.

It was all he could do not to explode right there, so vivid were the images and so intense the need to fulfill God's will and end this creature's corrupt existence. The anticipation brought cold perspiration to his brow as he unconsciously wiped his greasy, sweaty palms on his trousers.

That was when his mask had slipped. The whore sensed the change in him, her coy expression quickly disintegrating into a look of wariness, a half realization of just what she was sitting next to, of how close she was to death. It was subconscious, but it was there.

"I . . . I need to go freshen up," she stuttered, her coquettish demeanor transformed now to one of a cornered alley cat.

He could almost see the hair standing up on the back of her neck.

Confusion backlit her eyes as she pushed away from the bar and started to head toward the ladies' room. He grabbed her by her forearm, gently but firm enough that she would have to struggle to break his hold.

"Why don't I come with you?" he asked suggestively.

That's when the full realization had hit her, and she pulled her arm from his grasp.

"Stay away from me, you weirdo," she spat back, flecks of spittle landing against his face. "Stay the fuck away." Her face was contorted by fear; not by rage, by *fear*.

She backed away and then disappeared into the gloom of the bar. Byron stood up, trying to look as much like a disgruntled boyfriend as he could.

"Women," he said with an exaggerated sigh to the bartender, as if this single word could sum up the full complexity and confusion that was the fairer sex. He slapped down a five-dollar tip on the bar and made his way slowly out of the dive to the parking lot.

He was lucky that night, watched over by the one who had sent him the task, who had taught him this, his most valuable lesson. But for weeks after leaving Las Vegas, he expected to be pulled over every time he saw a highway patrol officer or a deputy, and *he* had been afraid. It was a first for him.

At first he had not understood what had happened that night. He spent hundreds of miles going over the event in his head, looking at himself through her eyes, analyzing the situation.

It had come to him eventually, a simple realization: on some lower level she had detected his intentions. During that momentary slip, as he had teased himself with the pleasure of his reward for the work that was to come, he must have emanated some kind of psychic energy, which she had picked up on—an aura was how he thought of it.

Since then he was careful to always wear his psychic mask when hunting. He slipped it on each time he stepped out of his cab, not letting any part of the real Byron Portia ooze out between the seams. Byron thought of it as locking himself away in a little room inside his head. It was like one of those interrogation rooms you'd see on the old cop shows, with one-way glass that he could see them through, but that showed the person in the room just a reflection of themselves staring back.

It had worked. No more whores causing commotions in bars. Simple and efficient.

And so here he was, years later, heading south on I-15 toward Los Angeles. Still undiscovered. Protected. With much work behind him but far more still to come.

It was New Year's Eve, and there would be an awful lot of people out celebrating. That was just fine by him. He could lose himself easily in a crowd, walking among those he had been given the task of watching over while searching for those he hunted. And tonight he felt the pull, the need, a powerful imperative filling his blood.

This was how it always started. That tingling sensation deep in the pit of his stomach telling him there was work for him to do. He needed to follow his gut, park his big, old truck and wait. It was like getting an e-mail straight from God. Inevitably, the person he was meant to find was going to cross his path.

Byron Portia's truck hurtled along the highway, surrounded on both sides by desert, the sun a liquid ball shimmering on the far horizon. He was just a couple of hours outside of LA, and if everything remained copacetic he would find somewhere near Burbank airport and park for the night. That would give him enough time to clean himself up and go see what he could see.

Tonight he would hunt.

THREE

St. Bartholomew's Church, West Hills, Los Angeles

Father Edward Pike pushed the great oaken doors into place, drew the two huge metal bolts closed, fastened the locks, and sealed off the outside world from St. Bartholomew's Church for the night.

With the final lock securely in place, the priest's face seemed to lose all strength, dragged as though by some sudden pulse of gravity toward the cold slab floor of the church. In its wake stood a hollow shell of the man he had imitated for the past twelve hours.

Through sheer force of will, he had managed to preserve his facade of normalcy; it was the least he could do for his parishioners, he supposed, to maintain the pretense he was what he claimed to be. It was the final selfless act of a lost soul.

His face now drawn and haggard, his green eyes dull and jejune, Father Pike took one painful step after the next, making his way along the aisle between the rows of lemon-oiled pews, the fragrance of incense still clinging to the air around him. He shuffled toward the chancel, the echo of each footfall his only escort through the now-empty church.

Not bothering to genuflect as he reached the communion table, he paused instead to stand at the head of the aisle, his eyes drifting upward before settling finally on the life-sized crucifix that was the centerpiece of the sanctuary.

During the day the natural light of the huge stained-glass window stretching from the floor to the ceiling nearly fifty feet above would light this emblem of Christianity. The window reproduced the fourteen Stations of the Cross, the images depicting scenes of suffering in each of the successive stages of Christ's passion. It was a design created to instill a sense of awe in all who entered the church, to humble the proud and spark joy in the hearts of the downtrodden.

The colorful mosaic of painted glass lent an otherworldly ethereal-ness to the church, sunshine pouring like wine through the beautifully colored scenes. But at night, without the sun's illumination, the window was black and lifeless.

Soulless, he thought.

The aged priest understood the dichotomy it represented.

To compensate for the loss of light once the sun set, hidden blue and red spotlights sparked into artificial life, tastefully highlighting the effigy of the Christ hanging from the cross, his face a mask of suffering. The sculptor had captured perfectly the man-god's torment: a vicious crown of thorns dug into his head; a spear wound in his side bled water and blood down over his hip. His agony was so obvious, his suffering so profound, no one looking upon the scene could fail to be moved by the enormity of the sacrifice it portrayed.

But this was not what the father saw.

He saw an icon of deception, a promise to the human race that would never be fulfilled, *could never* be fulfilled. It was an empty ves-sel of a lie, as hollow and dead as the very tomb the crucified man had finally been laid to rest within.

As empty as his own heart now felt.

Like a cancer, Edward's despair had eaten through him, eroding the foundation of his spiritual house until finally, with nothing left to support it, his belief had collapsed in on itself. And for the past three years, Father Edward Pike had been faithless. He no longer believed in the wonder, the resurrection, or any of the underpinning principles that had drawn him to the church and a life of service to God.

Despite this crisis of faith, he continued to perform his daily duties out of habit rather than devotion, even though he was unworthy to be a leader to his flock. Hoping against hope that it would pass.

But how could he be expected to lead when he was so lost himself?

He had so very many questions, and not one of them could he find an answer for within the pages of the book of books.

That first morning, he had awakened with a feeling of disquiet in the pit of his stomach. Stumbling through the morning prayers and service, he found himself distracted and unsure of his words, something he had never experienced before in his forty-two years as a priest.

For a while he thought he may be sick. And in a way he supposed he was sick, but it was a malady of the soul, not of the flesh. It would have been so much easier to deal with a life-threatening illness; instead, he was facing a much harsher future.

He had prayed every day for guidance, beseeching the Lord God Almighty to show him the way back to the path of enlightenment, to help him find his way home, to guide him back to divinity. Every day he awaited an answer, and every day he drifted farther away from his religion when no answer came.

Finally, he had stopped trying, too tired and too old to continue to bother. The church had priests, spiritual directors, who were trained to help those like him, but he knew that would probably mean he would be forced to step down from his position within the parish, surrendering his flock to another. The embarrassment would be too much for him. Besides, he had battled his inner demons for too long, and now he was tired. No, now he was *exhausted* and entirely depleted.

The feeling of disquiet only grew stronger with each passing day, until finally *today* he realized he was empty of all feeling for the church, for the religion . . . *and* for life.

Standing under the stone arch of the doorway that would take him from the transept to the vestry, he paused and looked back into the cavernous interior of St. Bartholomew's, his fingers hovering over the bank of switches that controlled the multiple sets of lights within the church. He had spent most of his life in service to God in churches around the country, the last twelve years here at St. Bartholomew's.

Looking out across the rows of pews that until minutes earlier had seated hundreds of parishioners, the priest waited for—hoped for—a flicker of some low-smoldering spark of belief that might remain hidden away deep in his heart, a final chance at redemption, a sign he was not forgotten. Instead, a bitter draft skulked through the doorway on frosty feet, sweeping any hope of salvation with it as it blew over him.

With a final sigh of resignation, the priest turned off the overhead globe lights and then flicked the remaining switches one by one, extinguishing the rows of footpath lights and the spotlights beneath the crucifix, plunging the church into darkness.

A row of dove-gray filing cabinets lined one wainscoted panel wall of the vestry. The metal cabinets held the parish records for the last sixty-five years, all meticulously recorded by Father Pike and his predecessors. A history of the priests and people who had lived, loved, and died in the parish. A rack of three simple shelves above the cabinets held various administrative supplies: reams of paper, pens and pencils, file folders and tabs, all needed for the day-to-day running of the church.

An ancient oak armoire, the original veneer long eroded, its dark wood scuffed and scraped through years of use, stood against the opposite wall. The squat, simple dole cupboard next to it originally contained bread and other supplies the priests would have distributed to the poor and needy of the parish, but the needy far outstripped the capacity of this simple wooden cupboard long ago. Now it held a few blankets and a pillow for when the father felt the need to spend the night.

Father Pike removed his chasuble and vestment and folded them neatly one on top of the other before placing them on the second shelf of the armoire. Stepping out of his cassock, he draped it over a metal coat hanger and hung it on a hook next to the door. He pulled on a pair of black, loose-fitting Lee jeans, slid his arms through the sleeves of his shirt, buttoned it, and then pushed his clerical collar into place. A mirror fixed to the back of the vestry door allowed him to check his clothing; he straightened his collar with stiff, arthritic fingers. Tufts of gray hair had puffed up when he pulled off his cassock and now protruded from his liver-spotted pate.

"You look ridiculous," he said to his reflection as he removed the plastic comb from his shirt pocket and forced his rebellious hair back into place.

In the center of the room, he placed the chair from his study. Plastic, with a high back lined with comfortable foam, and covered in a stain-resistant cloth that had faded over the years to a dull purple from its original red. He had written many sermons seated at this chair, he thought as he ran his hand slowly over the ridge of its back. Each of its four supporting legs had a caster fixed to it, allowing the chair to roll easily.

Kneeling slowly, his knees popping in complaint, the priest pushed in each of the four thumb-shaped plastic locks, securing the chair's casters in place, stopping it from moving. Satisfied the chair would not move, he raised one foot up onto the seat and again tested its stability before cautiously heaving the rest of his sixty-eight-year-old body up. He was no longer as spry as he once was, he reminded himself, so he kept a firm grip on the armrests with both hands. The chair wobbled a little, not designed to take so much awkwardly positioned weight. Instinctively, he threw out one of his arms to steady himself while he held grimly to the other armrest, catching his balance before he toppled over. Once he was sure his balance would not betray him, the priest raised himself gradually to a precarious standing position.

Earlier in the morning he had secured a length of strong hemp rope to one of the ceiling beams, fashioning a noose at the unsecured end.

He slipped his head into it and tightened the hangman's knot until it sat snugly against the bones of the nape of his neck, then reached a hand up to give a final tug on the rope. Satisfied it was still securely fastened to the heavy timber beam running the length of the room, he dropped his hands to his sides.

"God forgive me," he said, then kicked the chair from beneath his feet.

He jerked spastically at the end of the rope for over a minute until blackness finally claimed him.

FOUR

There was a certain gaudiness to Bourbon Street at this time of year, which, while it repulsed him with its cheapness on one level, was also a strange attractor, drawing Jim Baston like a priest to a potential convert.

Sitting at a street-side table of an out-of-the-way café, he waited for a server to fetch his drink. It was a kitschy little coffee bar with fake lampposts and piped accordion music, attempting—in vain, Jim noted—to recreate the ambience of a Parisian street café. But it was the only place he could find with any space left for him to sit; all of the other restaurants and clubs were filled to brimming, and he was averse to elbowing himself through a heaving body of youngsters just for the sake of some company.

The waiter, a tall twentysomething with a stubbly goatee and dressed in a long, white bib and apron, brought his drink: whisky and soda on the rocks.

"May I get you anything more, monsieur?" the man asked with a half-decent French accent.

Jim shook his head. "Thanks, but this will be fine for now."

Spiraled black bars of wrought iron, set firmly in a redbrick base, separated the sidewalk from the table area where Jim now sat. Perhaps this was why the café was less popular. People liked to be able to walk— or stagger—freely between bars in this town. Jim was glad of the space. He could sit unobserved with a clear view of the street and watch the world and its inhabitants wander by, undisturbed thanks to the cage-like bars.

From the breast pocket of his jacket, Jim pulled the cigar he had bought earlier at a small tobacco shop he'd come across as he strolled along Bourbon Street. A hand-rolled Churchill maduro; Cuban, clothed in a clear plastic wrapper that crackled as he rolled the cigar between his fingers. Cuban cigars had become widely available in the United States, the trade embargo finally lifted back in 2015. The owner of the store had been kind enough to give the cigar a cut and supplied him with a complimentary book of matches, the shop's logo and address printed in colorful relief on its cover.

He flipped the cover open, tore a match from the book, and struck it against the safety bar on the back side. The match flared, casting shadows on the ivy-lined bistro walls as the sulfurous smell of the match's ignition filled Jim's nostrils and he felt his mouth begin to salivate in expectation.

Jim tore away the plastic wrapper, placed the cigar between his lips, and twisted it close to the match flame while taking quick, deep puffs to ensure the cigar lit evenly. When he was certain the tobacco was lit, he inhaled a long draw from the maduro and allowed the smoke to fill his mouth, exciting his senses.

He shook the match to extinction. A billowing stream of blue-gray smoke drifted above his head as he exhaled slowly.

There were only two kinds of people in this world, Jim thought: cigar people and non-cigar-people. It was one of those smells and tastes you either acquired immediately or just never developed a liking for. He had never met anyone who had ever said they didn't mind cigar smoke or they thought cigars were okay. Invariably, on asking if his company would be bothered if he lit a cigar, they either enthusiastically encouraged him or gave a shudder of horror. Strange to say, he had always found women more accepting of cigars than men. Perhaps it was certain men's subconscious homophobic reaction to putting something so phallic in their mouths that turned them off.

At a nod from Jim, the waiter brought him another drink. Jim handed him his empty glass, took one more long pull off the cigar, and settled in to watch the old year die.

***

In the moments leading up to midnight, it seemed to Jim the city had found its full voice as thousands counted down the final seconds together at the top of their lungs.

Ten, nine, eight, seven, six, it exclaimed. *Five, four, three, two, one!* Fireworks erupted into the night sky, exploding in great flourishes of color, glorious in their beautifully short life.

Raising his half-full glass to the light show high above the city, Jim spoke quietly to the night air. "Happy New Year, Lark," he whispered, before downing his drink in one swift gulp and setting the empty glass back on the table.

***

Jim arrived back at his room just after one in the morning. His head buzzed pleasantly from the three drinks and the cigar, the taste of which still lingered agreeably on his palate. He dropped his raincoat over the back of a chair still dry, the threatening storm never having materialized. Maybe that was a good omen for the new year.

Standing at the window, he looked out over the city. It was almost silent now, the throngs of revelers having made their way back to their hotel rooms.

"Jim! You have a call from your agent in Los Angeles."

The sudden sound of his computer's AI voice made him jump. He was half tempted not to take the call. He knew Archie would be disappointed with his lack of progress, but he also knew if he did not take his agent's call, Archie would be pestering him until he got what he wanted.

"Put it on speaker," he said eventually.

There was a faint click, and then the voice of Archibald Krogh filled the room.

"Hey, Jim! Sorry to call so late, or is it early? Anyway, happy New Year." His voice sounded nasal; he probably had a cold.

"Happy New Year to you too, Archie. Don't you have better things to do than harass your clients in the middle of the night?"

His remark was met with a chuckle, which rapidly deteriorated into a coughing fit. "Good God," Krogh said finally. "I swear this flu is going to kill me one of these days . . . So tell me, how's the book coming along?"

Jim was not comfortable lying, but he decided that for the sake of both his own sanity and his overstressed agent's health, he would make the exception this time.

"It's doing just—"

Everything changed.

FIVE

A little Philosophy inclineth Mans Minde to Atheisme; But depth in Philosophy, bringeth Mens Mindes about to Religion.

—Francis Bacon

Project Tach-Comm Laboratory, January 1, 2042

At 1:30 a.m. the laboratory was finally prepped and ready.

The transmitter sat on a plain wooden table in the center of the lab. About the size of two paperbacks stacked one on top of the other, it was enclosed in a black, impact-resistant plastic case. It looked clunky and utilitarian. There were no sleek curves or shaded coloring, no logos or trendy advertising motifs, just a solid black box with a connector for a microphone on its front fascia. Next to that was a plug for a VR-keyboard, and from the rear of the box a two-inch-thick red high-voltage lead snaked across the floor to a huge transformer sitting in a locked cage in the opposite corner of the room.

A young woman wearing a white lab coat, her blond hair tied back in a ponytail that stretched down to the middle of her back, approached the table with a portable microphone in her left hand

and its corresponding stand in her right. She placed both items on the table next to the box, careful not to jostle the delicate piece of equipment.

"Prof. Lorentz, would you like me to connect the microphone now?" she asked.

Dr. Mitchell Lorentz looked up from his VR-comp and regarded the woman over his pince-nez glasses.

"Yes, please do, Dr. Drake. The sooner we get this over and done with, the sooner we can get on our way, yes?" He smiled warmly at his assistant before turning back to his VR-comp.

Lorentz was a distinguished-looking man—seventy, with long pure-gray hair matched by an equally gray but neatly trimmed mustache and goatee beard. Although Lorentz liked to dress casually, he always gave the impression he would have felt just as much at ease in a business suit or a tuxedo as in the khaki slacks and polo shirt he wore beneath his white lab coat. A full mouth that was quick to grin and rarely frowned complemented his lean face and long Roman nose.

Well known around the lab for being a stickler for his daily exercise, the professor would routinely break off a meeting if it interrupted his lunchtime workout regimen. Fit and lean, he was still a good-looking man for his age, his broad shoulders and toned arms often allowing him to be mistaken for a decade less than his actual age.

There was no Mrs. Lorentz. When asked why he had never married, he would reply in his most charming voice, "Not married? Have you not met my wife?" while gesturing around the lab with a sweeping hand.

Those close to him—of which there were few—knew he was too dedicated to his work to inflict his obsessive pursuits and eccentric timetables on a wife. Not that there had been a lack of interest on the opposite sex's part, but it became quickly apparent to any woman who entered his life that work was his first and only true love.

He had started out as a research assistant almost fifty years earlier, working for JPL out of California after graduating summa cum laude at Caltech with a degree in advanced applied and theoretical physics. Part of the original NASA team that formulated the design of the first manned mission to Mars, he had left the agency in 2018 and quickly advanced, thanks in part to his capability as a project manager, but also to his brilliant work on theoretical particles. Within ten years he had gone on to head up the R & D department at TachDyne Research Industries, where he had received his first of two Nobel Prizes in Physics.

In 2030, just a few years after leaving TachDyne to open his own research lab in Pasadena, he had received his second Nobel Prize for his company's work on superluminal propagation, proving finally the existence of that long-disputed particle, the tachyon.

The search for the tachyon was thought to be the scientific equivalent of a snipe hunt. Then Lorentz proved its existence beyond a doubt when he simultaneously disproved the paradox of Gödel's time travel in a rotating universe theory and proved the veracity of the reinterpretation principle, a theorem now known as the Lorentz effect.

A few months after receiving the second Nobel, he sold his company to Aberdeen Enterprises and used the profits (which were considerable) to create a small start-up in Reno, where he returned to his first love: hands-on physics.

Prof. Lorentz spoke into a lapel mic attached to his lab coat. "Edward, are you about ready?"

Lorentz's voice was calm and level, and that amazed his assistant, Prof. Adrianna Drake. Here they were on the cusp of an experiment that would revolutionize the communications industry, and the professor showed no signs of excitement at the prospect. She had worked with him for long enough to understand, she believed, why that was. He was simply one of those men who enjoyed the chase, the existence of the puzzle, rather than its actual solution. It gave little gratification to him to know he had potentially succeeded in his goal. She found that odd, alien even, in this results-driven world where she had spent her last few years.

Three rooms farther down the corridor from the lab, a similar box sat in a similar room. Instead of the connectors for the VR-comp and microphone, this box had only one connector for an ancient Bose speaker, which rested on the table next to it, connected by a length of twisted speaker wire.

A young man, his eyes owlishly amplified by his thick glasses, sat with the lid of the receiver resting next to him on the table. A soldering iron in hand, he was deep in the wiring of the machine, his shoulders hunched tightly as he maneuvered carefully through its electronic guts. A thin plume of gray smoke rose from a circuit board as he secured a new component in place, and the acrid smell of hot solder floated through the air.

"Just finishing up, Doc," he said in a basso profundo voice that belied his wiry body. "Give me about five more minutes and we'll be ready to roll."

Back in his room, Prof. Lorentz pulled up a second virtual display on the VR-comp. He used his index finger to highlight and capture the data on the first display and pulled a duplicate across to the second screen, which seemed to hang in the air a few feet in front of his face. Thanks to the holo-projectors located strategically around the room, no matter where Lorentz or any of his staff moved, the display screen of the VR-comp would follow them, always at the optimal position and angle for reading. As Lorentz walked around the room, the screens became transparent to allow him unhindered vision, coalescing back into visibility when he stopped moving.

Data generated by the experiment would be collected through sensors positioned throughout the room. The main CPU driving the system was located in its own room elsewhere within the laboratory complex.

"All right," came Calvin's voice over the comm-link. "Just running the diagnostics . . . and . . . couple more seconds . . . Okay, everything's kosher here, Doc."

"Thank you, Cal."

Prof. Lorentz pressed an icon outlined in red on the floating display in front of him and "Recording" began to flash at the top of the VR-screen.

"Okay, team, we are up and running. Everybody stand by, please," he said.

The computer now began churning through an automated program, displaying each step and its result on-screen. Although everybody on the project was receiving the same feed and the VR-comp was recording everything in real time, Lorentz still read each step aloud as the computer progressed—old habits died hard at his age.

"Phase one diagnostics: complete." And: "Phase two diagnostics: complete. System diagnosis: optimal."

The transformer in the corner of the room began to power up, emitting a low whine that rattled the protective bars of its cage like a monkey testing the security of its enclosure. The whine rapidly grew in pitch until it passed out of the range of human hearing, leaving behind a low thrum that reverberated through the walls and across the floor of the lab.

Then: "Power: engaged."

The old scientist's screen flashed a message in bold green letters:

System diagnosis: completed.

Power level: optimal.

And a few lines beneath that, outlined by a flashing red border, a single icon glowed.

Engage?

The word blinked on and then off repeatedly.

Lorentz regarded the screen for a few moments longer, savoring the moment. Finally, he turned to look directly at the black box on the table and his associate professor standing expectantly next to it, holding the microphone in her hand.

"All right, fire her up," he whispered, and pressed the "Engage" icon.

Everything changed.

PART TWO

THE SLIP

SIX

Rebecca Lacey woke up screaming.

Her fingers twisted into claws that grasped at the cloth of her sodden, sweat-soaked T-shirt, bunching handfuls of the material, until the shirt pulled up to expose the lean paleness of her damp belly. Her breath exploded in short, ragged, panting gasps, and tears spilled over her scarlet cheeks as beads of perspiration dribbled over her naked arms and legs.

She heard her words as if from a distance, more pleading than spoken: "Oh . . . God. Oh . . . God." A mantra of horror repeated over and over as her heart rattled behind her ribs, a terrified animal trying to escape its cage.

The dream—it felt *so* real—had started out quite wonderfully. She was someplace beautiful. The half-remembered sensation of running her hands through long grass. Warmth. A wonderful light permeating all things. And clouds. The scent of something so . . . As much as she struggled to remember, she could not describe the wonderful fragrance that filled her mind.

And then it was all gone, ripped away from her in an instant and replaced by a horror so profound, her breath froze in her lungs.

The *blade*.

She could still see it glinting in the light of the naked bulb hanging from the bare stucco ceiling of her apartment, the glass lamp shade shattered on the floor where her head had smashed it into a hundred pieces. The stranger had twisted the blade back and forth, back and forth, letting it glint and scintillate across her eyes, his face inches from her own and his breath hot against her cheek. She felt the frigid keenness of the cold metal as he traced its point from her forehead over the ridge of her nose and across her lips, sliding it down the curve of her throat until it reached her breastbone.

An everlasting pause and then: *snick*. He had sliced away one of the buttons of her blouse. In the dream a moan of terror had escaped her lips.

Snick. There was the next button.

"Oh, please, no. God. No," she had pleaded.

The man with the knife had worked his way through all of the buttons, his breathing becoming more and more rapid, and then—*Oh dear God*—and then he had . . . he . . . Rebecca threw herself over the side of the bed and heaved a steady stream of vomit that spread in a rank-smelling pool across the carpet and splashed against her ghost-white skin.

She kept throwing up until there was nothing left; dry heaves forced the breath from her until she thought she would choke to death. And when finally it was over, she started screaming. A shrill, horrified ululation escaped from deep within her very soul, shattering the calm of the room before petering off to a low, sobbing howl of pain and terror.

The door to her bedroom burst open. Between her wracking sobs she managed to lift her head toward the two people who now stood in the doorway and mumble through chapped, vomit-caked lips, "Mom . . . Dad . . . he killed me. He killed me."

In the doorway, Mr. and Mrs. Lacey stood in confused disbelief. As the early-morning sun shone through the bedroom window, framing them both in a beam of dust-mote-filled light, Jim Lacey, his eyes wide with shock, fell to his knees and began to weep like a baby. His wife, Sarah, her hair disheveled and tumbled, crossed the space between the door and her daughter in two quick bounds. She wrapped her arms around the weeping girl and pulled her close, until Rebecca could barely draw breath, all the while keening in her daughter's ear, "You're alive, praise Jesus. You're alive."

SEVEN

O, that great Jove would give me once again my vanished years!

—Virgil

". . . fine."

Jim Baston blinked at the sudden change of lighting.

His skin tingled as a light coat of static electricity played across it. There was an odd, fluttering sensation in his stomach, and he felt as though he had come to a sudden and abrupt stop after a long fall.

He breathed in. Leather, like expensive new shoes; the smell filled his nostrils.

The young store assistant stared back at him across the countertop. She looked to be about to speak. Her rouged lips opened . . . and then closed again as a cloud of confusion passed across her face. Her brow knitted above brown eyes, the pupils of which had suddenly and fully dilated. The left side of her mouth lifted, while the right side dipped down, her head tilted toward her right shoulder as though she was suddenly deep in concentration.

"I . . . I," she stammered as the cloud of confusion turned rapidly into a storm of bewilderment that billowed and rolled with her expression.

"I'm terribly sorry but I . . . What were you saying?" she asked.

There was a momentary pause, in which Jim could have answered but did not, his own confusion freezing his tongue, arresting any possibility of a reply as his mind furiously tried to understand what was going on. The silence between the two strangers stretched out before she asked in an apologetic, frightened voice, "Where am I?"

Her auburn hair whipped back and forth across her face as she glanced frantically left and then right, panic now superseding confusion. Her cheeks flushed as blood rushed to them, and Jim could see her breathing rate increase rapidly.

He regarded the confused woman standing across from him for a long second, his own head now cocked questioningly to one side. Jim was sure he had a similar look of confusion on his face, because he had no idea on God's good green earth where he was or why he was here. He could not even remember how he got here. Panic began to claw its way out of its hiding place in the pit of his stomach, crawling on taloned fingers toward his throat.

The last thing he *could* remember was answering the phone to his agent. He had been talking to him just a second ago—the phone had been in his hand. It was New Year's Eve. He had been out, had a couple of drinks, and made it home sometime after midnight; exactly what time he couldn't recall. A cold shiver of fear ran down his spine as a single thought filled his mind: Alzheimer's. They could fix it nowadays of course, but they had to catch it early enough to stop any damage. Once memories were lost to the disease, that was it: they were gone forever.

It had been four years since Jim had been to see his doctor for any kind of a checkup, and he mentally kicked himself for not keeping those yearly appointments. He swung around and took in his surroundings. He recognized nothing. This was not the comfortable hotel room in

New Orleans he thought he had been standing in seemingly only an instant before. Instead, he found himself next to a glass countertop, on the other side of which stood the woman who looked as confused as he felt. Three rows of display racks ran through a store lined top to bottom with expensive-looking leather luggage, clutch bags, women's purses, and crocodile-skin briefcases. A rotating display unit off to his left was full of men's wallets, and a sign fixed to the top of the stand proclaimed "Finest calf leather" in an elegant hand.

Behind the glass counter the young store assistant had started speaking again, calling out, as if to a lost child or dog, "Steven? Alison?" A disturbing edge of panic grew in her voice.

How the hell did I get here? he thought to himself again. *Where am I?*

"Do you think I could use your phone?" he asked, but the girl did not even register his question. Her gaze swept over him like a searchlight and moved on, having found nothing of interest.

"Steven? Alison?" The panic in her voice was now pronounced.

"It's just that I don't seem to remember where I am. It's just a local call," he said. He was disturbed to hear a note of desperation in his own voice.

"Alison? Oh my God." The young woman's voice was now so alarmingly tremulous he could barely understand what she was saying.

Something was not right here. There were three other customers in the store, all of them a lot younger than him, but as Jim regarded each in turn, he could see the same strange look of confusion reflected back from each of their bewildered faces. They looked as though they had all just walked into a room and then forgotten why they were there or what they had come to do; as though they had left something undone but just could not remember what it was.

There was a large glass window at the front of the store. Through it he could see a white marble-effect walkway running parallel to the store. Across the walkway he could make out two other shops: a Gap and a Pretzel Time. He was in a mall? How the hell had he gotten to a mall?

A reflective aluminum safety railing ran down the center of the walkway, guarding an open space that, he guessed, dropped down to at least another level below the one he was on. Several people had gathered in front of the window, milling aimlessly. Jim watched them looking around in the same confused manner. One of them—a young woman who until seconds ago had been turning in slow circles as she gazed up at the ceiling somewhere outside of Jim's vision—seemed oblivious to the baby stroller her left hand rested upon, its plastic hood concertinaed forward into the closed position. As the young mother completed one more slow turn, the purse slung loosely over her shoulder clipped the handle of the stroller and sent it rolling noiselessly away from her. Noticing it as if for the first time, she took two quick steps after it, taking hold of the handles with her outstretched hands to bring the stroller to a halt before stepping around to the front of it. As she knelt almost reverently before it, Jim was sure he could see tears beginning to flow down her face; her jaw was vibrating with emotion. Jim watched as she reached out, her hands disappearing inside the stroller. When they returned into his view, she held a baby no more than six months old. Her mouth began moving, but he could not hear what she was saying. Whatever it was, she was repeating the words again and again. A smile of utter joy lit her face as she stared at the child she now held cradled to her breast.

Jim's confusion deepened as two balding, middle-aged men who had been walking hand in hand now turned and faced each other, each regarding the other as though he had not seen him in many years. Almost in unison they threw their arms around each other's neck and fell to their knees, locked in an embrace.

A brown-skinned teenager sprinted up to the store window. He stopped for a second in front of it and placed his forehead against the glass. Using his hands to block the glare from the store's reflected light, he gaped at the people inside, a look of frantic desperation on his face as his eyes darted from one face to the next. Then, just as suddenly as he had appeared, he sprinted off out of sight, leaving only a grease stain where his forehead had contacted the glass.

Jim's attention was dragged back to the inside of the store by the weeping of a woman sitting cross-legged on the carpeted floor an aisle or so away from him. The woman's low, keening voice set a beat to an underswell of fear Jim could feel seeping into the air.

"What is going on here?" a large man in a business suit demanded, his voice loud and pompous.

The store assistant, still calling forlornly for Steven and Alison, ran past the fat man toward the exit at the far end of the store. Jim followed her.

He pushed through the glass doors and stepped out into the mall. A tsunami of sound struck him as a wave of anguished voices washed over him, soaking him in its confusion. Here and there, intermingled with the buzz of voices, Jim could occasionally make out an ecstatic cry of laughter or the rapid chatter of happiness. They floated through the confusion, emotional flotsam riding on a sea of panic, all accompanied by a soundtrack of Muzak that wafted down from hidden speakers set high up in the latticework of white metal braces that held the glass ceiling of the mall in place overhead. The discordant interference was amplified as it bounced from floor to ceiling and wall to wall, until it became a mind-numbing cacophony.

Disoriented, Jim took a few faltering steps forward to the aluminum safety railing that prevented shoppers from falling through the open space to the floor below. He took a deep breath and leaned on the horizontal grab bar like a nauseous passenger gazing sickly over the side of a storm-rocked liner. He could see he was on the top floor of a shopping mall, three stories up. The floors beneath were just as packed with people, all as equally disoriented as those around him.

A thought struck him: maybe this was a terrorist attack. He remembered back in the late nineties of the last century some Japanese religious cult had begun gassing people on the Japanese underground, and then in 2019 that homegrown terrorist group—what the hell was their name? Radical America? Freedom America? Whoever they were, they had managed to dump a ton of genetically modified respiratory syncytial virus into the water supply of some Midwestern town and killed all those people. Maybe *that's* what was going on here; a terrorist group had loosed a chemical agent in the mall. It would explain why everyone was acting so harebrained.

But, he reasoned, there hadn't been any real terrorist threat in the world for the last fifteen years or more.

Who the hell was there left with the capability to pull an attack like this off?

A subtle change in the air drew Jim's attention away from his thoughts of terrorist attacks. The demeanor of the crowd had begun to shift; fear had replaced panic, and that was quickly mutating into terror. He turned around, looked up, and saw a wave of horrified faces and bodies flooding toward him.

Jim was transfixed, his eyes flicking from face to face as the crowd rushed forward. The novelist in him observed with a detached, professional attitude, taking note of everything, from the wild look of panic in their eyes, to the way the front row of oncoming bodies seemed to ebb and flow into those behind.

The large, pompous man from the luggage store had left just after Jim and was making his way in the opposite direction, pushing anybody who stood in his way aside. Seeing the oncoming crowd, he tried to turn and get out of its way, but the mob swept over him as if he did not exist, trampling him underfoot. Others, faster than the unfortunate executive, dove for cover in shop doors or were caught up in the panicked throng and pulled along too. Those not so lucky ended up knocked aside or smashed through the glass windows of storefronts.

For a brief moment Jim thought about jumping over the safety banister, holding himself there while the mob ran past, but he doubted his arms would hold him long enough. His hands were too damp with perspiration for him to not expect to instantly lose his grip and fall the three stories to the ground below. No! He would take his chances with the mob, thank you very much.

Turning, Jim began to run in the opposite direction to the oncoming crowd, hoping to get his old legs up to some kind of competitive speed. To his utter amazement, he found he was sprinting like a teenager. His legs ate up the ground, his arms were pistons pumping the air, his heart thumped powerfully in his chest, and the blood thrummed through his veins.

He chanced a brief look back over his shoulder; he had a lead of five feet or so. If he could just make it to the stairs or the escalator before the horde, he might be okay. *Assuming there is an exit this way, of course.* Facing front again, he was just in time to see the bewildered woman standing directly in front of him.

In her eighties, she had wispy gray hair that hung in greasy clots around a face that had probably been remarkable in her younger days. Plastic surgery had stretched and pulled her skin, until it now looked so parchment thin it would tear and split if she should chance a smile. She wore a skintight catsuit that accentuated her overly large breasts, the silicone implants ensuring, even in this late stage of her life, that her boobs stoically resisted the effects of gravity.

"We don't care about you, only about Michael," she shouted incoherently as he collided headlong with her and sent both of them sprawling onto the cold floor.

Jim slid on his back across the highly polished tiles and felt the air slammed from his lungs as he collided with something solid and unyielding.

The old woman was on her hands and knees, her lank hair hiding her features, until she raised her head on a wrinkled stalk of a neck. Her face distorted into a mask of anger as she stared across the walkway at him, her eyes flashing a fury he could not fathom. Her lips moved, but Jim could hear nothing she said over the roar of voices and the thunder of approaching feet as she spat what he was sure were some choice expletives at him.

Behind her the crowd bore down.

Fear must have shown in Jim's eyes, because she twisted just in time to face the onrush of bodies as they smashed into her. A man in the front row, pushed along by the hundreds behind him, saw her, tried to leap over her scuttling body, but mistimed his leap and jumped too late. His foot caught the back of her head, sending him sprawling on his face. Those behind had no time to react. They stumbled and lurched, tripping over her and the sprawled man, grabbing at others as they went down. The old woman and the fallen man disappeared instantly beneath them. It was a train wreck: bodies flew everywhere as the onrushing mass stumbled and fell and screamed and cried out in pain and surprise or cursed in anger and fear.

Jim took that split second to quickly assess his location, whipping his head from side to side. He had landed near a molded plastic bench. Fixed to the safety railing of the mall, it allowed three or four people to sit in modest comfort on the curved, injection-molded plastic seat. There was a gap between the underside of the seat and the floor, no more than eighteen inches. If he could just squeeze into that gap, he might stand a chance of getting out of this alive. Hardly thinking, he pulled himself hand over hand on his belly and slipped between the floor and the base of the seat. A moccasin-clad foot smashed down on his left hand before he could pull it under the shelter. He screamed a curse and whipped his stinging fingers to his chest, scooting himself farther under the overhang of plastic until he felt the upright support bars of the safety railing pressing into his back.

The crowd thundered by, the floor shuddering with their passing. Jim felt the rolling vibration reverberate through his bones, forcing his teeth into an involuntary chatter. The fact that he was terrified did not help either.

A body crashed to the ground, smashing into the walkway with the sickeningly abbreviated sound of a melon dropped from a great height onto a metal spike. The bloody face of a teenage boy, his eyes lifeless and blank, faced Jim. The poor kid's body jerked and twitched as countless feet stomped over him, pounding him into the walkway. Unable to turn away from the horror, Jim knew he would never forget the look of terminal shock embossed on the kid's face.

Time passed.

Finally, the river of feet slowed, became a trickle, and eventually dried up completely. The dead boy, crushed and broken, gazed lifelessly at Jim, one shattered arm stretched out across the floor toward him as if pointing to Jim's hiding place. His mouth hung open, and a trail of blood leaked from his split and broken lips, his staring eyes accusatory: *Why did you live? Why you, old man?*

The sobbing lament of a woman broke Jim's trance, and he slid his cramped and aching body out from under his plastic sanctuary, careful to avoid touching the dead kid. A pool of congealing blood spread like a crimson lake over the stark, white tile of the floor. Jim rose to his feet and looked around. The source of the weeping was the young mother he had seen through the window of the luggage store earlier. She sat cross-legged in the recessed entranceway of an H&M store. She held her baby, wrapped in a pink blanket, to her chest, rocking back and forth. The baby stroller lay twisted and wrecked farther down the walkway.

The low keening of a nursery rhyme floated across the now deafeningly silent mall.

"Mama's gonna buy you a mocking bird," she sang as Jim began walking stiffly toward her. *"And if that mocking bird don't sing, Mama's gonna buy you a . . ."* She stopped singing when she saw Jim approaching.

"Are you okay, miss?" he asked quietly.

The young woman scooted farther back into the doorway, her face suddenly fearful.

Jim lifted his hands, palms out, to head height. "It's okay," he said gently. "I'm not going to hurt you. Are you okay? Is your baby all right?"

Her back connected with the door of the clothes store. From inside the store Jim heard the faint tinkle of bells. Unable to push herself back any farther, she instead rounded on Jim. Her eyes flashed a mixture of fear and anger. "Stay away from me," she yelled, her voice a high-pitched squeal.

"It's okay. I just want to help you. I'm not going to—"

"Stay away from me, you bastard!" she screamed. The fear in her voice was so overwhelming, Jim felt as though he had been physically struck.

"I just—" he tried to continue.

The woman dissolved into tears, pulling the child even closer to her chest.

Jim backed away from her. "I'm sorry," he said as he turned away.

The woman, her attention already refocused on the pink bundle in her arms, resumed her lullaby. There was nothing more he could do for the poor woman; he would just have to leave her here and hope the paramedics looked after her when they arrived. *If* they arrived, he corrected himself, before turning and moving reluctantly in the direction where he hoped he would find an exit out of this insanity.

***

There were a half-dozen dead bodies strewn across the mall walkway, their trampled forms smashed and crushed, broken limbs jutting at odd angles.

All was still.

Shattered glass from storefronts was scattered all over, crunching under Jim's shoes as he picked his way through the desolation. Bodies lay in a disheveled heap around the top of the escalator's gunmetal-gray stairway, and a second broken and blood-spattered mass of crushed bodies had collected at the bottom of the steps. They looked like care-lessly cast-aside dolls discarded by some hateful child. He avoided look-ing directly at the unfortunate souls as he stepped over them to ride the escalator down to the next level.

On the ground floor he found a large illuminated visitors' map of the mall. A fat, red arrow labeled "You Are Here" indicated Jim's loca-tion, and he traced the route from it to the nearest exit with his index finger before turning and heading in the direction the map indicated.

***

The sky, a perfect cerulean blue, stretched off into the distance as Jim Baston pushed open the glass exit doors of the mall and stepped out into the fresh air. He stood for a few moments, bent at the waist, his hands braced against his knees, sucking in lungfuls of warm air. The heat of the day was astonishing after the controlled, air-conditioned environment of the mall. It radiated up from the concrete sidewalk in waves, and within seconds of leaving the building, beads of sweat began to pop on his forehead.

A scattering of lifeless birds lay dotted over the road separating the sidewalk from the mall parking lot. Glancing up at the huge building he had just exited, Jim thought he could make out bloody splotches where the birds had collided with the polarized glass fascia of the mall.

This is all wrong, he thought, raising himself to an upright position and shading his eyes with his hand from the intense glare of the sun. The sky was too blue, the air far too warm. *Wherever* here *is, it sure as hell isn't New Orleans. Not even Louisiana by the looks of it.*

Blocking the road off to his right were three cars that had smashed headlong into each other. Steam or smoke rose from two of the ruined vehicles. Jim could just make out the body of the driver still slumped against the wheel of one of the cars, barely visible through the hissing fog rising from the vehicle's wrecked engine.

Every nerve of his body screamed at him to leave, run away, get the hell out of here. But he couldn't leave the driver to die. At the very least he had to check if he or she was just unconscious. *This is madness. Sheer madness*, he thought as he began walking cautiously over to the crashed vehicles.

Two of the cars were empty, their occupants having fled the scene. The third, an unrecognizable compact, was sandwiched between the other vehicles and had sustained the most serious damage. The driver, an elderly woman with blue-rinsed hair, was slumped against the steering wheel of her decimated vehicle. The airbag had deployed, and the woman's face rested against the deflated bag. Her jaw hung limply open; a thick clot of congealed blood filled her mouth. Jim assumed her severed tongue probably lay somewhere at her feet. A web of blood-splattered fractures radiated out from the spot where her head had connected with the car's side window. Jim was sure she was dead, but he stretched a cautious hand through the broken window, carefully avoiding the pieces of glass still in the surround, and placed two fingers against her throat for a few seconds.

Nothing. She was gone.

Jim stepped back from the destroyed vehicle and its dead driver. His left foot trod on something metallic, and he almost lost his footing as the object slid out from beneath him. He blurted an expletive as he barely managed to regain his balance, then looked down at what had caused him to slip. It was one of the vehicles' license plates. Though the license plate was battered and dirty and torn from its fastening on the rear of one of the cars, the blue letters spelling CALIFORNIA were still clearly visible.

Kneeling down, Jim picked up the piece of twisted metal and examined it as though he held some ancient scroll or religious relic; as though it held the key to his very existence. In a way he supposed it did hold an answer of sorts. He'd been wasting time wondering where he was when the solution was all around him, fastened to the hundreds of cars and trucks left in the mall's parking lot, waiting for their owners to return.

Still holding the warped piece of metal in his hand, he walked across to the nearest row of parked cars. Moving from one car to the next, he checked the license plate of each in turn. By the time he reached the end of the first row of vehicles, he knew where he was. There were a smattering of out-of-state license plates—Nevada and Washington, even one from Idaho—but the majority had the same blue-on-white plates as the one he held in his hand. California. And judging from the blue expanse stretching out above him, he would hazard a guess and narrow it down to Southern California.

The sun was past its zenith and easing toward the western horizon across the cloudless canvas of the sky. But in the distance, beyond the rows of waiting cars, a black plume of smoke spiked high into the upper atmosphere, as hard and expressionless as gunmetal. At its base, Jim thought he could make out the orange flicker of flames leaping high into the air. A faint smell of burning rubber reached his nostrils.

It looked like a big fire. Jim expected to hear the sound of emergency vehicles screaming along the roads toward the inferno. There should be helicopters and camera drones buzzing around the scene of the distant disaster like worker bees buzzing around a bountiful honeypot. But there was nothing in the air. Nothing on the ground.

A memory began to tug at his mind and a sense of déjà vu descended like a mist, confusing him even further. Everything *looked* so familiar. No, that was wrong: everything *was* familiar.

He knew this place. He was sure of it.

Taking a step out onto the blacktop, he craned his neck to read the name fixed over the mall's recessed entrance: "Fallbrook Mall."

The name rang a bell somewhere in his memory. He repeated the name of the shopping center over in his head a couple of times.

Fallbrook Mall? Fallbrook Mall?

"Got it," he said with a snap of his fingers. It was the name of the mall he used to shop at when he had still lived in California; when *they* had still lived out in the San Fernando Valley. There was a great little Italian restaurant he and Simone would eat at and a Cineplex they used to visit with . . . Lark.

His eyes dropped to ground level again, and he began to walk toward the low brick wall bordering the building, hedging in a bed of sad flowers that looked wilted and dry under the sweltering sun. From the corner of his eye, Jim caught a glimpse of movement. Someone was watching him.

On the other side of the doors, standing in the foyer of the mall, a man stared intently at Jim. Dressed in khaki pants, a white open-collared shirt, and a black leather jacket, the stranger looked to be in his thirties, brown hair swept back over his forehead, eyes locked solidly with his own. Jim took a step back in surprise. The figure took a step back too. Astonishment crossed both their faces. Jim raised his left hand; the stranger mimicked his gesture.

"Christ!" Jim whispered as he stepped forward and placed his hand flat against the door of the mall's entrance. The face that stared back at him from the door's mirrored surface was not that of the old man Jim had become.

It was the face of a man in his late thirties.

EIGHT

I must have fallen asleep at the wheel.

That was all Byron Portia had time to think before the road in front of him turned into a sea of shimmering red as drivers thumped brake pedals to the floor, their vehicles' brake lights suddenly glowing like hot coals.

This was all wrong.

An instant ago he was a half hour away from LA, his earlier plan of reaching the city before midnight delayed by an unexpected accident outside of Baker. Some fool kid with too much synthahol in his system or jacked up on the latest designer drug had forgotten to turn on his car's AI to get him home and had wound up smashed into the support of a bridge. The accident had spread both the car and the drunk driver over eight lanes of the highway. The backup had stretched all the way back toward Vegas for thirty miles and cost Byron three hours of his time. He had celebrated New Year's sitting in the cab of his 18-wheeler.

After that he had not bothered hurrying; he knew the time was past for him to find anybody suitable for his purposes that night. But that was all okay. Everything happened for a reason, after all. And so he had contented himself with abiding by the speed limit and tried not to dwell on the missed opportunity.

He understood; he was protected.

And then suddenly . . . this.

Darkness had been replaced by blinding daylight and blue sky. The sparse, industrialized outskirts of Los Angeles, shrouded in the comforting shadow of darkness, replaced by the urban sprawl of . . . where? He had no idea.

Cars were everywhere. His confusion was followed by a strange sick sensation of abruptly arrested motion in his stomach. He instinctively sucked in a gulp of air and held it as all around him vehicles began careening and skidding across the unfamiliar freeway in a slow-motion ballet of chaos. Clouds of smoke erupted from tires as panicked drivers brought their vehicles rapidly down to zero and stopped dead, only to be sent spinning in all directions by others behind them who could not react quickly enough to the wall of metal thrown up in front of them.

He saw one car lurch awkwardly into the air, corkscrewing gracelessly over the concrete median dividing his side of the freeway from oncoming traffic. The face of its terrified driver was plainly visible for a moment as the driver's-side window of the airborne sedan passed in front of Byron's windshield before disappearing in a massive ball of flame as it ripped through a stalled RV, then cartwheeled away out of his view.

Byron had no chance of stopping as his foot smashed into the brake pedal; it was instinctive, it was automatic and intuitive, but it was also stupid. The big rig he was riding wasn't a car: it took time to slow down. Gentle caressing of the hydraulic brakes was all that would bring one of these metal leviathans of the freeway to a safe stop. Hammering the brakes could only lead to one result, and even as the thought slipped through his mind, he felt the dynamics of his vehicle begin to change.

The forty feet of trailer hitched behind his rig began to slip sideways, torquing his cab to the left. He tried to compensate by turning the wheel into the skid, attempting to avert the oncoming jackknifing of his rig, but he could already feel it was too late. He was going too fast, and he had hit the brakes too hard. It wasn't going to matter anyway; there were too many damn cars ahead of him. All he could do now was hang on.

The inevitable impact seemed to happen gradually, taking place over the space of a couple of seconds. But it felt as though it were five or six times as long, time stretching out for him as his adrenal glands dumped their contents into his system.

He felt the potential energy building in his vehicle, the cabin begin to strum and squeal as the tension resonated through the tortured metal. Energy built furiously in those . . . long . . . drawn . . . out . . . seconds . . . before . . . the rig detonated.

His steering wheel whipped out of his hands, and Byron catapulted from his seat, exploding toward the roof of the cab. He smashed into the ceiling, knocking the stored air from his straining lungs. The windshield imploded into the interior of the cabin with the sound of a million shattered bottles, broken glass showering the leather driver's seat with diamond hailstones.

Through the newly punctured eye of his cab, he felt a numbing rush of hot air and saw the outside world spinning and tumbling as the scream of twisting metal and the cracking and splitting of plastic pummeled his ears. It was a strange but somehow fitting anthem for this disaster. He was heading down again, back toward the warped dashboard, as the strangely possessed steering wheel thrashed and turned, as if the driver's seat now belonged to some invisible, deranged demon driver.

Byron Portia, truck driver and one of the most successful serial killers to stalk the United States, plummeted toward the floor of his cab. His head smashed against the steering wheel with a sharp crack, and consciousness fled instantly from him like rainwater down a storm drain.

NINE

The store he was looking for—according to the map of the mall he had consulted earlier—should be on the ground floor on the opposite side of the mall to the exit. He found it just as the sign had said, nestled between a Sears and RadioShack.

"Barnes & Noble" the sign above the entrance announced. *Wow!* Jim took a moment; it was a real honest-to-goodness bookstore. He couldn't remember when the last time was he had seen one of these.

Jim picked his way through the literary rubble of spilled fiction, true crime, encyclopedias, dictionaries, and thesauruses. The occasional dropped briefcase or dumped school satchel was the only indication that the cause of the destruction both within and outside the bookstore was rooted in human panic and not some strange weather anomaly that had run its destructive course throughout the mall.

Against the far wall of the bookstore, Jim found what he was looking for. He reached for a copy of the *LA Times* from the rack, not bothering to read the headline or open the broadsheet. Instead, he quickly scanned the top of the front page, looking for the date: Monday, June 19, 2017. Tossing the paper aside, he grabbed a *New York Times*: same date, same year. One after another he checked the remaining newspapers. All of them read the same.

There was no way in hell this could be right. He had until what had seemed like only minutes earlier been over two thousand miles away in New Orleans, safely hidden away from the world in a cramped but comfortable hotel room in 2042. Yet now somehow he found himself standing in a bookstore twenty-five years in the past. And, judging from the commotion and confusion he had witnessed since his arrival, he wasn't the only one who had made the journey.

Goose bumps erupted down the lengths of his arms as a dizzying feeling of unreality washed over him. He leaned against a rack of books, waiting for the queasiness to pass, hoping he would not throw up, while sucking in deep gulps of air.

Although he was not aware of it at the time, from the moment he found himself standing in the luggage store, Jim realized he had been close to losing it. Panic had grabbed hold of him without his even noticing and had driven all of his actions and pushed all of his buttons. He had been on autopilot, his conscious mind forced into the background while his survival instincts took over. Now, as the adrenaline was finally dissipating from his body, his thoughts became clearer and his personality regained some control.

He began to think through the possibilities of just what was going on here.

He hadn't done any drugs since he was a kid, so unless someone had slipped him something at the bar last night . . . No, he had bought his own drinks and never left them unattended, so this was not some kind of a drug-induced hallucination. He wasn't tripping.

It wasn't a dream, either. The experience was too visceral, and the throbbing in his bruised fingers that had been trodden on by the mob removed all doubt this was anything other than reality. This—whatever "this" was—was actually happening.

The possibility he was suffering some kind of mental breakdown had crossed his mind, but that would not account for the panic and death that he had witnessed all around him. Maybe others were sharing his psychosis. Doubtful.

There were some very realistic virtual reality simulations available—he'd tried a few of them—but they could not come close to truly simulating the feeling of being somewhere other than hooked up to a machine. Although incredibly realistic, the environment still had a certain synthetic feeling; the virtual-population seemed a little too unreal in their responses when you talked with them. It took a personal suspension of your belief to truly immerse yourself into the program. The kind of processing power needed to create a scenario as real as what he had already experienced was still decades out of reach.

So, what was left? That he and God knew how many others had somehow been transported back in time into the bodies of their earlier selves.

Unbelievable! Inconceivable! Impossible!

But how did that old quote go? "When you have eliminated the impossible, whatever remains, however improbable, must be the truth." The only remaining answer he had left was that he was truly experiencing this event. That for some unknown reason, he and at the very least the rest of the people in this shopping mall had been thrust back through time twenty-five years into the past.

The implications were simply staggering.

So, if he was to accept that he had traveled back to 2017, the next question was: Am I stuck here?

Maybe it was a localized phenomenon. Perhaps even now emergency services were sealing off the perimeter and attempting to assess the situation. Maybe somebody out there actually knew what the hell had happened. And if somebody knew what was going on, then maybe they could reverse it.

That's an awful lot of maybes, he thought as he headed back toward the mall's exit.

TEN

Byron Portia smelled something burning.

Not only could he smell it, he realized, as he sucked in a lungful of smoke-filled air, he could also taste it. Thick, acrid, and cloying, it seared his throat with every breath he took as he struggled toward consciousness.

If there's smoke, then there's fire. That's what his daddy used to say. And Daddy was always right. You never argued with Daddy, not if you valued your hide.

Portia's eyes flickered open, and he tried to force his befuddled brain to assess exactly what had happened to him. There was a large gap in his memory. He had been on his way to Los Angeles—he remembered that much. It had been nighttime and then suddenly it had been day, and he could not remember what had happened in the blank space between dark and light. Of course, that was the least of his problems, he realized.

His world had turned upside down—literally.

He was lying on his back on the ceiling of his cab, staring up at the driver's seat and the floor. Where the windshield had been, there was now nothing but a few loose pieces of shattered glass hanging from the windshield's surround like rotten teeth in an ancient mouth. He could feel a warm breeze flowing through the space into the cabin. The breeze was pulling in smoke with it too—it was starting to fill the wrecked cab. Gray-black fumes snaked over the inverted dashboard.

There was almost no sound. He could hear a creaking, squeaking noise that reminded him of a rusty weather vane or the unoiled wheel of an old bicycle. Portia strained to listen for any other clue. There was another sound—a crackling, popping noise—and it was getting louder. As the crackling grew, so too did the smoke. It became thicker and blacker, filling the cab with creeping black tentacles.

Fire!

Portia's short-circuited brain finally made the connection. He was going to burn to death—or suffocate to death first—if he didn't get out of this cab.

Tendrils of fear wrapped themselves around his heart, and he sucked in another deep lungful of the choking black smoke. His eyes itched painfully, and tears welled up in response to the smoke, blurring his vision even further.

He had to get out.

Portia reached his arms out, placed his hands palms up against the body of the cab, and pushed. Pain coursed up his left side and struck his heart, paralyzing him with its intensity. A mewling whimper crawled from between his lips, and he collapsed back onto the ceiling, sucking in great puffs of air between clenched teeth. The fetid air made him choke and almost vomit; it was becoming less and less breathable by the second. Through the swirling smoke that now filled most of the cabin, he could make out yellow flames flickering dimly. He could hear the fire growing in intensity.

Terror sent adrenaline coursing through his body—he was not going to let himself die here, not like this—and with a snarl, he pulled himself up into a sitting position. The pain was horrendous. His vision swirled and darkened, and the urge to throw up was almost unstoppable this time, but if he blacked out now he knew that would be all she wrote: he would lose consciousness and choke to death on his own vomit.

"But I'm chosen," he whimpered as unconsciousness threatened to swallow him again.

With an almost-superhuman exertion of will, he fought back the darkness, pushed it away from him, until finally the interior of the overturned truck swam back into view. He was upright, his left hand braced against the inverted back of his driver's seat and his right hand holding the rim of the shattered windshield. His right foot was jammed in what was left of his truck's steering wheel. It had snagged through the gap between two of the wheel's spokes and was caught up against the dashboard and the steering column. The steering wheel had folded over on itself in the impact and trapped his foot in a clam-like vise. His foot, bent at a right angle to the ankle, felt numb, and as he strained his neck to get a better look at it, he could make out white bone jutting through the skin. The ragged point of bone protruded through the bloody, torn skin, an amateur carver's attempt at whittling a spear point.

Portia strained to reach his foot, but the angle was too obtuse and the pain from his ruined ankle too intense. His stomach muscles began to twinge and shudder with the strain of holding himself in this awkward position until finally, and with a frustrated yell of despair, his body collapsed back down.

The shroud of smoke swallowed him, leaking into his nostrils, flowing down his throat into his lungs. Oxygen-depleted, his brain struggled to remain alive but proceeded only to order his lungs to suck in even more of the poisonous fumes that were killing him.

Finally, consciousness began to leave him, and he knew he was going to die.

A pale hand thrust through the empty space where the windshield once was, its long, elegant fingers groping blindly through the smoke. It grabbed Portia's trapped foot and wrenched it free of the buckled steering wheel. The pain was incredible, overwhelming his nervous system and overloading every nerve in his body, to the point that he couldn't even scream.

The last thing Byron Portia's dying mind registered was the beautiful hand of God as it reached down through the swiftly approaching blackness to claim him.

ELEVEN

Jim Baston exited the mall and walked over to the parking lot.

There was no police cordon or sudden rush of emergency personnel hurrying to greet him with thermal emergency blankets in hand, concern stitched across their faces and a thousand questions about his well-being waiting on their lips. No cadre of reporters thrust microphones at him, asking if he had any idea what had happened, the lights from their cameras blinding him.

Instead, all that waited for him was what he first took to be snow. Holding out a hand, he allowed a flake to settle gently onto his palm. It was ash. Gray, evanescent ash falling in a flurry from the leaden sky, settling lightly on the hot concrete and bringing with it a reek of burning rubber laced with the campfire smell of wood and turpentine. Together they produced a sickly, syrupy odor that clogged his nostrils like tar, burning the back of his throat with each breath he inhaled.

Rummaging through the pockets of his jeans and jacket, he found nothing he could use to block the choking smoke. Placing his hand over his mouth, Jim jogged back inside the mall and zagged into a kids' clothing store near the exit.

The doors shushed efficiently open as he entered the air-conditioned store, the clean air a soothing relief to his already-raw throat. Child-shaped mannequins showed off the season's latest—and to Jim's future eye, quaint—styles, their unsettlingly still forms scattered around the store in various frozen poses. The place seemed eerie without the presence of human staff and customers, as though he had stumbled into the lair of the Medusa and at any moment might catch a glimpse of her and be instantly turned to stone.

If this were one of those old horror movies he grew up with, he'd be hearing single piano notes right about now. Unable to control his irrational fear any longer, Jim grabbed a handful of preteen dresses from the nearest rack and ran out of the store.

***

There was an oiliness to the air. It stuck to his skin, making it slick and dirty.

Jim's eyes smarted painfully. The torn strip of summer dress he now wore over his mouth and nose provided a modicum of protection against the pollution, but he could still smell the stench of burning rubber, and he felt its chemical tingle in his throat and tasted the acidic sourness in his mouth.

The thick plume of smoke he had seen rising into the air earlier now filled most of the southern horizon, like black and purple bruises forming on the skin of the abused sky. Most of the western skyline was gone too, buried beneath a black shroud of smoke, the sun a barely visible afterimage, and, he realized with horror, the buildings visible earlier had now disappeared behind the solid bank of smoke rolling inexorably toward his location. Jim could see unruly spires of flame leaping high into the air: the source of the Pompeian snowstorm that now fell on the city. Tendrils of smoke drifted free from the main body of the massive fire and hung over the mall, the advance guard of the rapidly approaching firestorm, blown by the high-altitude winds.

"Christ!" he said aloud.

The sense of disquiet he felt in the empty clothes store had not entirely dissipated. As Jim watched the rapidly approaching storm of smoke, his uneasiness returned with a vengeance. A cold surge of panic took hold of him.

"Get a grip on yourself, man." His voice was muffled by the makeshift bandana covering his mouth. He just needed to reason this out, not let the panic blind him to his situation. *I must have got to the mall somehow. So there has to be a car parked somewhere out here*, he thought.

Pushing his hand into his jeans pocket, he pulled out a three-inch shiny plastic car-shaped fob. He flipped it over. On the reverse side he saw the glittering, laser-etched hologram of the Tesla Motors company. *What car was I driving back then—back* now? he corrected himself. He stared at the plastic key in his hand as if it might be able to answer him.

Of course, it was the Model X. Simone had bought one for him for—when was it?—his thirty-fourth? No, his thirty-fifth birthday. They had still been living in California. He was still working for JPL, and they had the place in the San Fernando Valley.

They were still together back then too. They were still a family, back before everything had fallen apart; back before the accident had taken Lark and destroyed their marriage.

Jim froze. Simone! He hadn't dreamed she might be caught up in the event. But if it was as widespread as he was beginning to suspect it might be and he had truly traveled back in time somehow—well, *then* was *now*. They still lived in the house in the Valley at this point in time. They wouldn't put it on the market for another two years, and Simone would be there. God knows what she might be going through.

He hadn't talked to his ex-wife in years, but if there was even a slight chance he was correct about the event, then there was no way he was going to leave her alone. He had to get to her.

Now, if he could just figure out where the hell he had parked the damn car.

***

It took Jim nearly forty-five minutes of walking the ranks of parked cars waving the Tesla key fob back and forth before he finally found his vehicle. He caught the flash of the Tesla's lights through the swirling mists of smoke one row across from where he stood. He pulled open the door, climbed inside, and closed his eyes for ten seconds, allowing his mind to quiet.

When Jim opened them again, he noticed a smartphone sitting in the center cup holder, tossed there, he guessed, when he had parked the car. It had power. He scrolled through the list of saved telephone numbers, found the one for the house landline, and tapped the "Call" button. The phone beeped the tone for each of the numbers rapidly in his ear, then . . . nothing. Not even an engaged tone. The screen flashed "No Signal" repeatedly at him.

"God damn it," he hissed, tossing the useless phone onto the back passenger seat.

He shifted the Tesla into reverse and pulled out of the parking spot. The dashboard computer glowed with electronic luminescence, and a synthesized voice swam unexpectedly from the car's concealed dashboard speakers.

"Hello, James. Please fasten your safety restraint," it said in a husky female contralto.

Jim pulled the safety belt into place across his chest, knowing this would be the only way to mollify the eternally persistent onboard artificial intelligence of the car. Besides, if he didn't comply with the AI, it would not allow him to engage the drive, and he would be stuck here until the fire reached him.

"Thank you, James," the disembodied voice said as the clasp of the seat belt clicked into place.

The Model X came equipped with an onboard navigation system as standard. Its display was set into the dashboard within easy reach and view of both the driver and passenger. It had already identified his location, displaying a graphical representation of his vehicle in the center of the screen. The surrounding streets and roads, along with places of interest, were all illustrated and labeled as well. Jim tapped an icon on the screen. Instantly, a box popped up with his current location: 21207 Topanga Canyon, California, 91614.

Quickly, Jim tapped through the menu system until he found the "Directions" button. He was relatively sure he knew the general direction of the house, but it had been so many years since he had last made this drive, and he did not want to get lost out here. He was going to need a little help from the GPS.

Choosing "Current Location" as the point of origin for the trip, he pressed the "Home" button as the destination and waited for the navigation system to calculate the fastest route to get him there.

"You are now off track," announced the car's AI.

"Yeah, yeah, yeah," mumbled Jim as he slipped the car into drive and edged out of the parking spot.

"Turn right ahead," the car instructed him as Jim drove the car to the junction leading out of the mall's parking lot and onto Topanga Canyon Boulevard.

According to the navigation computer, the house was twelve miles away. If he was lucky, he would make the trip in less than thirty minutes.

TWELVE

His eyes opened to blue sky overhead and pain throughout his entire body; a relentless sharp throb made his hands spasm and clench involuntarily.

Grass: his hands had grabbed a fistful of grass. His fingers dug deep into cool, loose dirt.

Byron Portia sucked in a lungful of clean air and coughed violently, the wave of pain that washed over him so intense he willingly accepted the black sheet of unconsciousness that rippled around the edges of his mind, longing for the painless embrace of oblivion. Instead, the pain subsided a little and with it the darkness, replaced by a glow filtering through his tightly shut eyelids. Light motes swayed and eddied across his vision.

His eyes fluttered open. He was alive.

Overhead the sky stretched limitlessly, filling his vision, summer blue and still, undisturbed by either cloud or aircraft. Carefully, with no wish to experience another nauseating bout of agony, he raised his head from the soft earth.

He found himself on the grass verge running alongside a freeway. Eighty feet away he could see the burning wreck of his big rig, jack-knifed diagonally across most of the lanes of the freeway. It lay on its roof, wheels pointing into the sky, looking like a giant dinosaur, dead under a Jurassic sun. Surrounding his decimated truck was a fortification of mangled metal that jutted out in a chaotic display of torn steel and plastic, tattered flesh and splintered bone. The cab of his truck erupted suddenly in a brilliant ball of flame that sent a pillar of flame, smoke, and debris skyward.

A gentle breeze swept the smoke from the burning vehicles away from Byron's side of the embankment, exposing the destruction in all its glory.

It was a magnificent sight, an earthly manifestation of the power of God. The evil and unclean—sinners one and all he was sure—struck down in one lightning act of might. It was truly beautiful in its power and terrible in its swiftness.

And he had been spared.

"Beautiful," he whispered, the emotion slipping from him as though he were seeing his newborn child for the first time.

His pain all but forgotten now, Byron tilted his head to the left, scanning the full extent of the aftermath of the crash, absorbing the grandeur of the mass of destroyed vehicles that stretched off into the distance on either side of the highway. It was horrifyingly arousing. That heap of twisted, burning metal, of smashed, burnt, and crushed lives. It made him feel alive.

The pain in his leg began to fade, inconsequential when compared to the ecstatic excitement coursing through his veins. He felt giddy, but this time it was with joy.

A giggle of wicked pleasure rose to his lips.

"How are you feeling?" said a voice off to his right. He whipped his head in the direction of the sound.

Nearby, a man in his forties, stocky with a mass of disheveled hair, stood staring out at the concrete river of devastation, his arms folded across his chest. When he spoke, he did not turn his head to look at Byron; instead, he calmly continued to watch the freeway.

"I have been given a sign," the stranger continued before Portia could answer him. The stranger turned to face the injured killer, the white clerical collar of a priest clearly visible now around his throat. Regarding the exhausted Byron Portia with cool, piercing, intelligent eyes, he raised his right arm and extended a long, well-manicured forefinger directly at him. "And you, you will be my first disciple."

"Who are you?" Portia asked, his voice a barely audible croak over the crackling of the freeway fire.

"My name," the stranger said, "is Father Edward Pike."

THIRTEEN

It did not take long for Jim Baston to realize that it was going to take a lot more than the thirty minutes he had originally estimated to get to West Hills. He had managed just over two miles so far, and that had already taken him over twenty minutes.

The Valley was a battleground.

Cars littered the roads. Some were smashed beyond recognition, just smoking heaps or burned-out wrecks. The majority seemed to have been abandoned, as though the drivers had suddenly vaporized into thin air, forcing Jim to pull off the road and onto the sidewalk to avoid them.

Pedestrians were everywhere, some walking dazed in the street, others screaming at each other over collisions or stepping in front of his car as if he did not exist. Most had a stunned, uncomprehending look, and it seemed like they could barely manage to put one foot in front of the other. He saw a couple of cops looking as confused as the rest.

Other, less scrupulous individuals seemed to have grasped the situation quickly. More than once he saw the smashed windows of stores, merchandise scattered across the pavement as looters took advantage of the confusion, store alarms ringing shrilly in an attempt to alert emergency services that either didn't care or no longer existed.

He had passed several bodies lying in the street, sprawled in twisted poses, congealed blood pooling around them, flies already buzzing expectantly around the still forms. Those unlucky pedestrians who had found themselves crossing the street when the event occurred, he guessed.

Farther on, Jim passed a European-style sidewalk café, the kind where patrons could sit at tables on the sidewalk, beneath large colorful umbrellas, while they sipped cappuccinos and lattes. A large tow truck had plowed through the sea of umbrellas, cutting a swath of destruction, sending the people sitting in their shade and the tables in all directions. The truck had continued on its deadly journey into the café, until finally it had come to rest against an interior wall. The truck's rear end jutted obscenely from the café's front, the tail hook still swinging gently back and forth. Jim counted nine bodies lying in the heat, scattered like pins in a bowling alley.

Several other vehicles were trying to make their way through the wandering jaywalkers and abandoned vehicles, but it was like trying to drive through a Middle Eastern bazaar—painfully slow and ultimately futile.

The throng of humanity became steadily worse the farther into the Valley he drove. Jim slowed the car to a crawl and, finally, to a standstill. If he kept trying to maneuver the car through the crowd, he would hit someone for sure, and anyway, at the rate he was traveling he would be better off traveling the rest of the way on foot. It might not be safer, but he would make quicker time, and Jim had a nagging feeling time was definitely of the essence today.

He pulled the car as close to the sidewalk as he could, grabbed the cell phone from the backseat, where he had tossed it, and stuffed it in his trouser pocket. Jim checked his position on the GPS one final time, making a mental note of the roads he would need to take to get to the house, before he put the car in park and stepped out.

***

Rising high above the stores and tree line, the plume of smoke snaked ominously into the air, a dark harbinger of doom. Jim felt a growing unease creep over him, setting his skin tingling and his pulse throbbing, as he realized the smoke and fire emanated from ahead of him, directly in his path.

Outside a deserted Ralphs food store on Roscoe Boulevard, a soft drink machine thrummed in the growing heat. In the shade of the store's overhang, he fished through his pockets until he found what he was looking for. He dropped the seven quarters into the machine and selected spring water. The plastic bottle of H_2O rumbled through the machine's metal innards and fell into the dispensing slot. He took a long swig from the icy bottle and felt the water ease the stinging sensation at the back of his throat.

The air was thick and heavy, the sun just a dim light shrouded in the blackness of the smoke. The temperature was rising, and in the near distance Jim could now clearly see the flames of multiple fires. Houses and trees burned brightly and intensely, the flames dancing like crazy imps at the gates of hell, free to run rampant with no fire service to check their spread.

The crowds began to grow thinner as he reached the edge of the Valley's commercial area and headed into the residential section of the San Fernando Valley. A mile later and the crowds had evaporated altogether, driven away by the poisonous air and flames.

Jim did not miss the panicked eyes and the thousand-yard stares of his fellow humans. He was glad to be alone again, happy to be making headway without the hindrance of the zombies the majority of the human race seemed to have become.

He began making better time, and his confidence surged as he began to recognize the occasional street name. There was a cigar store on the junction of Fallbrook and Saticoy, its large walk-in humidor a regular hangout for Jim when he had lived here, and across from it a Taco Bell—Lark's favorite fast food. He had passed by both as he made his way west along Saticoy. He knew he was less than a mile from his home when he finally crossed over Woodlake.

There had been a strip mall set back from the street at the junction of Saticoy and Woodlake. It had contained the usual smattering of convenience stores: a large supermarket, a hair salon, a discount liquor store, and a gas station.

That was all gone.

In its place a smoking gash ran diagonally across Saticoy, slashing through Woodlake, a smoldering pit thirty feet deep and at least the same distance across that extended into the flaming ruins of what had once been a gated housing community. Now it was so much rubble and broken timber.

The tail fin of a Boeing 787 Dreamliner jutted incongruously out of the remains of the food store, its charred skin blackened and smoking. Jim guessed from the devastated housing development and fields of fire he could see in the distance that the jet had collided with the ground right here, tearing away the tail section and sending the body of the plane careening off, before finally coming to rest somewhere west of the housing community that now lay in ruins.

It had all but obliterated the road ahead of him. If he wanted to reach his home, he was going to have to get across the massive trench running between him and his destination. He could walk around it, but that would add too much time to his trip, and the fire was spreading rapidly. If he didn't get to the house soon, then there might not be a house left—assuming it hadn't already been consumed by the fire.

His decision made, Jim moved to the edge of the pit and peered cautiously over the edge. A chunk of blacktop broke free under his weight and slipped into the hole, escorted to the bottom by a cascade of gravel. He stumbled back, barely in time to save himself from following the rubble into the crevice.

"Shit!" he said, scuttling away from the lip of the pit on all fours.

Heart thumping audibly in his chest, Jim waited for his pulse to slow before flipping over onto his belly and sliding carefully forward until he was able to look safely down into the pit.

On the opposite wall of the fissure, halfway down the wall of dirt, a broken water main spewed a torrent of water the ten remaining feet to the bottom of the pit. Below, a muddy lagoon had formed, and a river of brown mud sluiced off downhill. The action of the water against the dirt walls was rapidly eating away at the soft earth, forming an overhang in the fissure. The outcrop of road did not look like it would support the weight of the ground above it for very much longer.

As Jim watched, assessing his next move, a six-foot-long piece of the overhang collapsed with a giant splash into the water below, sending waves rolling downstream and splashing him with dirty droplets of muddy water. The gap was gradually increasing in width as the water eroded the sides. If he was going to get across, he was going to have to do it now before it became too large.

Pushing himself a little farther over the edge, Jim looked down at the wall of mud and clotted earth on his side. He could make out the sister piece of fractured water piping below. It jutted out from the wall of earth about a foot, enough for him to get at least one of his feet onto. A slight incline in the pit wall would allow him to slide down and onto the exposed piece of pipe.

Jim said a quiet prayer that it would hold his weight and swung himself around until his legs dangled over the edge, flipped himself onto his belly, and began to inch out. When his midriff reached the lip of the fissure, he dropped his legs until he felt his toes rubbing against the loose soil. He kicked at the wall, chipping away chunks of earth to create toeholds he was confident would support at least some of his weight while he shifted his torso out far enough to see whether he was positioned correctly over the pipe.

Pebbles of gravel sliced at him as he slid his upper body cautiously over the edge. He glanced down; his left foot was positioned directly over the pipe, about four or five feet above it. This next part was the difficult bit. His nerves sang their discomfort as he slowly allowed his body to drop down, his elbows taking the majority of his weight, until his arms were fully extended. At this point the only thing stopping him from falling the remaining ten feet to the floor of the pit below him was his tenuous hold on the thin crust of road above him.

Less than a few hours ago, he was talking on the phone to his literary agent. If someone had told him back then he would soon be attempting the equivalent of a rock climb while trying to avoid a fiery death, he would have laughed in their face. But with his newly regained vigor, Jim felt as though he could achieve virtually anything; he let go of his handhold.

His knees scraped painfully against the sides of the pit as he slid downwards. He felt a nail on his right hand fray and break as he tried to grab at the wall to slow his slide. He felt his right foot connect with the pipe, and his downward slide stopped abruptly and jarringly.

Jim's breathing came in quick, ragged bursts. He buried his face into the cool soil, and a bitter laugh escaped him. He was halfway down. Glancing down to his right, he could see that the wall of the gully dropped away sharply toward its base. He cautiously repositioned his right leg on the pipe, maneuvering his body until he faced the opposite wall.

Crouching down as carefully as he could, Jim swung his right foot off the pipe and allowed his hands to take the weight of his body as he lowered himself to a sitting position. Then, slipping himself slowly off the pipe, he slid the remaining few feet down to the bottom of the scree-strewn slope.

From the bottom of the massive furrow, the walls looked a great deal higher than the thirty feet he had estimated. Looking up at the sky, filigreed with gray strings of smoke, he imagined this was what it would look like to gaze up from one's grave. Dismissing the morbid thought from his mind, he turned his attention to escaping from the gully.

The lagoon of water was growing rapidly, fed by the waterfall cascading down the side of the furrow from the broken water pipe. The ground along the edge of the newly formed stream was sodden, waterlogged, and his shoes sank deep into the muck, up to his ankles.

Jim stopped to catch his breath, and he felt the mud sucking at his feet, pulling him deeper. This quagmire would drag him down until he had no chance of escape if he didn't keep moving, and then this hole really would become his grave.

His foot came free with an obscene slurp as he pulled it out of the mud. If he headed upstream away from the source of the water, he would eventually reach dry ground. Trying to stay as far up the crumbling bank of earth as he could, Jim edged his way along the margin of the growing pool of water. In the minute or so he had been at the bottom of the pit, the water level had increased by over two inches, eating away at the thin vein of flat ground he had expected to be able to use to move freely upstream. Now the water was lapping at his knees, and with each step his foot slipped down the loose scrabble of earth and deeper into the water.

Finally, he stepped onto firmer ground. His feet and lower legs were saturated and frozen, his sodden trousers flapping like rain-soaked flags as he rubbed furiously, trying to get some feeling back into the blocks of ice he had once called legs.

As feeling returned, Jim began moving farther upstream, away from the cataract of water. Up ahead he could make out a feature he spotted when he first reconnoitered the fissure from up top. A large piece of the road had collapsed, due, he surmised, to some underground geological abnormality exposed when the jet had carved out the land.

The collapsed road had formed a steep ramp from the bottom of the pit, and, standing at its base, he could see it reached all the way up to ground level and the newly formed corniche.

The giant chunk of tarmac and bituminous solids had broken into three pieces and now formed a set of giant steps Jim was sure he could use to climb up to the road. Reaching one mud-splattered hand toward the first handhold he could reach, he began to pull himself skyward.

***

A billowing gust of wind almost knocked Jim back down over the precipice as he tried to pull himself up onto the safety of the road, but with a final effort he threw one leg up onto the asphalt and pulled the rest of his body up after it.

He was exhausted, and for a couple of minutes he just lay at the side of the precipice, feeling the warm road beneath his back. The wind was beginning to pick up, and smoke from the fire swirled and eddied through the disturbed air above him.

A sickening sense of urgency spurred Jim on. The wind would drive the fire with even greater ferocity. If the house was still standing, then he had to get to it quickly. He was sure he had very little time left.

Gathering what was left of his strength, Jim pulled himself to his feet and began jogging the remaining distance to his home.

***

The crash had spared his home—barely.

The airliner had come down a hundred yards south of the house on Keswick Street, and as he made the final turn onto the cul-de-sac, he could see the house was still standing. It had not escaped scot-free, however. The big oak that had for years stood in the front garden had toppled over, smashing into the front part of the house where the upstairs den had been, removing a portion of the roof in the process and exposing the interior of the room. The trunk of the tree lay diagonally across the front of the house, blocking both the garage doors and entrance into the home.

Glowing ash floated on the currents of warmed air like deadly orange fireflies. Jim could see smoke rising from many places on the shingle roof of his home, but there didn't seem to be any fires burning from within. He offered a silent thank-you to whatever God was watching over him.

His neighbors' homes had not been so lucky. They burned fiercely, adding to the smoke hanging heavy as morning London fog in the air. The heat from the fires was incredible, the air virtually unbreathable.

He soaked the now soot-caked bandana in his remaining water and tossed the empty bottle aside. Pushing the wet cloth to his mouth, he dashed toward the house.

***

A heat-induced current of hot air wailed down the cul-de-sac. It turned the narrow street into a wind tunnel, dragging twirling eddies of smoke over the road. A bright-yellow inflatable emergency life raft had caught on the lamppost outside his house. It danced and jittered like a hanged man as the wind whipped against it.

A first-class passenger seat from the downed aircraft had come to rest in the middle of the street. Upright and incongruous, the seat's decapitated, business-suited occupant was still strapped securely to it, but Jim barely registered the body as he jogged toward the house, swiping at the burning ash smoldering in his hair, singeing his scalp.

Standing on the concrete driveway leading up to the three-car garage, Jim yelled, "Simone. Are you in there?" His voice was hoarse, brittle, and barely audible over the roar of the fires consuming the other homes on the street.

There was no answer.

The trunk of the fallen oak tree completely obscured the front door to the house. He would have to either climb over it or go around the back and get into the house that way. If the back door was locked, then he would lose time he did not have. Deciding a direct approach was the best, he pushed his arms through the thicket of branches, forcing them aside as best he could. Grabbing a thick branch, Jim used it to pull himself up and onto the trunk of the tree. Trying not to poke an eye out on one of the innumerable tiny spiked twigs that protruded at every conceivable angle, he tucked his chin against his chest and pushed through the remaining web of tangled branches until he could finally squeeze himself onto the porch.

The front door was ajar, knocked open by an eight-foot-long tree limb that jutted into the brown-marbled entranceway of the house. Easing between the door frame and branch, he stepped over the threshold and into the house.

The thing he had always loved about California-style homes was the openness. It created a spacious, airy atmosphere he had always found welcoming. If it hadn't been for the tragedy that had taken place here, then he imagined he, Simone . . . and Lark would still have been living here well into their old age. *Don't delude yourself*, his inner voice said, but he ignored it, choosing instead the familiar deception that everything had been fine between him and Simone.

The foyer, lined by a teak banister, led into a living room that swept back toward a swing door, which in turn led into the expansive kitchen. From the kitchen you could step through into the family room. A generous stairwell curved up to the second floor and the master bedroom, a spacious den, an office, and . . .

And Lark's room.

Spacious and light in his memory, the house now seemed claustrophobic and dark. The smoke flooding in through the open front door gave it a gray, unreal feel.

"Hello?" Jim yelled as he walked into the living room. "Is there anybody in here?"

Silence.

"Simone! Are you here?" And then after a pause he added, "It's Jim."

Still nothing.

Moving quickly from room to room, he checked each for signs Simone had been in the house when the event had happened. The lower floor was in order except for a few magazines scattered carelessly on the glass coffee table of the living room. There was no sign of her in the backyard or in the swimming pool, so he made his way up the stairs to the top landing.

Jim checked the office first, then the master bedroom. Both were empty, with no obvious signs anyone had recently occupied them.

The upstairs den was a wreck.

The felled tree had smashed away the majority of the right side of the room, opening up a gaping hole in the floor and exposing the garage below. The L-shaped sofa they had used to watch movies on a giant plasma screen on the opposite wall had tipped into the hole, one end pointing in the direction of the exposed sky and the other resting on the concrete garage floor below.

Jim edged near to the lip of the hole in an attempt to peer down into the garage, but the fractured floorboards squeaked in protest, sagging as he stepped on them. Made wary by his earlier experience on the street, he backed away from the edge.

That left just Lark's room.

He did not want to have to look in this last room. The thought of viewing his child's bedroom was the first thing he could honestly say frightened him on this strangest of days. But he had to check, had to make sure Simone was not in there. Mentally bracing himself as best he could, Jim opened the door to his dead child's bedroom and stepped inside.

FOURTEEN

They were arguing again. Simone had started as soon as he told her that he had to go to the lab.

"But it's Saturday, for God's sake. Can't it wait until Monday?" Her voice sounded whiny to Jim, but he knew it was really pleading.

"We hardly see you as it is. Please . . . Just for today can't we be a family?" she continued as tears began to run down her cheeks.

Jim had almost agreed . . . almost.

How different his life would have turned out if he had just shrugged, taken off his jacket, and said "Sure, love. You're right" and parked his ass on the sofa for the rest of the weekend.

But of course he hadn't. Day late and a dollar short.

Instead, he mumbled an excuse about the lab needing him and headed toward the door. Toward his mistress—his profession.

And that's when Simone got up in his face. Screaming at him that he was tearing their family apart, that he cared more about his precious lab than he did his own wife and child. What about Lark? She was growing up without a father. Didn't he realize what he was doing to them both?

He had protested . . . weakly, his excuses melting under the intensity of her words. Finally, he yelled some dumb response back at her and stormed out.

His Model X was sitting patiently in the garage, and he angrily got behind the wheel.

What the hell gave her the right to get on him like that? Who did she think she was? Didn't she realize *he had responsibilities, for Christ's sake?*

Jim pressed the garage door opener button and waited until he heard the metallic thunk of the roller door locking into place overhead. He slammed the car into reverse, so angry he didn't even bother to check his rearview mirror.

There was a dull, soft thud and rattle of metal. The car bucked as the rear left tire rolled over something.

"Jesus Christ," he shouted angrily, banging his clenched fists against the steering wheel as he pushed the gear lever into park.

Now he was pissed. Lark had left her bike in the drive again. *How many times did he have to tell the kid not to leave the* goddamn *bike in the* goddamn *drive?*

The door from the garage into the laundry room flew open. Simone stood in the doorway, her face a mask of anger—she always had liked to get in the last word. Bracing himself for the torrent of abuse at this, his latest screwup, he saw instead her eyes move from him to the car and finally down to the ground, the stream of vitriol perched on her lips left unspoken.

Simone's face had paled in an instant. One second flushed and ruddy with anger, her face was, the next moment, as white as a winter morning. Her facial muscles seemed to lose all elasticity as her jaw fell open, leaving her mouth sagging in a frozen O.

Her scream was silent, but it was there.

"Lark," she had finally choked, her hands flying to cover her mouth as if she could pluck her child's name from the air and cancel what she saw.

Jim looked slowly toward the driver's-side mirror. He could see the handlebars of Lark's bike protruding from under the tire, twisted and bent, the pink tassels he had fixed to each handgrip still swinging gently back and forth.

A little arm protruded from the mangled remains of his daughter's bike, pale and twisted at an awful angle. A large pool of blood was spreading slowly across the gray, leaf-strewn concrete drive.

He looked away then, tore his eyes from his child to stare instead at his wife. Her eyes were blank, but a quizzical expression moved over her face like molten wax.

"What did you do to my baby?" she asked, her voice hushed to a whisper.

The question had haunted him for the rest of his life.

What did you do, James? What did you do?

There was an inquest, of course. Both parents exonerated of any blame. However, Jim knew the truth. He saw compassion in everybody's eyes, but when he looked into his own all he saw was guilt.

Before the accident, he and Simone had been teetering on the edge of divorce, but for a while, strangely, the death of Lark brought them closer. But when the tears finally dried up and he still could not assuage the burning sense of guilt that throbbed in his heart, he started to drink. He found the bottle gave him some solace, and as each day passed he realized he no longer needed his wife; his newfound friend would do him just fine.

Yup! With the help of his namesake Dr. James Beam, he could anesthetize himself against the pain and, finally, against all of life itself.

Six months after the accident, he didn't go home. Instead, he moved into their cabin at Shadow Mountain Lake and hired an attorney to file for divorce.

At the hearing, Simone had pleaded with him not to go through with it. She told him she knew it was an accident, as much her fault as his, and she knew how much stress he was under. If it wasn't for her insisting on him staying, the accident would never have happened. Did he see what that meant? That it was as much her fault as it was his. He ignored her plea to give their marriage one last try, and just like that they were divorced.

FIFTEEN

Jim stood outside the door to his daughter's room; his hand was shaking visibly as he reached for the knob. The guilt of almost twenty years had come rushing back to him. As he eased the door open, he half expected to see his daughter sitting on her bed, dead eyes peering out from behind a matted curtain of blood-encrusted blond hair, to hear her say through a mouth clogged and matted with gore, "Daddy, why did you kill me?"

But Lark's room was empty.

After the accident they had cleared the room out. They donated most of her toys and clothes to a charity, and the rest had gone to family and friends as mementos. Simone had objected at first, but eventually she had submitted to him, and they had removed all that had made the room Lark's. He scrubbed it clean of any memory of her in the vain hope that removing the constant reminders of his little girl might in turn help him overcome his grief and self-loathing.

Standing here now, her room restored and the accident still so far away yet so keenly remembered, brought back the aching loss of his daughter. Her bed neatly made, a cuddle of soft toys collected on the pillows, her books and DVDs resting in racks against one wall. Her iPod speakers sat high on a shelf; below it, her TV.

It was all so . . . pristine, so untouched—it was Lark's.

He slammed the door shut, unable to face this particular ghost from his past. Now was not the time, he told himself. The voice in the back of his mind whispered back, *When will it ever be time, Jim-boy?*

He pushed the thought aside. What he had to concentrate on now—what was *important*—was finding Simone. She wasn't at the house, so where would she most likely be? She would try to get to someplace safe.

If she had been anywhere near their home, then she would have seen the devastation and gone elsewhere, unless of course she was so close she had become a victim of the crash herself, engulfed by the fireball that had surely accompanied the unscheduled landing of the massive airliner in the middle of their housing development.

He could not allow himself to think that. She *had* to be alive, and he *had* to find her.

Simone's parents! Of course, they lived in Thousand Oaks. Maybe she was visiting them. She used to hop over there most weekends when they were still married. Perhaps she had made it to them. It made sense. It would be the logical place for her to go, he supposed. After all, he and Simone were divorced, would be divorced, or whatever. This flip-flop of time was confusing enough without having to think about present and future tense.

On the off chance cell service might be working again, he activated the smartphone, scrolled through the list of names until he found the number for Simone's parents, and hit the "Send" button. He got the same "No Service" message as before. In the master bedroom he tried the phone next to their bed—nothing. It was dead too.

Thousand Oaks was over eighteen miles away. It would probably take him a day or more to walk it, and with the current state of madness there was no guarantee he would make it alive. He needed transportation, and he knew exactly where to find it.

**

They had bought the bikes the previous year with a plan to take rides on the weekends up into the nearby San Fernando Mountains. There were so many great trails lacing through the San Fernandos and surrounding hills, but for some reason the weekend excursions never materialized. Jim knew why—he was just *too* busy at the lab—and the bikes had stayed in their racks. Simone had talked about selling them, but he had promised her they *would* use them—*someday* they would.

The bikes were stored in metal overhead racks attached to the ceiling of the garage. When the tree had fallen into the den above, part of the upper floor had collapsed down into the garage below, burying the three bikes under a six-foot-high mound of splintered wood, stucco, and furniture.

Jim picked up a pair of leather gloves from the shelf where Simone kept her gardening tools and rose food, and began digging through the debris.

The heat was beginning to take its toll. His muscles ached with each piece of debris he moved from the pile to the clear side of the garage. He was covered in grime and dirt; dust had crusted inside his nostrils and scoured his dry eyes. He was exhausted, but within minutes a glint of chrome rewarded his toil. Kneeling down on the pile of rubble, Jim hurriedly threw the remaining debris aside, uncovering Simone's bike still attached to its storage rack, its four fastening pins locked to the remnants of the plasterboard that had once been the ceiling.

With a final tug, he pulled the bike free of the mangled storage rack and hefted the scratched and bent bicycle over to the opposite side of the garage.

A broken floorboard had punched through the spokes of the bike's badly buckled rear wheel, ripping them from the wheel's rim. Now they protruded outward like the staked ribs of a vampire. The front tire was flat, and with the back wheel so badly damaged, the bike was useless. He would just have to hope for better luck with his own bicycle. Jim leaned the bike against his workbench, then headed back over to the pile of debris.

His bike was in a little better condition, and by the time he pulled it free of the remaining wreckage he could see the front tire had ragged gashes in several places, and the front fork, instead of jutting forward as it should, now slanted back until it almost touched the pedals. Other than that the bike looked to be in working condition.

Between the two damaged bikes, Jim realized he had one working one; it would just take a little cannibalization. Rummaging through a toolbox, he pulled out a couple of wrenches that looked like they would fit the locking nuts keeping the wheels fixed in place. He released the front wheel from Simone's bike and switched it out with the one from his. Next he grabbed the hand pump and started inflating the flat tire.

Ten minutes later—and much to his relief—the tire remained inflated.

***

The fastest route to Thousand Oaks from where he was would be via the 101 freeway west, and as Jim Baston headed onto the on-ramp that fed off Valley Circle Drive and onto the 101, he could see it wasn't going to be an easy ride. Jim guessed he had probably about an hour of light left. The first hint of dusk was already discoloring the sky, turning the blue to a deep purple.

Completely blocked by a line of abandoned cars that snaked around the curling on-ramp and down to the freeway below, Jim left the road and pedaled his bike up onto the grass verge running alongside the road, skirting around the crush of vehicles.

Things were worse on the freeway.

Cresting the gentle rise of the on-ramp, he brought the bike to a hasty stop, gazing out over a sea of glittering quicksilver.

The ghostly light of the setting sun glinted off the roofs of thousands of crushed, burnt-out and abandoned cars, trucks, and big rigs, lending an eerie orange cast to the terrible panorama that shimmered and stirred in the heat haze floating above the river of destruction. The smell of melted plastic—like toy soldiers left too long under the midday sun—wafted to him on the breeze.

"Jesus wept."

It was the most terrifying thing Jim had ever laid eyes on; this total annihilation of thousands of vehicles spoke more poignantly to him of the frailty of human life than all the bodies and devastation he had seen that day. It reminded him of news reports he'd seen when he was a kid during the Persian Gulf War. Toward the end of the war, the coalition air force had bombed the Iraqi army as it retreated along the open road to Basra. The resulting annihilation had left miles of eviscerated, burned-out vehicles. The charred bodies of Iraqi soldiers had been barely distinguishable as having once been human.

The 101 freeway had become a road straight to hell.

Drivers had found themselves suddenly and inexplicably behind the wheels of vehicles speeding along some long-forgotten highway on trips that had been almost a quarter century distant, for reasons that had become ancient history. Only an instant earlier they had been busy getting on with their everyday lives twenty-four years into the future. Caught utterly by surprise—and with the advances in vehicle AI safety protocols that would virtually eliminate highway accidents still a distant invention—those unfortunate enough to find themselves in their vehicles on this fateful day had attempted to avoid other cars and trucks. Most had probably instinctively hit the brakes or simply waited for their vehicles' nonexistent AIs to kick in and bring them to safe stops. Instead, they had careened across each other's lanes and this . . . this carnage was the result. Fires had erupted and swept rapidly over the vehicles, with many of their occupants still trapped inside and unable to escape from the oncoming firestorm.

Maybe Simone is in one of these tin-can coffins.

No! He could not contemplate that. If she was, he would never know.

It had taken years of pain and denial, the mental equivalent of self-flagellation throughout those years, but finally he realized Simone had been right. Consumed by his own anguish and self-pity over the death of Lark, he had used all that negative emotion as a wedge to drive Simone and himself apart. *Youth is wasted on the young.* Boy, was that ever right, but now he had a second chance to prove he was wrong, and he *knew* that Simone was not one of the dead who lay in this vast metal tomb.

She was alive—she had to be—and he was going to find her.

***

Whispers!

The mass of twisted metal had found a voice, and now it murmured constantly to Jim as he rode his bike between overturned campers and the shells of burned-out cars.

Beneath the lavender California sky, the cars had begun to finally cool. As they surrendered their heat to the evening air, their metal bodies began to creak, squeak, and crack. Each expansion and contraction of the daylong-heated metal sent a million vowels and consonants soughing and sighing into the air like dying butterflies.

It was an uncanny sound. To Jim Baston's exhausted mind, it sounded as though the occupants of the cars were chattering in their metal coffins, an eerie susurration of which he was certain he was the subject.

Who are you?... Help us!... Why did you live? the dead whispered.

The questions skittered through the air to him, a mirror of his own exhausted mind's thoughts of why he had survived when so many others had not.

He avoided looking into the brutalized wrecks after the first few; the seared bodies of the occupants were mostly unrecognizable, the fire having thoroughly removed any trace of humanity from its victims. The remains were naked, sexless lumps of charcoal resting on beds of springs or melted into dashboards . . . for the most part. Here and there a glimpse of a bloated arm jutting through a window space or a badly burned torso illustrated the fact that not all of the day's victims had died quickly or quietly in their vehicles.

The stench was truly awful, detectable even through his muck-caked nostrils. The pungent, reeking miasma of dead humans and dead machines hung in the noxious air, overwhelming his senses. It seemed that in death the fusion of burned human flesh and boiled bodily fluids had comingled with the oil and gasoline, melted rubber and seared metal to form a smell that had never before existed on this planet; it was the stench of defeat, of the destruction of mankind and its servile machine culture.

***

The sun had finally dipped below the horizon. A pair of sun dogs stretched skyward on either side of it like lopsided rainbow guardians of that dimming orb. Jim watched as it sank without a trace, replaced by the crescent of a skull-white new moon, the setting sun's distant orange glow swapped for the cadmium lambency of the freeway gantry lights.

Ahead of him still lay a freeway littered with vehicles of every size and description, scattered haphazardly across the lanes at every conceivable angle. Sedans, tankers, coupes, pickups, vans, SUVs, car carriers, motor homes packed so tightly together in places Jim could not tell what the original vehicles had been.

It was impossible to pedal in a straight line because of the sheer number of vehicles blanketing the road. The machines had spilled over into the central median, crashing through the separating barriers. They had overturned in the breakdown lanes that skirted both edges of the freeway, many even lurching over onto the grass verges and through the fences designed to block the daily noise of traffic from the businesses that lined the freeway's shoulders.

Jim found himself zigzagging through the maze of metal as though it were an obstacle course. The road was scattered with small pieces of detritus, sharp pieces of metal that ranged from tiny slivers to parts of engines and other *things* he tried to avoid looking too closely at. In the past few hours since leaving the house in the Valley, he had dismounted several times and been forced to carry the bike rather than risk a puncture.

All it's going to take is one of those metal splinters in a tire and I'm walking the rest of the way, he thought as he applied his brakes, slowing the bike to a crawl to negotiate a particularly hazardous stretch of road. Once clear, Jim remounted and began pedaling.

The road ahead became suddenly and completely blocked by a burned-out, jackknifed big rig; its trailer lay on its back, wheels pointing into the air. Littering the road around the truck was a wall of decimated cars concertinaed into so much scrap metal. The hill of vehicles blocked all of the lanes ahead. Other drivers, not caught in the initial carnage of the crash, had swerved left and right in an effort to avoid the barrier. Their vehicles blocked both the breakdown lane and grass verge as well as the median, so he couldn't simply maneuver around it.

It was no problem. He'd already encountered similar accident-induced barriers. All he had to do was dismount, shoulder the bike, and climb over the mountain of metal as carefully as he could. In the twilight darkness cast by the freeway lighting, he was going to have to be extra careful. He didn't want to fall and break anything out here. Help would never arrive.

Jim glanced at his wristwatch as he jumped off the bike and prepared to climb. The display glowed 20:35. He had made good time considering the circumstances, helped by a strangely deserted stretch of road along the Agoura Hills section of the freeway.

The last sign he had passed had indicated he was only a mile or so from the Greenwich Village turnoff, which put him close to three miles away from his destination, and Simone's parents. They lived a few blocks down on El Dorado Drive. If he took the East Janss Road exit, he would be there in an hour or so.

A man waited in the road ahead of Jim.

He looked to be in his twenties, dressed in a business suit that fit his linebacker-sized frame just a little too tightly. The suit was expensive looking but torn in several places along one arm and covered in spots of dirt and oil and blood. The man had fashioned a tourniquet out of his equally expensive-looking silk tie and fastened it around his left calf just above a large black stain of dried blood.

The man held a baseball bat.

Jim lowered the bike cautiously from his shoulder as they stared at each other across the ten feet of asphalt separating them.

Jim broke the silence. "Are you okay, buddy?" he asked with as much concern to his voice as he could muster.

The suit looked hard at Jim, summing him up. *Gauging my threat level*, Jim thought.

When the man spoke, it was in a voice thick with Southern syllables. "Give me the bike," he drawled, making the word "bike" sound more like "bark."

Jim shook his head. "Can't do that. I have to get to my ex-wife. I have some water. I can—"

The stranger covered the distance between them with lightning speed. Jim barely managed to duck as the man savagely swung the baseball bat through the air where his head had just been.

Christ! This guy is going to kill me over my bike, Jim thought as he ducked the blow. *Is this what it's come down to?*

The momentum of the missed strike propelled the stranger forward, past Jim. The guy had put all his energy into a one-shot deal to get hold of some transportation, he guessed. That wound on his leg must have sucked a lot of the energy from him. The assailant now stood panting and gasping from the exertion of the attack, his bloodshot eyes lupine in their wariness of him.

Jim had dropped the bike instinctively when he leaped away from the incoming bat, and now the attacker had managed to maneuver himself between Jim and it.

He could just leave the bike, give it over to this stranger, and avoid anybody getting hurt, but who knew where he would be able to lay his hands on another? Bikes would be like gold dust for as long as the freeways and roads were blocked.

"I don't want to have to hurt you," Jim said, and then added, "But I will if I have to."

The suit must have thought this was funny because he grinned insanely, raised the bat to his shoulder, and stepped up to the bike. He spread his feet wide and waited in a stance that clearly said, *Try it.*

The guy easily had fifty pounds on Jim, plus he had a weapon. Of course, it looked like his attacker was injured, but Jim couldn't be sure how debilitating that might be.

Jim scanned the ground around him, searching for anything he might be able to use to defend himself. The remains of a VW Beetle rested beneath the overturned body of an SUV, its domed roof crushed almost beyond recognition, its neo-hippy owner now surely nothing more than pulp behind the compacted steering wheel. The Beetle had collided with the upturned truck that blocked most of the lanes, but it had been in a skid when it hit, because the car had come to rest sideways against the truck. The chrome front bumper had been torn from one of its mountings by the impact and now lay glinting in the gloom, beckoning to Jim.

Jim took a step sideways. The thug in the suit matched him but didn't move away from the bike. Certain he wasn't going to be suddenly battered, Jim backed the few remaining feet to the VW. The suit didn't move, guarding his prize like a lion who had just stolen a kill from a hyena.

Casting a nervous glance over his shoulder, Jim turned his attention to the bumper. The impact of the crash had torn one of the metal L-brackets holding the bumper to the car's chassis free. That side now rested loosely against the ground, but the second bracket was still fixed firmly by its welded joint. It was going to take the application of some brute force to separate it.

With a final look over his shoulder to make sure his attacker wasn't going to jump on the bike and attempt to ride off into the darkness, Jim braced his foot against the hood of the Beetle, grabbed the bumper, and pulled. The already stressed and twisted metal of the mounting squealed and screeched its resistance, but Jim felt it give a little. He was going to have to twist the joint to get more torque, and that meant pushing the bumper upward and leaving no question in his assailant's mind he was trying to obtain a weapon.

Squatting down, Jim spread his legs wide for better leverage, took the free end of the bumper in his hands. Pushing from his knees, he wrestled the length of chromed steel toward the sky. As he heaved, he felt the resistance increase, until finally he had to set his feet back a step and lean *into* the upright piece of metal, his entire body weight now pushing against it. With a squeal the bumper slowly began moving toward its apex until, with a final effort from Jim, the metal fixing snapped.

Jim hurtled forward, his right knee catching the curved hood of the destroyed Beetle. He slid off the hood to the ground, sprawling onto the freeway, the now-free bumper clattering and clanging to the ground beside him. Scrambling hastily onto his knees, Jim reached out and grabbed the bumper, hefted it to his chest, and tested its weight. Using the remainder of the bracket fixings as handles, he held the bumper in front of him like a staff as he climbed back to his feet.

A guttural roar alerted Jim to the oncoming stranger as he ran full charge at Jim, the baseball bat in position for a devastating upward strike at Jim's head. Instead, the bat connected with the bumper as Jim thrust it out in front of him. The metal bumper rang violently in his hands as the bat smashed into it, the energy of the impact reverberating painfully through his fingers and up through his elbows to his shoulders.

Jim gasped as pain spiked through his hand. *Dear God, this guy is strong.*

Afraid his traumatized fingers would drop his only protection, Jim switched his hands from the stubby remains of the fixing brackets and took an overhand grip of the curved chrome of the bumper, exposing his fingers to his assailant's bat but assuring his grip.

The suit raised his bat for another attempt, this time an overhead swing. Jim saw the man's eyes flick to his exposed fingers and instinctively knew the next strike would target them. He would be no use in a fight once his protection was gone, and with his fingers broken or crushed the battle would be over and he would be at the mercy of this psychopath.

It was now or never, Jim realized, spying his only chance to end this uneven fight. He feinted a blow toward the man's exposed crotch, and as his attacker instinctively dropped his guard, Jim brought his metal staff around in a powerful sweeping strike to the left side of his head. The makeshift weapon sang in Jim's hands as it connected with a thrumming twang against the attacker's cheekbone. The man's eyes glazed over for a second as he staggered back. Unbelievably, the big man regained his senses almost immediately and, with a shake of his bloodied head, began advancing on Jim once more.

Jim smashed the bumper into his head again, this time sending the dazed man to his knees. Still conscious but swaying like a willow in a breeze, he tried to use the bat as a crutch to push himself back to his feet.

What is this guy made of?

Jim hit him once more with all the remaining strength his arms had. This time the man went down and, with a final groan, stayed down.

A panting, sweating Jim Baston kicked the aluminum bat clanking and echoing away into the wreckage of cars. Gasping for breath, he tossed the dented and bloodied VW bumper to the ground, well out of reach of the felled giant.

Jim tentatively reached out two fingers to touch the unconscious man's neck. Good. There was a pulse. At least he hadn't killed the idiot. There was a lump of purple broken skin on the man's forehead, and blood trickled from a cut across the bridge of his nose.

Reassured that the disabled man wasn't going to be getting up anytime soon, Jim forced his own exhausted body over to where his bike waited and gave it a cursory once-over. It looked okay.

Is this the kind of world I have to look forward to? he wondered. One where a stranger would be willing to beat in his head for a bike.

And with that thought, Jim Baston hefted the bicycle onto his bruised shoulder and began to climb over the ruined truck that lay between him and the remainder of his journey.

SIXTEEN

Thousand Oaks was oddly untouched by the events of the day. As Jim Baston rode his bike onto his ex-wife's parents' street, it struck him how strangely normal it all seemed here. The fires and chaos were distant, there were no wrecked cars, and no bodies lay bloated in the heat.

The streetlights' luminescence pushed back the darkness of the road ahead of Jim, and here and there decorative garden lights, buzzing with moths and bugs, cast their meager glow over deserted driveways and empty garden paths.

Not one light was visible behind the drawn curtains of the houses lining both sides of the cul-de-sac. Jim knew people were home; he could see the occasional twitch of a drape or curtain as the occupants of the single-story homes watched him make his way down El Dorado Drive.

It was so quiet. A sudden hiss and blur of movement sent Jim swerving on unsteady wheels off the sidewalk and back out into the middle of the road. He let out an embarrassed laugh when he realized it was just a lawn sprinkler spluttering into life in a nearby garden. It took all his control not to allow the laughter to disintegrate into tears;

his frayed nerves had been pushed well beyond their breaking point by the day's events, and his grip on reality was tenuous at this point.

Thomas and Jessica Shane lived in an alabaster-white bungalow on a quarter acre of landscaped property at the end of the little street. Jim pulled to a stop outside their home with a squeal of objecting brakes. Resting with one foot on a pedal and the other against the raised curb, he could see the house looked just as he remembered it. Its green lawn was so well manicured it looked sprayed into place rather than planted. The drive leading from the road up to the two-car garage was spotless; the rosebushes and flower beds glowed in luxurious color, accenting the crazy-paved path leading up to their front door. Jessica Shane had always loved her roses. Her death had left a vacuum in all their lives.

When she died, Thomas had been heartbroken, but he had taken on the responsibility of caring for her flowers. He had told Jim in one uncharacteristic moment of vulnerability that it made him feel close to his wife, to be able to continue to do something for her, to continue to raise the flowers she had thought of as her surrogate children.

Jessica had been a truly wonderful woman. When first introduced to her, Jim felt an instant rapport with this gentle, caring woman. He could see where Simone got her beauty. When he heard the news of her death back in '33, it had hit him hard.

Standing on the porch of their home, he could not help but remember the great times they had all shared here before everything went to hell. Jim knew he was lucky: it wasn't every man who could count his ex-wife's parents as friends.

Thomas had carried on his life after his wife's death. But after his Jessica's passing, he had always seemed so much less than whole, and Jim had the impression life no longer held any sparkle for Thomas Shane. Simone had tried to fill the void, but her father had taken her aside one spring day and gently told her that he appreciated her kindness and he loved her very much, but she could not replace the woman he had spent the last thirty-eight years with and she shouldn't try. Simone had been upset, but Thomas hugged her close, knowing the emptiness he felt was as great for his child as it was for him.

Casting those memories aside, Jim rapped gently on the front door and waited, illuminated in the dull glow of the twin lamps fixed to either side of the entranceway. There was no sound or sign of movement from inside the house, so Jim knocked once more, this time a little harder. There was still no answer.

His hand had raised to try one final time when he caught a hint of movement out of the corner of his right eye. The front-room window blinds had moved, he was sure of it, and he turned to face whoever might be watching, stepping a little farther into the light so they would have a clearer view of him.

"Thomas? It's Jim . . . Jim Baston," he hissed, his voice rising barely above a whisper.

The slats of the blinds parted, two fingers pushing them apart. There was a pause while whoever stood on the other side of the window took a good look at him; then the fingers disappeared and Jim heard footsteps coming to the door.

"Step back from the door," demanded a stern voice.

"Thomas, it's Jim," he reiterated.

"I don't care who the hell you *say* you are. Step back from the door."

Jim did as the voice demanded, stepping off the porch and back slightly into the shadows. He heard the sound of dead bolts sliding back on the other side of the door. It opened with a slight creak of unoiled hinges.

Thomas Shane stood in the doorway—at least Jim assumed the dark silhouette was Thomas—but there was no mistaking the outline of the pistol in his hand, leveled at Jim's chest.

"Keep your hands where I can see them," the figure demanded, the usually gentle Midwestern voice now sharp and commanding.

Thomas Shane had been a big man in his prime. He stood six two and had the build of a professional athlete. When Jim had last seen him, he was in his late seventies, and time had taken its toll on the man. But as his ex-father-in-law stepped out of the shadow and into the meager light cast by the exterior lamps, Jim could see that the same strangeness that had returned his own youth had also worked its bizarre magic on Simone's father.

Here stood a much younger Thomas than the one Jim had last seen all those years ago. All signs of decrepitness had evaporated. His bright-blue eyes peered at him from beneath a full head of gray hair. He was still muscular but had a slight paunch that hung over his belt.

Thomas had been a cop in LA for most of his life; he had a quick intelligence and a sharpness of insight, honed by years of life as a street cop, that allowed him to sum up people's characters with a single glance. Jim could feel that intuitive skill at work now as the man's gaze swept over him.

Jim caught sight of his own hands. They were black with soot and grime; blood from a cut on his left hand—he couldn't even remember where he had gotten it—had congealed into an ugly-looking scab. His clothes, he realized, were in no better state, dirty and torn in multiple places, and Jim guessed his face was just as messed up.

"Thomas. It's me, James Baston," he said, then added, "Your son-in-law."

Apart from his vehicle's AI, Jim's father-in-law was the only other person who called him James. Thomas was a stickler for using full names. He hated anyone calling him Tom or Tommy or any other contraction of his own name, and he believed in affording others the same courtesy he demanded. So from the first day they had met, no matter how often he had hinted his father-in-law should call him by his preferred moniker, he had remained James.

Thomas took a step forward and scrutinized Jim even more closely. A smile of recognition spread across the man's face as he closed the gap between them, throwing his arms around him in a bear hug.

"Boy, you look like shit," said the big man, stepping back to regard Jim's disheveled appearance. "Come on into the house. Let's get you cleaned up."

***

"Is Simone here?" asked Jim as he stepped into the Shanes' home.

Thomas regarded Jim with barely hidden unease before answering. "I had hoped she had been with you when . . ."—he seemed to be searching for the right word—"the *miracle* happened."

"No. I found myself in a store. I thought—hoped—that I would find her here with you."

Jim knew his father-in-law was not an overly religious man. Thomas attended church on all the right holidays, had raised his daughter with a respect for religion, but he had encouraged her to find her own path to God. So the use of the word "miracle" to describe the day's events did not jibe with the horror and cataclysm Jim had just experienced on his bike trip.

Thousand Oaks seemed to be an oasis in a sea of destruction; perhaps Thomas had not ventured very far from the house and had not seen the awfulness of the highways or the distant pillars of smoke rising from the burning city of Los Angeles.

Thomas rested his hand reassuringly on Jim's shoulder. "Don't worry. Simone's tough. If she's caught up in all this, she will find a way to get to us."

"I wish I had your optimism. If you had seen what I have today, you might think a little differently," Jim replied, unable to keep the weariness from his voice.

"Come with me. I need to show you something." Thomas led Jim down the hallway and through the kitchen.

"Hello, Jim dear," said a familiar female voice as he stepped into the comfortable living room.

Smiling pensively from her favorite easy chair was Jessica Shane, pale but most definitely alive despite the fact she had been dead for the past twelve years.

SEVENTEEN

Jessica Shane was a strikingly beautiful woman.

As Jim looked disbelievingly at his resurrected mother-in-law, it struck him just how much Simone had resembled her. Same high cheekbones; an oyster-white complexion that needed no blusher or foundation; blond hair that streamed down to her shoulders, a streak of gray adding an elegant look to her already exquisitely chiseled features. Her soft blue eyes seemed able to delve deeply into the souls of those she observed.

Her hug almost crushed his vertebrae to powder. "But," he said. "But—"

"I know. I know," said Jessica, her voice a soothing lullaby as she led a shocked Jim over to the sofa next to her chair. Sitting on the arm of the chair, she grasped Jim's hands in her own and looked deeply into his eyes.

"I know you must have questions for me, Jim. And I know that you are as confused as we are, so why don't we just let Thomas explain what happened?" she said soothingly. "Okay?"

Of all the Kafkaesque events Jim had experienced during his first day in the past, this was the most bizarre, the most personal for him, overwhelming in its emotion. Afraid that if he opened his mouth his brain would simply stall and refuse ever to start again, he contented himself with a simple nod of acquiescence.

Thomas took that as his cue to begin explaining exactly what had happened.

***

"I was at my brother Jed's in Miami," Thomas began. An eddy of emotion rippled beneath the surface of his crisp accounting of the resurrection his long-dead wife, but a smile from Jessica allowed him to gather his emotions before continuing.

"He asks me over there every year, so this year I figured, what the hell? I'd take him up on the invite. The family was all there. We'd seen in the New Year, and I was on my way upstairs to bed." Thomas paused before continuing. Jim knew he was rerunning the split second just before the event through his mind. "Next thing I know, I'm in our back garden, it's the middle of the damn day, and I've got the water hose in my hand and I'm watering Jessie's roses. I always loved to do that, 'cause of that look she'd give me when she saw me doing it. I thought I was dreaming. Thought maybe I'd had a stroke or some mental problem. Thought something might have snapped inside here." Jim tapped his forehead with a finger.

"Anyway, I had no idea how I got back home, but the sun was shining and the bees were buzzing and it was too real for it all to be a dream. And then here she comes, like nothing ever happened, like she'd never . . . never . . ." His words trailed away to nothing, and Jessica reached out her hand, grasping her husband's in her own and giving it a tight squeeze to accompany her reassuring smile.

Thomas squeezed his wife's hand back and wiped away the tears from his eyes. "Anyway, here she comes walking down the path toward her roses like she hadn't been gone more than a minute. I guess that's all it's been for her after all—just a minute. She had this confused, odd expression on her face. She just walks up and stands there, right in front of me, looking straight into my eyes, and I can't say a Goddamn thing."

"His mouth was hanging so far open it about touched the ground," Jessica interjected with a wry smile. "I swear, for a man who has so much to say, he's been pretty damn quiet today."

Thomas continued as if he hadn't heard the fun his wife had just poked at him. "Next thing I know my leg is freezing cold and soaking wet from the damn hose. That snapped me out of my dumbness and I just grabbed her."

"You about broke my back you hugged me so hard, you big brute you," said Jessica, throwing a playful punch at her husband's arm.

"She kept asking me what was wrong over and over. I couldn't speak a damn word—mouth kept moving but no sound came out. She was saying that she didn't remember how she got home. That she might have had a blackout, and all I could do was hug her and cry my damn eyes out like some big old baby."

Jim's father-in-law's voice became sober. "But James, I knew any second I was going to wake up, that I'd find out this was just a dream. But it's not, James, it's a miracle." Thomas's lower jaw quivered. He was on the verge of tears again. "An honest-to-God *miracle*."

Jessica took over: "The last thing I remember before finding myself back at the house was taking the car to do some shopping. It was raining, and I stopped at an intersection about to turn into the lot of the Albertsons out in the village. There was a bang, and I remember being jerked against my seat belt and this . . . screaming sound. Next thing I know, I'm standing in the kitchen peeling carrots, and I don't have a clue how I got there."

Jim could still remember the sheriff's account of the accident that killed Jessica Shane: the driver of an SUV lost control as he approached the set of traffic lights where Jessica had pulled to a stop. The SUV hydroplaned on the rain-covered surface right into the back of her Toyota with so much force he knocked Jessica's smaller car into the center of the intersection. She was hit driver-side on by an 18-wheeler doing fifty plus—at least ten miles over the legal limit, the sheriff had explained. She didn't stand a chance.

Died instantly, the sheriff had assured him.

Jim went with Thomas to identify her body. He volunteered to make the identification himself at the morgue, but Thomas said he had to do it; otherwise, he would spend the rest of his life never really knowing if it was his sweet Jessica or not. The sheriff's deputy who accompanied them had already warned Jim it might be best for him to make the ID rather than the deceased's husband, and he tried his best to persuade Thomas, but the older man was having none of it.

He'd escorted his father-in-law to the viewing gallery, and the attendant pulled back the sheet covering the corpse on the gurney. Thomas had broken down, collapsing into Jim's arms at the sight of his wife's decimated body.

But now here she was.

Remade and looking just as she had years before she had died. It truly did seem to be a miracle.

Jim was still too stunned to comment.

After the initial shock of their reunion, Thomas had walked Jessica into the living room, sat her down, poured them both a drink, and insisted she finish hers before he sat down himself to describe what had happened. He explained to her about the accident, how she had been gone for so many years, and how every day he had prayed it would be his last. That he would be able to join her so the pain her absence had left could end—because he loved her; he loved her more than he could ever possibly say.

"I told her something wonderful had happened. That God had brought her back to me," said Thomas.

"I don't know if it's a miracle or something else," Jim replied, finally finding his voice. "There's so much death and destruction out there that I have to believe this is probably man-made rather than divine intervention."

"Of course it's a miracle," insisted Thomas, a broad smile crossing his face. "James, don't you understand? Don't you realize what this means?"

Jim shook his head. "What are you getting at?"

Jessica reached out and took his hand. "Jim, if I'm alive, then what about all the others who died between now and 2042?"

"What about Lark?" said Thomas.

The realization hit him like a hammer blow to the chest. "Dear God Almighty," he whispered, instantly on his feet. "I've got to try and find her. What if she's out there? What if she's alone?"

The panic that overcame him was total and choking. He was going to fail his kid again. She was out there somewhere in the night and he could do nothing to help her.

Jessica was with him in a second. Her arms enfolded him, pulling him to her. "It's okay—Lark's okay," she insisted, the words spoken with such sincerity and certainty he found himself believing them too. This event was too big, too huge for it not to hold some kind of cosmic meaning. For it to be just a random act of an uncaring universe beggared belief. The universe could not be so cruel—could it?

"I have to find her," he said.

"We know, and we are going to help in any way we can, but the best thing you can do right now—the *only* thing you can do—is wait here," said Jessica, holding him tightly. Her voice was adamant and strong, a lifeline for him to grasp and hold on to, to ease him back to the shore of sanity away from which he was inexorably drifting.

"But what if she's out there alone? What if she's running around those streets lost . . . or worse?" His voice was a panicked bleat.

Thomas joined in, laying a reassuring hand on his back: "James, you know she's with her mother. Where else would she be? You checked the house; you know she wasn't there. Was her car in the garage?"

Jim thought back to the garage. "No, it was empty."

"Then you know Simone was not home when this happened. Would she leave Lark on her own in the house? Would she?"

"No."

"Lark is with her mother, and you know our daughter will do her very best to keep her safe. Don't you?"

"Yes," was the best answer he could muster.

"What we need to do is stay calm," Thomas said. "Stay calm and just wait for her to come to us."

Jim just looked at him. "But what if—?" he started to say.

"No what-ifs. They are going to be just fine."

Jim did not think his father-in-law sounded convinced.

***

It felt good to be clean again. Jim hadn't realized how disgustingly filthy and smelly he was until he'd caught sight of himself in the mirror of the Shanes' entertainment unit. His face looked like it was painted with camouflage: blotches of black and gray, with streaks of white where sweat had dripped. His clothes stank worse than he did, and he felt a pang of shame at having spent the last hour in the company of his ex-wife's parents in such a state of dishevelment.

When he stepped out of the shower, he found a pair of Thomas's jeans and a fresh T-shirt neatly laid out for him on the guest room bed. His own clothes had disappeared, but he could just hear the faint rumble of a washing machine from elsewhere in the house.

It all feels so normal.

Catching sight of his rejuvenated body in the mirror hanging on the back of the bedroom door, Jim reminded himself of just how abnormal his world had actually become. Gone were the wrinkles and gray hair. Back was the muscle tone and, he noticed approvingly, his hairline.

Slipping into the two-sizes-too-large jeans, Jim made his way downstairs.

***

"Has anybody tried the TV?" Jim asked as he walked back into the living room.

Surprisingly, they had not.

"You know," said Thomas, "we hadn't even thought about turning it on. The day has been so . . . earth-shattering."

The first few channels they surfed were playing movies, reruns of old sitcoms, wildlife documentaries, a prerecorded infomercial for cutlery; one just aired cartoons.

"Try one of the local stations," Thomas suggested. He told Jim the station's channel number, but when the screen flicked over, an unrecognizable picture filled the screen.

"What's that?" said Jessica, tilting her head to her shoulder as if it might give her a better idea. "Looks like some sort of fabric."

The screen had filled with what looked to be fur under magnification. As they tried to fathom what they were looking at, a low sobbing began to filter from the TV's speakers.

"Is that someone crying?" Jim asked.

Faintly, as if from a distance, Jim could hear what sounded like the sorrowful sobbing of a woman. He reached over and turned the volume up, and the woman's weeping filled the room.

"It's the back of a chair," said Jessica suddenly after she had switched her head to the other shoulder. "See? It's fallen over on its side, and I guess the camera must be zoomed in really close . . . but it's definitely a chair. You can just make out the back support up there." She pointed to the top of the screen, but her excitement wilted as another wave of mournful weeping filled the room.

It felt to the three of them gathered around the TV as though they were the unwitting witnesses to a terrible tragedy; it was at once fascinating and repulsive.

"The poor woman," said Jessica after a minute had passed, and then she reached over and changed the channel. "Are you hungry?" she asked, glancing at Jim.

He hadn't even given food a thought. But at the mention of it, his stomach gave a rough, loud grumble. *How long had this day been?* Jim gave Jessica a look of thanks and nodded his appreciation. Jessica smiled and headed into the kitchen, shouting back over her shoulder, "Ham and cheese sandwiches okay for you two boys?"

"Sounds great," he replied. After she disappeared into the kitchen, Jim turned to Thomas. "How you holding up?"

Thomas took a second to consider Jim's question before answering. "I'm afraid," he said candidly, and continued to scan the channels for signs of life.

EIGHTEEN

Jessica was fetching their sandwiches—thick chunks of sourdough bread with what must have been half a pig packed between each slice—from the kitchen into the living room when they finally found a live broadcast.

On the screen a man in his late forties, his graying hair brushed meticulously across his forehead, the hint of a day's worth of stubble peppering his jaw, sat behind a horseshoe-shaped presenter's desk with room for another two people on either side of him, the logo of WWN, the World Wide News network, fixed prominently to the front of the desk. The man seemed to be talking to someone off camera as he rearranged papers on his desk. Although he was obviously speaking, no sound came from the TV. The newscaster looked vaguely familiar, and it was Jessica who finally identified him.

"Norm Jones?" she said as she handed Jim his sandwich.

"Right," said Jim, drawing the word out to twice its length and snapping his fingers in recognition.

Norm Jones had been an anchor with the local Los Angeles WWN affiliate for as long as Jim could remember. He had retired a few years back (or a multitude of years from now, depending on how you chose to view it). Now here he was, looking tired, looking confused, looking a helluva lot younger, but the familiar face was a reassuring sign normality had not completely disappeared off the face of the earth. This newsman had become an anchor in a much higher sense of the word.

"Did you turn the sound off?" Jessica asked.

"Nope," Jim said, checking the volume control. "They must be having technical problems."

A sudden burst of static from the television was quickly replaced by a strong, sonorous male voice. *". . . on yet? . . . Okay . . . Apparently, you can now hopefully hear me."*

The presenter seemed to relax a little, some of the stiffness leaving his stress-lined face as he settled back into his chair.

"I have to apologize for the rough construction of this broadcast, but as I'm sure you are all aware, this is not a normal day. We here at WWN are trying to pull together as much information from around the country and the world as we possibly can. Unfortunately, we are operating with limited staff due to the"—he paused, searching for the appropriate word—*"event. And folks, it's been ten years since I last sat in this chair, so if I seem a little rusty, please bear with me.*

"We have pulled as many news feeds from the network satellites that are operational as possible. As you can imagine, there is a lot of confusion, so we can offer no definitive conclusion on the events of today other than they are unprecedented in the annals of human history. In summary: this does not appear to be a localized event. From the limited contact we have had with other news networks—and I must stress that it has been very limited—both here in the US and worldwide, they are experiencing similar, and in some cases far worse, circumstances to our own.

"The consensus seems to be that there is no current explanation for the event, but it does seem clear that an extraordinary occurrence has taken place. We have attempted to contact government authorities both here at home and around the world but have received no reply to our calls. If

anybody watching this broadcast is able to explain this situation, then we would be most happy to hear from you."

Norm rifled through a pile of papers on his desk until he found one he was looking for.

"Here is what we have learned so far, and I must repeat that all of this is of course unsubstantiated at the moment: the country is in chaos. Emergency services seem to be nonexistent. Most telecommunications seem to be down, although some areas do appear to have telephone service. There are reports of several large aircraft crashes throughout the state, including several within Los Angeles Airport and its outlying areas. Fires are burning uncontrolled in many parts of the city. Freeways appear to be impassable due to the large number of vehicular accidents; the same applies to most main streets throughout the city.

"We are receiving similar reports from . . ." The newscaster stopped midsentence, his left hand moving to his ear as if he was listening to someone whispering to him.

". . . and I'm just getting new information, so please stand by . . . Yes . . . ladies and gentlemen, we are about to receive a special feed from the White House—are we ready? Do we have the feed lined up? Okay—the White House."

The presenter's image disappeared, replaced by one of a lacquered teak lectern, the presidential seal of the United States of America visible on the wooden upright and echoed in a larger form on the wall in the background.

A door opened somewhere, and a commotion of people entered the room. A man walked toward the lectern, flanked by two big men in dark-gray suits. Their glances at the few members of the press crowded in front and behind the camera, along with their flatline expressions, immediately betrayed the two men as members of the Secret Service.

The man at the lectern shuffled a few papers before pulling the microphone closer to his mouth and then looking directly into the camera. A shock of black hair highlighted a narrow face watched over by carefully manicured eyebrows. Dressed in a black business suit with a bloodred tie, he looked to be in his fifties. A century before he would have been described as dapper, but tonight he looked drawn and gray: haggard. Pale puffed flesh under his eyes, and pink-tinged conjunctiva striated with blood.

A white caption appeared in capital letters at the bottom of the screen: *VICE PRESIDENT NATHANIAL RODERICK.*

"My fellow Americans," Roderick began, staring deep into the lens of the camera. *"I must first inform you that President Sarandon is incapacitated and that I, as vice president, have been appointed as president pro tem until she is able to resume control."* Roderick's voice carried a certain lofty tone bordering on arrogant as he delivered the news of the president's absence.

"As you are all by now no doubt aware, a catastrophic event occurred today. It appears that the United States and our allies have suffered some form of terrorist attack. At this point in time we cannot say with any certainty who the perpetrator of this cowardly attack is or why it was carried out, but you can rest assured we are already taking all of the necessary steps to ascertain the full implications of the situation.

"We do not know if this is a temporary effect or whether it is permanent, but you should have the utmost confidence that the best American scientific minds are now applying themselves to understanding precisely what occurred today.

"Just as you, the people of this great nation, are experiencing a time of transition and confusion, so too are we, your elected leaders, and it is with that information in mind that for your safety I am imposing a state of martial law for the time being. As of today a curfew will remain in place between the hours of 6:00 p.m. and 10:00 a.m. until further notice.

"Please, for your own safety stay in your homes. This situation will be resolved as quickly as possible. In the meantime I ask that you all be patient." He paused before adding, *"And may God bless the United States of America."*

The broadcast from the White House faded, replaced once more with the image of Norm Jones, looking even more confused than he had before the broadcast. *"Well, ladies and gentlemen,"* he said to the camera, *"make of that what you will. But it appears—"*

Thomas pressed the power button on the TV remote and the screen went dead, cutting the commentary off in midsentence.

***

Jim, Thomas, and Jessica discussed the vice president's speech into the small hours of the following morning. Truth be told, it was less of a discussion and more a primer to bring Jessica up to speed on world events after her death.

Originally, 2017 had been presided over by the first female president. President Sarandon had run on a vehemently antiwar platform (the right painting her as anti-American). She had run for office in '16 and had gone on to serve two full terms, a respected and strong president, helping to lift the country further out of the recession that had blighted it starting in '07.

President Sarandon's VP was a different kettle of fish altogether. It was well known that a wide political rift separated the president from her running mate, their two offices often finding themselves in conflict.

A graduate from the Bush school of diplomacy, Roderick allegedly opposed President Sarandon's light-handed approach to politics and non-confrontational attitude to policing the world. Seen as a hardliner within the party, he had been deemed the perfect choice to balance out Sarandon's perceived weaknesses. He was often portrayed as a closet megalomaniac who had surrounded himself with some of the best PR firms money could buy.

In an exposé after his retirement, he was portrayed as a dangerous man with expansionist ideals, a potential warmonger who had only been kept in check by the powerful personality of President Sarandon.

A biographer would later quote one unnamed source that had worked closely with him as saying, "Not since Machiavelli has the political sphere seen a more dangerous, cunning, and potentially disastrous politician."

"The man was . . . *is* crazy. I shudder to think what he has up his sleeve, given the current state of the world," said Thomas.

In 2042 the president had been—would be? Could be?—Jerome Faulkner, the country's second African American to hold the seat of power. He was a well-liked man, with nothing to mark or mar his presidency other than how truly unremarkable it had been to the date of the event. He was the duly elected president, but of course he was not going to actually *be* elected for many years yet.

"How the hell will they deal with *that* situation?" Jim asked.

"It's beside the point," Thomas said. "How old was he when he was elected? Forty? Forty-five?"

Jim nodded that the figure was close enough and, after a pause while he digested what Thomas was getting at, realized his point. Somewhere out there—in Maine, if he remembered correctly—the man who would in the future history of the world be elected president was now eighteen years old.

"Strange times," said Thomas as he saw the realization spread over Jim's face. "Strange times indeed."

It had been a strange day that had now moved into a surreal night. Eventually, exhaustion and fatigue flowed over Jim's body like a wave, and he excused himself.

"Good night, James," said Thomas.

Jessica hugged him and whispered in his ear, "In case all of this is gone in the morning."

NINETEEN

Rebecca was not surprised when her parents had explained to her in tones so hushed they were almost a whisper that her nightmare had not been a dream. Just thinking about it made her want to vomit, and it was all she could do to keep the urge under control.

Her mother and father sat across the breakfast table from her in the cramped kitchen of their double-wide trailer, an almost-beatific look of wonder on both their faces. Rebecca's mother must have realized her thoughts had strayed back to that moment again, because she reached out and quickly took her daughter's hand in her own, toppling the bottle of maple syrup they had just used with their pancake breakfast.

"Are you okay, Becky?" she asked, concern stitched across her face, ignoring the bottle and the pool of sticky syrup that had begun to leak onto the tabletop.

Rebecca swallowed hard and managed a weak smile. *I probably look like a grinning corpse*, she thought to herself. She forced the images of the glinting knife out of her head and asked her question again: "Please, Dad, tell me what happened. I need to know."

It had been three days since Rebecca had found herself so suddenly back in her childhood bedroom: three days of utter confusion, not only for her but also for the entire world. No one really seemed to know what had happened, what had caused billions of people to suddenly find themselves thrown so violently into the past. Even though the provisional government would have liked everybody to believe they had some idea, it had become patently obvious that they were as perplexed as the rest of the world. Of course, the news that President Sarandon was dead had not helped. She had been on board *Marine One* when whatever had caused the event had happened. The burned-out wreckage—the president and her entourage still strapped inside—had been found twenty miles from the White House. Vice President Roderick now held the reins of the country in his hands.

At least there was something resembling television coverage now. On the first day after the event, other than the occasional broadcast by a news station that had managed to overcome the initial shock of return—albeit only a mishmash of confused mixed messages and conjecture—there had been virtually no definitive information on what had happened. But now the networks were getting their acts together, and most of the channels that had been nothing but static or automated emergency broadcasts were now transmitting coverage of the event.

The news was not good. Telecasts and news reports from around the world showed humanity in utter chaos. Death, destruction, confusion, horror, and disbelief blanketed every nation.

It was odd to contrast the images beaming into the Lacey home to the peaceful, almost tranquil, oasis of small town Water Rock, Nevada. A little less than sixty miles west of Las Vegas, this hardscrabble town of forty thousand souls was isolated, surrounded on all sides by mountain ranges and desert.

There was no airport to speak of, just a private strip that saw the occasional light aircraft fly in or out of town. There was a hospital that according to Dr. Weaver, who lived a few doors down from Becky and her family, had seen only a few cases on the day of the event: a couple of heart attacks (one of those turned out to be just a mild case of angina) and a car wreck or two. Amazingly, there were no fatalities and certainly nothing to compare to the devastation they had seen in the large metropolitan areas of the US. Becky had also learned from Doc Weaver that she wasn't the only resurrectee in town. There were others who had "passed away," as the gentle doctor had put it, only to find themselves alive again, but they had all been older residents. At twenty-three, Rebecca was the youngest. He wasn't aware of anyone else who had returned after suffering through what the good doctor referred to as Rebecca's "unique set of circumstances." The news that there were other cases of the dead returning to life was comforting, even though there was no mention of any resurrectees who had died in as violent a manner as she apparently had.

Looking south through the kitchen window of her parents' double-wide, past the backyard toward Mount Charleston, she could still see the cloud of smoke that had gathered in the sky over Las Vegas.

The city of sin had been hit hard on the day of the event. McCarran International Airport had been devastated, and most of the hotels that lined the strip close alongside the airport had been destroyed when an incoming jet had cartwheeled through Terminal 1 and into the nearest casino. The local TV news had shown images of the resulting firestorm that had swept through the town, devouring most of the classic landmarks and reducing them to little more than ashes and skeletal corpses. The fire had been so voracious it had quickly overwhelmed the few confused Las Vegas Fire & Rescue Department members who had managed to respond.

Rebecca's parents had avoided answering her pressing questions for most of the three days after she had miraculously reappeared back at their home. And that had been okay at first. Her mind had been so confused, so off track, that her questions had been limited to trying to understand where she was and why she had no recollection of getting home. But now her mind felt clear, anchored in this reality. And she wanted answers to her questions.

"Mom. Dad. Please? I *need* to know exactly what happened," she repeated, almost pleading.

Her parents regarded each other across the breakfast table. They were not complicated people, and she knew she could not expect a definitive explanation of why the last thing she remembered before waking up in her bedroom was a man with a knife to her throat, but they could at least fill in the blank spaces for her. Help her illuminate the dark spaces that seemed to fill her mind; that was all she wanted.

Finally, after a long moment of speechless communication, a pale Kimberly Lacey nodded faintly to her husband, and he began to explain what had happened to his daughter.

***

As her father recounted the missing events, Rebecca confirmed most of what the cops had managed to piece together by themselves during their investigation: the girls' night out with her friends from work; the club where she met them for the evening, talking and laughing. And when the night was over, Rebecca had hailed a cab outside the club and taken it home to her modest apartment. Her last memory before she found herself immersed in her nightmare had been pushing the key into the lock that would open the security gate that kept out unwanted visitors from the grounds of the apartment building. Everything after that moment was a confused mess of images and thoughts.

The very last thing she remembered with any clarity was lying on her kitchen table . . . and the man. And the knife. She remembered the knife.

Her father filled in the blanks, while her mother sat stone-faced, tears trickling over cheeks.

"The police think he followed you home," her father said, choking back a sob before continuing. "From the autopsy report, they think he hit you with something while you were trying to get through the security gate. They found some of your blood on the ground near the gate, and you had blunt-force trauma to the back of your head." He reached up and tapped the corresponding spot on the back of his own head.

"The officer said whoever had done this to you had carried you to your apartment. They thought he had probably been watching you for weeks. That it might even be somebody you knew . . . know."

"I didn't know him," Becky interjected. "I saw his face. I didn't recognize him."

Becky watched her father take a deep gulp of air and hold it in before continuing his account.

"Somebody from the apartment called the police because . . . because . . . it was three days before anybody knew you were missing and . . ."—her dad scrambled to find the right words—"there were complaints from your neighbors. They thought maybe the sewers had backed up. When the apartment manager opened up your door, that's when they found you and called the police.

"That was—*will be*—two years from now, sweetheart." Her dad's eyes glazed over momentarily as he tried to navigate the confusing reality of past events that had been unwritten, yet still existed within his memory. "And not one day went by that we haven't talked about you. We were . . . we *are* so proud of you."

"We missed you so much, baby. And now you have been brought back," said Mrs. Lacey, reaching out to touch her resurrected daughter's cheek. "It's a miracle," she added in a tight whisper. *"A miracle."*

***

Rebecca did not share her parents' belief that her resurrection was the result of anything supernatural. They were good people; describing them as salt of the earth would have sounded like a cliché if it was not for the fact that it applied to her parents one hundred percent. Her father was a lineman for the local power company; her mom drove one of the school buses ferrying children from the north end of the Valley to the high school in the south. They led a below-average lifestyle on a below-average income. Raising a child could be a hardship for all but a lucky few, but it was doubly so in this small, rural, dirt-poor town. But early on, Rebecca's parents learned that their daughter was nothing less than exceptional.

She aced every aptitude test from the first grade on up, and it wasn't long before the young Rebecca Lacey's parents were informed that their daughter was not just exceptional, she was *special*, bright beyond her years. A prodigy. So special in fact that the school had recommended Becky be placed on the academic fast track. It was their recommendation that she move from the tiny public school to one that would challenge and help develop her intellectually—a private school with personal educators. They recommended a school where her full potential could develop and where the very best teachers would coach her, allowing her nascent intelligence to flourish and grow. *She'll receive the best education money can buy*, the counselor had said with a smile.

Her father had quietly informed the counselor that they could not afford to do that. The counselor had looked at him sympathetically over the rims of her glasses and told Rebecca's parents they did not need to worry about the funding; there were scholarships available for individuals in their financial situation, and she would be happy to give them the forms to fill out. With their daughter's test scores, they would have no problem, she was sure. Money would never be a consideration in their daughter's future education.

Rebecca had not wanted to leave her school and her friends. The other children liked her, and unlike most geniuses of a similar age she had the social graces to match her intelligence. She had spent many years being brilliant at not showing her peers that she was brilliant.

However, even at the age of ten she heard the call of something bigger than herself and the tiny valley that she was growing up in.

Mathematics.

Numbers, figures, formulae. She could see them in the flight of the hawks that sometimes circled above her home, in the random fall of gravel that made up the drive to their front door, or in the billowing clouds that hung over the mountains surrounding the town.

While other kids watched MTV and read the umpteenth Harry Potter, she was watching *Nova* on her local PBS channel and reading Sagan and Hawking, devouring anything by Gian-Carlo Rota and Julian Barbour. She appreciated mathematics as others loved poetry: she could hear the meter in a constant, feel the rhyme in an integer, and sense the prose hidden in quantum foam. It created a stunning sense of wonder in her, a wonder that never diminished.

With that sense of wonder came an awareness of something intangible, of something beyond the math; something outside intelligibility that, just as a molecule consisted of electrons, protons, and neutrons, made mathematics something greater, imparting a rhythm and a meaning to the figures and equations that she could not quite understand.

To Rebecca, it was a sense of God.

No formula could express what she was experiencing. Like a woman who lived in a two-dimensional world trying to grasp a third new dimension of reality, she did not possess the senses needed to interpret the undercurrent she felt rippling through each and every equation. Its ineffableness at once frustrated, terrified, and excited her.

And now, in this reconstituted world, here it was again, the same sense that something was at work behind the scenes of her life, an undercurrent pulling at her mind again, catching it in its tow and sweeping it out into a sea of uncertainty and mystery.

No. She did not believe that this was a miracle at all.

PART THREE
TOWARD YESTERDAY

CUTTING FROM THE
LOS ANGELES HERALD

March 22, 2018
Adventure Park

An estimated thirty-seven thousand people turned out today to hear the leader of the Church of Second Redemption, Father Edward Pike, preach at Adventure Park, Whittier.

While no arrests were made, Chief of Police John O'Donnell said that the sheer number of devotees who turned up to hear Father Pike's sermon caused traffic problems for the small residential area of Whittier.

Father Pike could not be reached for comment.

TWENTY

If you didn't know the path was there, you could easily drive right past it. It was just a narrow dirt track leading through the forest to the cabin on the lakeshore. Simone had asked Jim several times to get the trail paved. He had steadfastly refused; he liked the fact the place was off the beaten path—quite literally. Instead, he had agreed to spread gravel the last hundred yards or so to the house so they wouldn't track mud inside after one of the storms the area often experienced.

It took Jim twenty minutes of driving back and forth along the same strip of road before he spotted the track, obscured by a year or more's growth of juniper and sage. As Jim turned off the main road and onto the rough dirt track leading up to the cabin, he finally felt that he was leaving the events of the past year behind him. The forest was a boundary between the strange new world and him. A living fence of birch and oak separated him from harsh reality.

Jim pulled the truck to a stop outside the cabin. It was a quaint Colonial-style affair, built completely with local trees sometime in the early twentieth century. Surrounded by thick woods on three sides, the cabin sat on the shore of Shadow Lake, a seven-hundred-acre natural body of water. Jim and Simone had bought the place within a year of getting married, escaping to its tranquility every chance they could. As he exited the truck, he could hear lake water lapping at the supports of the old wooden dock out back and see their paddleboat bobbing languidly on the water's ebb and flow, just as it always had.

Of course, Simone was not with him this time. Jim had come to terms with the fact that both his former wife and Lark were in all probability dead. Killed in the first few chaotic days following the Slip—as the event had eventually become known. Along with the president, Simone and Lark were undoubtedly two of the estimated seven million Americans who had lost their lives in the US on that fateful day. Hundreds of millions more had been killed across the globe, and millions more perished in the weeks following the event, mostly in undeveloped countries, as their fragile governments and infrastructures collapsed around them.

Jim half expected the cabin to be occupied, claimed by one of the many displaced families that the Slip had created in its wake. But as he walked up the weatherworn steps onto the front porch, he found the door still locked. And peering through the grubby window, he could see the place was empty and just as he remembered it.

After Lark's death and the subsequent separation and eventual divorce from her mother, the cabin had become Jim's hideaway. In that first life, it had also been his bar and his confessional. But mostly Jim liked to think of it as his pupa: the place where he had entered as a broken, disheartened, self-hating child killer and emerged as an almost-whole human and critically acknowledged novelist.

Right now it was just somewhere to start over.

Safe. Secluded. Quiet.

He had stayed with Simone's parents for the first few weeks following the Slip; it seemed like the sensible thing to do, until some kind of normalcy returned to the world. Eventually, he had moved back to the house on Keswick Street. Their house had survived the fire mostly intact, so he spent his time repairing the damage where he could, waiting and hoping for the moment his ex-wife and child would show up at the door.

As the days had turned into weeks with no word from Simone, and the repairs on the house were slowly completed, Jim had volunteered for cleanup duty. By this time he had pretty much come to terms with the fact that they were probably dead, so he volunteered in the hope he might uncover some clue to Simone and Lark's fate.

It took eight months to clear the freeways and streets of Los Angeles, to remove the bodies from the cars and trucks and bury them in mass graves. With each body he had pulled from the burned-out shell of a vehicle, he wondered if it was maybe Simone or his daughter.

It fell to the operators of the mobile cranes and heavy lifters to clear the tin-can corpses of the hundreds of thousands of vehicles from the roads and freeways. The work had been soul destroying, painful, heartbreaking, and horrible. But it was also a test of fire for Jim, a bridge from the old reality to the new, and Jim had made his way through it, coming out the other side more complete than when he had entered. The same couldn't be said for many other survivors. Suicide rates in the first few months had grown to such massive levels that authorities had finally stopped counting. The media, in a rare show of clear-headedness in Jim's opinion, had stopped reporting on it.

The cabin's creosote-stained logs looked welcoming and familiar after all the disquiet and horror he had experienced in those times. The air was redolent with the smell of sap and dry leaves.

Jim pushed the key into the lock and opened the front door. He stepped over the threshold to the accompanying *brak-rak-rak* of a woodpecker somewhere deep in the surrounding forest. Dust sheets covered the furniture, and the scent of undisturbed air hung heavy in every room. In the kitchen the refrigerator hummed patiently. *Well, at least the electricity is on*, Jim thought as he carried his luggage into the front room. Later he'd need to take a trip down to the store and grab some supplies.

Jim had always thought there was an odd sadness to a house that had been left vacant for a long period of time, an echoic air that extended far beyond the empty rooms and silence. It was temporal, as though the very walls had gone into hibernation, waiting for the owner to return, while at the same time all the events that had ever taken place within them seemed frozen and available. It was as though he could reach out and pluck a single experience from the stillness. Jim felt that melancholia now as he moved from room to room checking the lights and windows, making sure all were working and intact. The place had a stillness that seemed more appropriate for a church than a home.

"Welcome home," he said to himself.

***

For the next few weeks, Jim kept pretty much to himself. He explored the woods, fished the well-stocked lake.

Since he'd arrived at the cabin, Jim had found his thoughts frequently returning to the cause of the Slip. How had it happened? Was it man-made or some never-before-seen glitch in the clockwork mechanism of the universe? Or was it as the Church of Second Redemption believed, that God had given humanity another shot, a second chance at their lives? The answer eluded him, but the simple application of Occam's razor meant he was erring on the side of man-made. Beside humanity's ability to quickly adapt to new situations, Jim had long ago observed its propensity to royally screw things up just as easily.

When he distanced himself from the carnage that had been inflicted on the world, what was left was a fascinating conundrum that constantly plucked at his physicist's mind. *Time travel! Who would have thought it?* It had long been seen as impossible by the scientific community, relegated to science fiction novels and movies. But now it had been proven possible beyond a shadow of a doubt. Admittedly, it hadn't played out in the way most science fiction writers had imagined, but it *had* opened up a whole new frontier of possibilities for science. If it could be controlled, it would become the most powerful tool humanity had ever created. Equally, it could also be the most terrible weapon in the wrong hands.

That was assuming anyone could ever figure out just *how* it had happened in the first place.

Strange how quickly the human mind can adjust to even the most seemingly outrageous of situations, Jim thought as he walked back from the lake. He had a four-pound trout stowed in the cooler he carried in one hand, a tackle box and fishing pole in the other. Still deep in thought, Jim mounted the back steps to the cabin, kicked off his boots and waders, and set his fishing pole and equipment down on an easy chair where he spent his evenings watching sunsets.

His fingers reached for the top pocket of his shirt and the pack of cigarettes that he expected to find there, but the pocket was empty, and the gesture was simply the remnant of an old habit. In the weeks and months after the Slip, he hadn't once felt the need for a cigarette. He had been just too busy, and by the time he wasn't, the urge had faded to almost nothing. *At least something positive had come out of all this*, he thought as he pulled open the screen door and stepped into the mudroom.

As if sensing his presence, the phone in the living room began to ring, demanding his attention. He strode toward the noise. He hadn't given the landline number to anyone, so it had to be a wrong number.

"Hello?" said Jim into the phone's receiver.

"James Baston?" a man's voice asked.

"Who is this?"

At the other end of the phone line, the voice paused for a second before continuing. "My name is Dr. Mitchell Lorentz, and I have an offer that I hope you will not want to refuse."

TWENTY-ONE

The sound of gravel crunching under tires alerted Jim to the arriving vehicle. It was exactly 11:00 a.m.—his visitors were precisely on time—and Jim wondered whether the car had been idling on the approach to the lake house just so they could put in a punctual appearance.

Jim opened the front door and raised his hand in acknowledgment to the man exiting the passenger side of the vehicle as it pulled to a stop in the driveway. The car was a black Lincoln Town Car with government plates and tinted windows that obscured the driver. The passenger was a tall, well-built man in army dress uniform, who strode across the gravel approach with the confidence and bearing that only comes from years of military training and intense discipline.

"Dr. Baston? Colonel Geoffrey DeWitt," he said, thrusting out a meaty hand. "Do you have any baggage, sir?"

"Just these," said Jim, pointing over his shoulder to a suitcase and a travel bag leaning against the wall of the hallway.

DeWitt picked them both up and took them to the back of the car, placing them in the trunk as Jim followed behind him.

"Prof. Lorentz has asked me to give you this, sir," said DeWitt, handing Jim an oversized manila envelope with the outsized words TOP SECRET stamped in thick, bright-red ink across the face of it and an embossed US government seal in the top right corner. "He would like you to read it en route," continued the colonel as he opened the rear passenger door and indicated for Jim to climb in.

"If there's anything at all you need, Doctor, please don't hesitate to ask. Just press the intercom and you will get right through to me up front."

DeWitt closed the door behind Jim as he climbed into the backseat of the Lincoln. A smoked-glass window separated the passenger compartment from the front section of the vehicle. A TV monitor embedded into the paneling behind the driver's seat gazed at him like a blank cyclopean eye.

As the car rumbled and crunched its way back toward the main road, Jim relaxed back into the exquisitely comfortable seat. It was going to be a long trip.

***

The briefing papers DeWitt had handed Jim—outlining a secret military communications project by the name of Tach-Comm—only added to the mystery of why he had been singled out by the enigmatic Prof. Lorentz. Despite rereading the papers three times, Jim still could not see how there could be any connection between him and the project.

It took three hours to make the drive from Jim's place at Shadow Mountain Lake to the government installation on the outskirts of Reno. It was an inconspicuous-looking building, but as the Lincoln pulled up to the security gate, Jim noticed the security protecting the complex was extraordinarily high. It was subtle, but it was there if you looked.

The guards staffing the security booth both had sidearms in brown leather holsters fixed to their belts and, he noticed, a row of assault weapons were stashed within easy reach on a wooden rack toward the back of the booth. A chain-link fence topped with razor wire ran around the entire compound perimeter. Fixed periodically along the fencing were red-bordered triangular warning signs. The icon on the signs depicted a body struck by lightning, with the words "Warning—High Voltage" printed in bold letters both above and below the image, clearly indicating what would happen to anybody stupid enough to touch the fence. Several low-key cameras were scattered strategically around the base, nestled surreptitiously between the lamps of overhead gantry floodlights, observing all those who entered and left as well as monitoring the movements of those who were already on the grounds.

In the distance Jim could see an electric cart as it patrolled around the perimeter of the fence. Two burly men dressed in the same taupe uniform as the gate's guards occupied the two seats. The complex was ostensibly a civilian site, but it was obvious to Jim from the level of security and the demeanor and professionalism of the guards—not to mention the smart salute the guard had executed when he saw Colonel DeWitt—that the military played a grand part in the running of the place.

Jim's window whirred quietly into its recess as DeWitt's voice came over the internal speaker: *"This won't take a second, Doctor."*

The security guard peered in through the open window, comparing Jim's face to a picture attached to a clipboard he carried. He scrutinized Jim for a few seconds, then turned to his partner in the control booth. Satisfied that the car's passenger matched the information, the guard nodded once, and the security gate that blocked the entrance began to rattle open. Jim noticed several vicious looking spikes protruding like punji sticks from the hot tarmacadam of the road retract back into metal lined holes.

The car engine engaged, and they pulled silently forward onto the long black drive leading up to the complex.

***

It was a low black building.

It reminded Jim of a squat, fat, black spider sitting at the center of a web of roads that led off and encircled the complex.

Hopefully, he was not the fly.

The Lincoln pulled to a halt outside the canopy-covered steps leading up to the glass double door of the building's entrance. DeWitt climbed out and opened Jim's door.

"Here we are, sir," he said as Jim exited the vehicle. "I'll get your bags and make sure they arrive at your apartment."

"Can't I just take them with me?" asked Jim.

"Sorry, sir, procedures. Security will want to give them the once-over before they are allowed into the main building," was DeWitt's reply, delivered with a tolerant smile.

The doors to the building swung open, and a woman dressed in a two-piece gray business suit descended the five concrete steps, a professional, well-practiced smile on her face. She was close to six feet tall, but at least three inches of that was due to her stiletto heels, the wearing of which she was obviously accustomed to, as she strode confidently down the steps toward him. Her shoulder-length black hair was pulled back into a topknot, accentuating a face with a firm jawline and a minimum of makeup. *Attractive*, Jim thought, *in a stern sort of a way.*

"Welcome, Dr. Baston," she said, offering her right hand. The woman's voice was the epitome of distant professionalism, the considered aloofness of one of Mr. Tolkien's famous elves. "My name is Mina Belkov. I am Prof. Lorentz's personal assistant."

Jim shook the proffered hand; she had a strong grip with none of the looseness he had been expecting. Her voice was a surprise too: very soft, very feminine, belying the austerity of her dress and the rigidity of her posture.

"If you would like to follow me," she continued, gesturing toward the entrance, "I will process you and show you to your apartment. This way, please."

She ushered him up the steps, through the smoked-glass double doors, and into the building's reception area. The exquisite parquet floor and brass fixtures of the building's interior were a stark contrast to its bleak, utilitarian exterior. Here and there large pots held what Jim guessed were probably real ferns. A waterfall cascaded serenely into a pool full of koi and water lilies near the base of a wide, open-backed stairway leading up to the second floor.

Belkov escorted Jim up to the marble-paneled reception desk. The pretty, blond-haired receptionist behind the desk raised her head in acknowledgment of their approach. She placed a guest book on the counter for Jim to sign, which he dutifully did, filling in his name and time of arrival.

"Now if you would just step over here to this spot, please," said the receptionist as she guided him to a red X taped to the floor next to her desk. A few feet away stood a tripod and digital camera, the lens of which the young woman now asked him to look directly into as she stepped behind it. "Say 'superaccelerated particles,'" she said with a wry grin, which extracted only a disapproving glare from Ms. Belkov.

A few seconds later a photo popped out from a printer sitting on the reception desk. Peeling off the backing, the receptionist placed it sticky side down onto an ID card that already contained Jim's name printed in bold black capitals.

"Now if I could just get your thumbprint here," the receptionist said, pointing with her manicured index finger to an inkpad and a blank box below his image on the card. "And finally," she continued, handing him a tissue for his blackened thumb, "just sign here at the bottom, please."

Placing the completed card into another machine, she finally handed Jim a still-warm laminated security badge, which Mina fastened to his shirt pocket for him.

"You will need to keep this with you at all times. If you lose it, please contact me immediately," said Mina, her tone indicating the loss of the card might well herald the end of the world as it was currently known. *Well, a little too late for that*, Jim thought absently. He smiled his understanding back at the woman as she continued talking.

"Okay, let me take you to your apartment."

***

By the time Mina Belkov had escorted Jim to his quarters, his bags had miraculously already arrived, considerately placed in the bedroom next to the nightstand.

"I know a few airports that could learn a lot from your baggage handlers," Jim joked, his quip bringing only a mechanical smile to the face of his escort. Mina gave him a perfunctory tour of his new home: one bedroom, a living room, and a well-equipped kitchenette. A small office off his bedroom held a computer she assured him connected to their mainframe LAN, along with a desk and a single filing cabinet, so he could work at any time he chose, she explained.

"I doubt that you will have much need for the cafeteria," said Mina, "but it is open twenty-four hours a day, and I think you will be pleasantly surprised by the menu range." Leading Jim back into the living room, Belkov continued: "You will find a list of all the facility's extensions next to the phone over there. If you need anything, please feel free to dial zero; that will get you through to reception, and they will be able to help you locate anyone or anything you need. You should also have received an itinerary in the package given to you by your driver." The last sentence was a statement rather than a question.

Jim nodded as she continued: "There will be a formal meeting tonight at six thirty, where you will meet Prof. Lorentz and the rest of the team."

"How many other . . ."—Jim's eyes focused to the right as he searched for the right word—"*guests* are there?"

"Besides the original group members? There are two new people, including you of course."

"Of course," he said with a smile.

Belkov began to walk to the door. Over her shoulder she said, "Is there anything else I might help you with, Dr. Baston?"

"No . . . thank you."

"See you at six thirty then."

And with that she was gone and he was once more alone.

***

Jim quickly settled into his new accommodations. He took a nap, followed by a shower, before changing into a pair of fresh slacks, button-down shirt, and jacket. It always amazed him how a shower and change of clothes could rejuvenate an exhausted body.

By the time Mina Belkov knocked on the door just before six thirty, he was sitting comfortably—if a little nervously—on the sofa.

"All set?" she asked.

Jim gave a nod and joined her in the corridor.

TWENTY-TWO

Three people stood chatting quietly in a group as Mina Belkov led Jim into the meeting room. A highly polished cedar conference table occupied the center of the floor with seating for fifteen. At the farthest end of the table from the door, a projector pointed at a blank white screen on the wall. A recording device—Jim presumed—sat on top of the table.

A tall man broke away from the group talking in the corner and moved toward Jim and Mina, his hand extended.

"Welcome, welcome," he said, grasping Jim's proffered hand in his own. "It's a pleasure to finally meet you, Jim."

"Dr. James Baston, this is Dr. Mitchell Lorentz," said Mina by way of introduction.

Lorentz was not what Jim had expected. He had a full head of hair, sparingly peppered here and there with the odd brushstroke of gray, which he insisted on keeping slicked back. He had lively blue eyes and a mouth quick to smile.

"It's a pleasure to meet you too, Doctor," said Jim.

"Let me introduce you to the rest of the team." Lorentz took Jim by the elbow, leading him over to the group, who had stopped chatting and now turned to face the two men.

Horatio Mabry insisted Jim call him Harry. Horatio's name was exceeded in exuberance only by the man's sheer size—Jim estimated Mabry weighed in at a minimum of two fifty, probably closer to three hundred. The man was an absolute bear.

"It's all relaxed muscle," Mabry maintained with mock sincerity as he patted his overflowing paunch, a guilty smile lighting up the rubicund face of the man Lorentz described as the team's resident electrical engineer.

"I keep telling Harry we have a perfectly good gym that he's free to take advantage of at any time," said Lorentz with a knowing smile.

"True. True," the big man retorted. "Unfortunately, you also have a wonderful cafeteria. Besides, the one thing we have all learned from the Slip is what our future holds if we continue down the same paths we originally took, and I for one like to know exactly where I am heading."

"And here," said Lorentz, turning his attention to the young woman standing quietly next to Mabry, "is another new acquisition to our team. James Baston, I would like you to meet Rebecca Lacey."

Rebecca was a striking young woman in her late twenties. Her chestnut-brown hair fell to her shoulders, highlighting a face that, while not classically beautiful, held an attraction on a level Jim could not immediately grasp. But there was something else about this woman, an intimation of pain that moved across her features like a mist across a morning field, hinting at a hidden hurt that ran deep.

"Rebecca is new to the installation, just as you are, Jim," continued Lorentz, "and we are hoping she will become a permanent asset to our team."

If Rebecca had noticed Jim staring, she did not let on; instead, she smiled politely—a smile that reflected in her emerald-green eyes. "I'm very pleased to meet you, Dr. Baston," said Rebecca in a voice full of melody.

Jim managed to answer, even though his tongue felt immobile in his mouth. "A pleasure," he said. *A pleasure? What am I thinking?* It made him sound like a Victorian villain from a bad vid-flick.

"Ah!" exclaimed Lorentz, breaking the spell as he peered over Jim's right shoulder toward the doorway. "I see the final member of our team is here. Please come in and join us, Prof. Drake."

Jim turned to greet the new arrival.

A child no more than six years old walked into the conference room. Her wispy blond hair was cut in a bob that outlined a face that would make an angel weep at its sweetness. Sparkling blue eyes assessed Jim Baston with a cool intelligence.

"Hello," said the girl in a voice little more than a squeak as she offered Jim her extended hand. "I'm Prof. Adrianna Drake."

***

Jim realized his mouth was hanging open. The little girl standing in front of him had a querulous, almost-disdainful look on her face. It was a look that said she was more than aware of the effect her childlike appearance had on adults but was well and truly bone tired of it. *Yes, yes*, she seemed to say. *Just get the gawking over with.*

Here was as fine an illustration as any of the many oddities this new version of an old world had created. For the majority of humanity, the millions of resurrected dead who had suddenly and inexplicably found themselves alive once more had been the hardest aspect of this new-past world to accept. They had collectively been labeled with the politically correct nomenclature of the "revivified."

But for Jim, he had the most trouble accepting the other extreme of the scale: the children who had until the day of the Slip been living normal adult lives in the future. After the Slip, anyone in their late twenties to mid-thirties had found themselves suddenly back in their childhood body, the event having wiped decades from their lives. Now they were all little again, but their consciousness was still that of their future self. They retained all the intelligence and memories of their adult lives.

Jim found it hard to grasp the fact that the child he saw walking down the street could have at some point in the future held down a job or been somebody's lover. They had attended school, college. Grown up, married, had perhaps even raised and now lost a child of their own. They had experienced everything that differentiates most adults from the children they used to be.

And now here they were again, trapped in a child's body, with all of the associated problems that brought. It must have been torturous in those first few months for them.

The exogenous children of the United States handled this most unexpected regression with varying degrees of adjustment. Some tried to make their way on their own, attempting to reacquire jobs they had held when they were adults, but that was difficult because most adults had an ingrained attitude toward children. Jim had read reports in several newspapers of attempts at organizing a child labor union. Others had grabbed eagerly at the chance to be kids once more, throwing themselves completely into experiencing their childhoods over again. Some went back to school (though not many); they played with toys, made friends, climbed trees, scuffed their knees, and enjoyed a second chance at life. Most, however, just accepted the fact they would have to once more rely upon their parents until they were of a sufficient age where they could step back out into the adult world.

Of course, not all the children were ex-adults; some had died before they left childhood. And it was these kids that Jim had the hardest time accepting. It meant that Lark had also had a second chance at life, only to have it torn from her again. It meant that he, her father, had failed her for a second time. It was a failure that tore at his heart every time he saw a child of Lark's age.

Prof. Adrianna Drake did not fall into any of these categories, Jim thought. He could see intensity behind her eyes, and a drive that was motivated by some source he suspected even she did not truly understand.

"I'm very pleased to meet you, Dr. Baston," the diminutive scientist announced before Jim could say anything.

"Don't be put off by Adrianna's . . . appearance," Lorentz chimed in. "The professor probably knows more about this project than the entire team put together. If it had not been for her brilliant work, we could not have succeeded in our original experiment."

"And that would have been a bad thing because . . . ?" said Adrianna with a sarcastic smile.

TWENTY-THREE

"Welcome," began Lorentz, resting both of his hands flat against the surface of the conference table. "Thank you all for attending. I'm sure that our two newest members are wondering exactly what they are doing here and why they were chosen to join our little team. And I'll get to that in just a moment. But first I must apologize to you both for the cloak-and-dagger tactics we employed to get you here. As you are about to find out, I was forced not to reveal any of the information you are going to hear before I was absolutely certain that you would attend this meeting."

Lorentz remained still for a moment, gathering his thoughts and inhaling deeply, before he resumed his oratory.

"I am responsible for the Slip," he admitted bluntly, a hint of unease in his voice. "I know Adrianna will tell you otherwise—that the team I assembled to work on the project that caused this calamity shared equally in the blame—but *I* was the instigator, and I *must* place the blame firmly and completely on *my* shoulders."

There was a stunned silence from Jim and Rebecca.

"Approximately twenty-five years from now, in a government-funded laboratory in Southern California, I will assemble a team of some of the most brilliant young scientists this country will have to offer. An original team of whom Adrianna is the only surviving member, by virtue of the fact that she was my eldest recruit. We were—*will be*—contracted to work on a secret government project that would revolutionize communications between military command-and-control centers and their units in the field.

"This project involved the sending and receiving of messages and signals using tachyons as opposed to regular radiotelegraphy. Project Tach-Comm, as we called it, was supposed to eliminate the need for encryption of messages and make the use of radio networks and systems, as we knew them, obsolete. How? By virtue of the fact that, given the innate nature of tachyons to travel backward through time, any message sent from our transmitter would effectively be received by the message's recipient before it was even sent. It would guarantee that only the unit in possession of the receiver would be able to receive the transmission—a guarantee which the military were more than eager to obtain at the earliest opportunity."

"You built *Dirac's radio?*" said Jim incredulously.

"Essentially, yes. But we had no intention of communicating through time per se, although theoretically speaking we knew the message would actually be received only seconds before it was sent. The real goal was to utilize that effect to create an unbreakable, uninterruptable communication device the likes of which the world had never known."

In 1938 Paul Dirac, a Nobel laureate, had devised a theory that allowed for the possibility of backward transmission of radio waves through time without the possibility of creating a causal loop. If correct, his theory meant that a radio transmitter could be constructed that would allow the future to speak with the past.

"As you may have guessed, our first major test of this new technology took place on New Year's Day of 2042. The unexpected consequence of that experiment was the Slip. Like everyone else, I was left confused and stunned by the event, but over time, as I managed to analyze exactly what had happened, I became convinced that my experiment was to blame. I was lucky enough to have contacts within the government in this time, and I convinced them that my experiment, Project Tach-Comm, was the catalyst for the Slip. I also believed that I could reverse the effects, and thankfully the government was willing to believe I could too.

"I say 'thankfully' because if we had not been given the opportunity to study the effect, we would not have learned that the consequences of the Slip were *far* greater than we first believed. Within three months of beginning my investigation into the event, I realized the Slip was not a unique occurrence. I have strong reason to believe that when that first experiment took place in the future, it initiated a cascade effect, one that will occur again on the exact date of the first experiment—January 1, 2042."

Jim began to ask a question, but Lorentz silenced him with a raised hand. Lorentz's voice had gradually grown less substantial as he explained the depth of the misfortune he believed he had set loose on the world. To those gathered around the table, he appeared to slowly crumple into himself as he recounted his part in what was surely the greatest catastrophe ever to occur, an event Lorentz felt was entirely his fault.

"On that date," he continued, "we will once more be thrown back in time twenty-five years. Everything we learn in the coming years, all life born during that time, every step forward we make will once again be wiped clean. We will all be thrust back into the chaos and destruction that accompanied the first Slip." Lorentz paused before adding, "Although I think the despair will be even greater the next time around, the devastation too great to even begin to imagine."

Rebecca eased the miasmal air of doom hanging over the room with a question: "What evidence do you have to support your theory of a recurring effect?"

"A very good question," said Lorentz. "Why don't I let Adrianna answer that for you?"

Adrianna switched places with Lorentz. The scientist slumped in his chair, gray with the weight of responsibility he had placed on himself. The child scientist's head was only just visible above the table, so a frustrated and embarrassed Adrianna climbed first up on to her chair, then stepped up onto the conference table and proceeded to sit cross-legged on the tabletop.

"That's better," she said, blushing. "When Prof. Lorentz and I first began working together again after the event, we decided that the only way to truly determine whether our experiment was the originator of the Slip would be to find a measurable effect . . . We found one. Our instruments detected residual tachyon . . . fallout is as good a word for it as any. This fallout consisted of traces of tachyons with the same entropic signature as those we created just before the Slip occurred. Although it isn't exactly incontrovertible proof that our experiment was responsible, it does strongly suggest to us our first test was the initiator for the event. We named it T-fallout.

"A few months after we detected the first signs of T-fallout, we took another measurement. And that was when we discovered we had an even bigger problem. Instead of decaying as we would have expected it to, the signal was increasing in strength. We checked our instruments—triple-checked them; they were calibrated perfectly. So we set up a regular regimen of T-fallout sample measurement and collation. The data we recovered reinforced our initial observation: over a period of six months there was a discernible increase in the amount of T-fallout residue detected. Also, the level of power that we were witnessing was way off the scale, far in excess of what we believed we should be reading at this temporal distance from the incident."

"And we don't understand why that is," interjected Lorentz from his chair. He looked to Jim and then Rebecca. "That's what we need you two to figure out for us."

Jim was quick to respond. Leaning forward in his chair, he said, "Look, Prof. Lorentz, I haven't worked in physics in over twenty-five years. I don't know how you expect me to be of any—"

"James," Lorentz cut in before he could finish his sentence. "Your early theoretical work on superluminal particles is still the yardstick by which all new theories are tested. It is genius . . . absolute genius."

"But it's been *twenty-five years*," Jim reiterated.

Lorentz waved his hands, dismissing Jim's objections. "It doesn't matter. Thanks to Ms. Belkov's superhuman efforts"—he smiled at his personal assistant, who sat two seats off to his left—"we have assembled a massive library of contemporary physics, both electronic and paper based. It's accessible via any terminal in the compound. Everything you could ever need is here Jim . . . *everything*. Of course, that also includes all notes and transcripts of our work so far. All we need from you is your commitment to help us."

Rebecca smiled at the professor. "I'm with you," she said.

Lorentz paused, looking Jim straight in the eye. "Please . . . as clichéd as this sounds, the very fate of the world relies on the few people gathered here in this room." Then he added with a grin, "No pressure, eh?"

There was a pause as Jim contemplated the request; then he nodded. "Okay," he said. "You can count me in."

TWENTY-FOUR

October 5, 2018—Stephen Goodmore Live

Transcript of an interview between talk-show host Stephen Goodmore (SG) and Father Edward Pike (FEP), head of the Church of Second Redemption.

SG: Welcome, Father.

FEP: Thank you, Stephen. It's very nice to be here.

SG: Now, for those viewers who may not be familiar with Father Pike, he is the founder and head of the Church of Second Redemption.

FEP: That is correct.

SG: Tell me, Father. Your church has seen a tremendous surge of converts in the twelve months since the Slip occurred. If my researchers have done their job correctly, then you have seen your flock go from a small group of devotees in the first month or so after the event to a following of over two point five million—a tremendous jump and an unprecedented increase. Why do you think so many people are devoting themselves to your branch of religion?

FEP: It's an easy question to answer, Stephen: people are looking for an answer to what happened, and we offer them the truth.

SG: And just what is it about your brand of the truth that makes it so special? What draws so many to you in these confused times? I'm sure there are many businesspeople out there who would love to know your secret.

(Laughter)

FJP: Again, it's a very simple answer. It is no secret I was without faith in my previous life. Even though I was a leader in the religious community, a priest without faith is unworthy to lead. I was unable to help redeem the very people whose souls I had been entrusted with. I became an instrument for evil rather than for good. I took my own life . . . but . . . I was given a second chance by God—

SG: Yes, but—

FEP: A second chance to redeem myself and to offer that redemption not only to those already within the Catholic Church but to those outside of it too. That is why we are nondenominational: you only need to believe to be forgiven.

SG: It has been said that the majority of your congregation are revivified—is that true?

FEP: Yes, that is correct. A large number of the reborn have found themselves drawn to our church.

SG: Why?

FEP: Are you familiar with the Book of Psalms?

SG: I can't say that I am, Father.

FEP: Psalms 111:9—"He has sent redemption itself to his people. To time indefinite he has commanded his covenant." God has given them—as he has given all of us—a final chance at redemption. Each of my flock is in a unique position to understand the implication of life eternal. They are God's reborn warriors, here to bring his word and fight for him. Armageddon is upon us, Stephen, and it is time for us all to choose a side.

TWENTY-FIVE

Project Tach-Comm Facility—Five Weeks Later

"Jim? Look at this."

Rebecca's voice contained a hint of suppressed excitement. Jim turned away from his computer. He saw the mathematician staring at her own computer screen.

"What is it, Rebecca?" he asked as he stood and made his way to her side.

"This," she said, pointing to a row of figures on her screen sitting alongside a line graph. She tapped a key, and the figures magnified to three times their original size. "There's something not right with these figures," she continued. "See here." She pointed with her index finger at a small group of numbers. "They shouldn't be there. Look." Her fingers flew across the keyboard, and the computer zoomed in closer on the line graph of the figures, isolating the numbers causing her concern. "This represents the numbers I just showed you. See how right up until this point things are just as you would expect?" She traced the curve of the graph with her finger, leaving a light smear on the screen. "No distortion in amplitude at all, but then when we get here there's this . . . bump, for lack of a better description. It shouldn't be there."

"Maybe it's interference. Some spurious emission." He leaned in closer. "Have you run diagnostics on the receivers?"

"Yes. That was the first thing I did. All the results came back clean. I cross-checked the data against the paper records in case the information has been corrupted somehow—that came back negative. Then I checked the maintenance logs for the monitoring receivers; nothing unusual there, either." She leaned back in her chair and folded her arms across her chest, biting her bottom lip as she gazed at the screen. "It just doesn't make any sense," she said.

Jim went back to his own desk and wheeled over his chair, steering it next to Rebecca's. They had been sitting in front of the computers for the past seven hours straight, and Jim caught the faint aroma of her musk floating across the narrow space between them as he sat down next to her.

"Well, it's not like we have anything better to do," he said through a smile. "Let's see if we can't figure this out."

Rebecca half turned in her chair and faced him, her own smile matching his, before turning back to her keyboard.

Jim felt a growing respect for the woman who sat at his side. In the five weeks since both he and Rebecca had agreed to join the team, he'd had little personal time with most of his new colleagues. The work had been intense and relentless. But not long after he had arrived at the lab, Mitchell Lorentz had pulled Jim into his office and explained to him that Rebecca was one of the tens of thousands of revivified who had originally died at the hands of another in their original timeline. At first Jim hadn't understood what the professor was telling him, but eventually the realization of what had happened to her sank in: she had been murdered. Lorentz had not disclosed the details of how she had died, and Jim wasn't sure he really wanted to know them, not yet anyway.

After Lorentz's revelation, Jim found it incredible she could function at all, but his incredulity had quickly turned to admiration as he witnessed the single-minded dedication with which she immersed herself in her work. Lorentz also told him that part of the reason Rebecca had accepted the position on the team was that the professor had promised her that once they had ensured the safety of humanity, the government would turn its attention to locating and apprehending the man who had committed the wicked crime against her.

"I even offered to have the investigation commence immediately," Lorentz had said, "but she said no. She wanted to wait until this was over. No distractions. That's a dedicated woman." Jim was not sure whether that was an indication of her strength of will or of her grasp of reality, but after spending the past few weeks in her company he was leaning toward the first explanation.

What he *did* know was that he liked being in her company, and he found himself taking advantage of any opportunity to be with her that presented itself.

For six more hours they worked at the keyboard of her computer, running over the data collected from the period just after the Slip occurred through to the present day. She was indefatigable, checking and rechecking data. They cross-checked all the information collected by the mainframe system with the paper printouts she had pulled from the systems. Those systems were linked directly to the tachyon receivers that monitored the ether, pulling in the tachyon fallout from the Slip.

Sitting next to Rebecca now, listening to the soft lilt of her voice as she read data to him from the computer printout, Jim realized his respect was turning into something more. It was normally just a fluttering in the back of his brain, but *this* close, his attraction to her became overwhelmingly diverting, and he felt his concentration wavering. Instead of focusing on verifying the figures on the screen, he found himself tracing the outline of her face with his eyes as she read from the computer printout resting on her knees. He allowed himself to follow the curve of her nose to the fullness of her lips. From her lips his eyes flowed over her chin and traced the arch of her throat until—

"Jim? Are you all right?" She was staring right at him, a perplexed smile on her lips, her head tilted questioningly to one side.

"Umm!" Jim felt his face redden. "Hey! It's getting a little late, don't you think?" he said, glancing at his wristwatch. "Maybe we should call it a night."

"Okay. But are you sure you're all right? You look a little flushed."

"I'm fine. Just a little bushed," he said, standing. "How about we pick up from where we left off in the morning?"

Rebecca smiled up at him from her chair. "It's a date," she said playfully, and Jim couldn't help but let out a stutter of laughter.

Halfway to the door, he turned and looked back at her watching him leave and then after a moment's pause asked, "Are you hungry? Would you like—?"

Before he could finish, she was standing and making her way to join him. "I thought you would never ask."

***

It was eleven fifteen at night and the refectory was cloaked in darkness, save for the green electronic glow of the digital clocks of several microwave ovens. Jim stood in the open doorway, allowing the light from the corridor to illuminate the room while he searched the wall for the light switch with his free hand. Finding it, he flicked the bank of switches, and the overhead lights flickered on, pushing back the darkness.

"Welcome to Chateau Baston," he said in his best mock-French accent while holding open the door for Rebecca.

They made their way over to a rack of glass-fronted refrigerators. Peering in at the shelves holding an assortment of ready-made sandwiches, pies, cookies, and candy, Jim continued his impersonation: "On tonight's menu we 'ave . . ."—he pushed the button to rotate the plates of food around the cabinet—"bologna sandwiches, sans mayo. Fruit pie and . . ."—after one more row of plates whirred into view—"the pièce de résistance, macaroni and cheese."

Through a half-suppressed fit of the giggles, Rebecca managed to blurt out her choice: mac and cheese.

"An excellent choice, mademoiselle, if I do say so myself. Let's make that two."

Jim carried the cardboard containers of ready-to-heat food over to the bank of microwaves and placed them inside.

"Not bad. Not bad at all," said Jim a few minutes later as he tasted his nuked meal.

"So tell me something about yourself, Jim," Rebecca asked as she sipped from a can of diet cola.

"What do you want to know?"

"Anything," she said, then added, "We've worked so closely since we got here, but I know so little about you. Mina said you were a writer. What did you write about?"

Jim swallowed the remainder of the food in his mouth and patted his lips clean with his napkin before replying, all the time keeping his eyes focused on the beautiful young woman who sat across the table from him.

"Science fiction . . . mostly. That was what I was well known for, but when the Slip happened I was finishing up a personal work."

"Your autobiography?" she guessed.

"I suppose you could call it that. It was more an accounting of my life. I never really intended to publish it, but don't tell my agent that. Like I said, it was a very personal book for me. I felt I needed to bring some strands of my life together that had slipped away from me. Do you know what I mean?"

She nodded.

"I didn't realize just how many strands there were, though, when I first started," he continued. "It's strange how over a lifetime you can lose track of . . ." Jim realized the woman who sat before him could not personally understand what he was talking about, because her life had been cut so tragically short. How could a man who had lived a life almost to its end convey that vast experience to someone who had not even made it out of her twenties?

He changed the subject. "I'm sorry," he said. "I didn't mean to travel down that road." He tried to sound cheerful: "Your turn to tell me something about yourself."

"Well, there's not much to tell," she said. "I come from a small town in Nevada. I majored in applied mathematics at college. My first boyfriend's name was Frank, and I had a dog named Fido."

"Fido?" Jim said incredulously, a forkful of macaroni stalled halfway to his mouth. "Really?"

"Really," she said, laughing.

"Well, ten out of ten for originality . . . I guess?"

As the laughter subsided, a silence descended between them. Not the awkward silence that can develop between two people who have nothing more to say to each other; this was more of a warmth that filled the space between them, something that only they could feel, alleviating the need for conversation.

Rebecca broke the silence a few minutes later. "I suppose you know about my death." Her brows crinkled, and her mouth drew down on one side. "That sounds so strange. I've never said it that way before. Odd."

Jim paused before replying. "Yes. I know."

When he next spoke, his question caught her off guard. Occasionally, someone asked whether she remembered anything about her final moments: Did she know who killed her? What did he look like? Had she been frightened? How did it feel to die? But no one had ever inquired past that point, so when Jim asked her "Do you remember anything after the time you died?" she was surprised. A fleeting memory played across her mind, more an emotion than anything, but it faded before she could hold on to it.

"Have you ever woken from a dream that was so vivid it seemed *too* real?" she asked. "A dream that's so intense you feel sure that you will remember every detail of it. You fall back to sleep and when you next wake up, all you can remember is a *sense* of it. It's not even a memory, more a *feeling* of how the dream made you feel." She turned her eyes away from the empty food container and looked up at the man sitting across from her, locking her eyes with his, challenging him to laugh or contradict her, searching for any sign that he may be mocking her. "That's what I felt when I first woke up after the Slip—like I had forgotten a wonderful dream."

Jim reached out across the table and squeezed her hand. "I believe you," he said matter-of-factly.

Later, as they stood at the door to Rebecca's apartment, after they had said good night for the third time, Rebecca turned and kissed Jim gently on the cheek before stepping into her apartment.

Jim stood outside her door for a while, unable to move, confused emotions tingling and his heart racing. Finally, he turned and made his way back to his own apartment.

TWENTY-SIX

The sun was liquid gold, melting into the eastern horizon as Rebecca Lacey walked out onto the diamond-etched field. She headed toward the batter's box, swinging the thirty-ounce Louisville Slugger in her right hand like a scythe.

The crowd—Mina Belkov waving a bright-red pennant—went wild, while over on the pitcher's mound, Mitchell Lorentz limbered up with some practice balls that curved and zigzagged impossibly like Sidewinder missiles to the catcher's mitt of Horatio Mabry. The big man's bulk cast an elongated shadow across the field, like a gigantic sundial.

In the outfield Adrianna Drake jumped and cartwheeled excitedly, tripping and falling over a uniform that was several sizes too large for her. Catching sight of Becky, she stopped her cavorting and instead began waving excitedly at her, a smile of pure childish joy lighting up her angelic face and making the baseball cap perched jauntily on her head jiggle. Jim Baston, resplendent and dashing in a beautiful black tuxedo, stood respectfully in center field, exuding a demeanor of debonair sophistication that removed all sense of incongruity from his choice of clothing.

Kicking sand off the plate with her toes, Rebecca swung the bat once, twice, three times to stretch the muscles in her arms before very deliberately glancing both left and right.

"Batter up," drawled Mabry.

Oddly, all the bases were empty, as were both players' benches in the home and away team dugouts. Looked like it was all up to her then!

The huge scoreboard, looming ominously in the distance, was counting backward, its home team score clacking down from ninety-nine in a painfully slow countdown to zero like some giant timer.

None of that mattered now. It was all up to her. The fate of . . . something . . . Something she could not quite put her finger on but which she knew carried a great responsibility hung squarely on her shoulders.

Becky fixed her steely gaze on a golden, glowing Lorentz out on the pitcher's mound as he wound up for the first pitch.

He let fly.

The horsehide-covered ball sped toward her impossibly fast, a bleached-white blur . . . and she hit it high and steep.

Lorentz, Adrianna, and Jim all ran to the same spot in the center field. They stood together in a huddle with their eyes turned skyward, watching the ball reach its apogee before it began a slow descent. All three raised their hands above their heads, ready to catch it as the ball plummeted toward the ground.

The counter on the scoreboard began rotating faster as the ball fell toward Lorentz's, Adrianna's, and Jim's outstretched hands. Numbers flew by in a blur; the mechanical whir of the scoreboard became a clatter like wind blowing through wooden wind chimes.

Their arms reaching high into the air, Lorentz, Adrianna, and Jim waved confidently at Becky as they waited expectantly for the ball to arrive, to fall into their waiting mitts.

There was a dull thud.

Rebecca turned to see a ball identical to the one she had sent soaring into the sky roll to a stop near her feet. Another thud as another ball dropped to the ground from nowhere. Then more balls fell, seemingly from nowhere, until a path of white baseballs lay between her and the group of her colleagues, who were still waiting patiently for the original ball to finish its descent. As Rebecca watched, more and more balls fell, carpeting the field. Finally, her original baseball fell straight into the waiting mitt of Mitchell Lorentz.

Jim leaped into the air, pumping his fist in victory. Lorentz grabbed Adrianna and swung her around and around as she giggled and snorted. Her baseball cap flew off, carried by a wind that swept it high into the air. The cap disappeared into a swiftly approaching darkness that had somehow crept up unseen, swallowing the horizon and now devouring the boundary of the outfield. The darkness brought with it a sense of impending disaster that began to chew and gnaw at Rebecca's stomach.

Horatio Mabry let out an exultant whoop of joy, tossed his catcher's mask carelessly into the air, and ran past Rebecca to join his celebrating friends in center field. But they had missed the ball. Couldn't they see that? Why were they celebrating?

Rebecca dropped the bat, which floated toward the ground in slow motion. Turning, she began to follow Mabry toward her colleagues, but her legs felt as though the air had turned to molasses. Barely able to move through the gelatinous air, she began waving her arms, desperately trying to attract their attention, but the group was caught up in its own celebration and did not notice her. Panic coursed through her body and she felt her heart begin to pound and pound and pound and—

The numbers on the scoreboard finally reached zero just as the sun disappeared into the darkness. The single deafening clang of a bell reverberated through the ground like an earthquake, and the world went dark as the blackness that had encroached unseen suddenly swallowed the remaining light.

***

Rebecca woke from her dream with a cry caught in her throat. Throwing back the sweat-dampened comforter, she swung her glistening legs over the side of the bed and glanced at her alarm clock: it was 3:38 in the morning.

She grabbed her dressing gown from its hook on the back of the door, then quickly crossed to her computer and turned on the screen, which cast its iridescent glow through the darkened room. Her fingers began to fly across the keyboard as she entered set after set of complicated mathematical equations into the system. Finally, after she tapped the last of the data into the computer, she set the program to calculate mode and waited impatiently, her fingers drumming anxiously on the desktop as the machine worked toward its resolution.

A minute later an electronic ping sounded from the computer's integrated speaker system, and the screen changed to display the results of its calculations. Rebecca's eyes followed the scrolling data. When she reached the final figure, she double-tapped the screen with her finger.

Rebecca reached for the phone and quickly punched in the numbers that would connect her with Mitchell Lorentz's room.

TWENTY-SEVEN

Jim's phone chirruped insistently, dragging him to wakefulness. Bleary-eyed, he reached a hand blindly toward the phone, his fingers searching for the speakerphone button.

"Yeah? Hello," Jim mumbled into his pillow.

"Jim, I'm sorry to wake you but it's urgent," Lorentz's voice crackled from the speaker. "Can you meet us in the cafeteria in ten minutes, please?"

"Sure," Jim slurred back. "What's up?"

"I'll explain when you get here."

The line went dead.

***

Nobody is supposed to look good at five in the morning, but as Jim walked into the now brightly lit cafeteria, he decided he would have to amend that belief, because as he stood in the doorway looking in at those already assembled, somehow Rebecca managed to look radiant.

Her hair was tousled and tangled, and she hadn't bothered with makeup, yet she was the most beautiful sight he had ever set eyes upon, Atlantean in her beauty and otherworldliness. She was talking animatedly to Lorentz, who looked exhausted, but his eyes seemed to reflect an excitement and spark Jim had not seen before.

"This had better be good," said a sleep-gruff voice from behind Jim as Harry edged his bulk through the space between Jim and the doorjamb. "I need all the beauty sleep I can get."

When she caught sight of Jim walking in her direction, Rebecca seemed to become suddenly aware of her appearance, running a long-fingered hand through her hair.

Adrianna was already in the room. She passed Jim and Harry cups of lukewarm black coffee as they sat at the Formica table.

Jim knocked back his in one gulp and grabbed a refill from the dispenser before sitting back down. "Now you have my undivided attention," he said as he sipped from the Styrofoam cup.

Rebecca's eyes met his, and she gave him an almost-invisible smile.

"Sorry for getting you all up so early. You can blame Miss Lacey for that," said Lorentz in an attempt at humor, his face betraying the true gravitas of the early-morning meeting. "She has something she wants to share with us that I think you will all agree is important."

Rebecca stood, took a sip from her coffee, then began recounting the images she had seen in her dream. Several minutes later, her story complete, the confused eyes of the team stared at her.

"You got us all here at"—Adrianna paused to glance at the large clock fixed to the wall behind her—"five in the morning to tell us about a dream?" The diminutive scientist's voice was heavy with incredulity, and she ended her question with a frown and a dismissive shake of her head.

"You will have to forgive Prof. Drake," Lorentz said. "I sometimes think that the trauma of the Slip caused her politeness to be left behind in the future."

Adrianna let out a humph and sat, with her arms crossed, sullenly.

"It's okay. I think I need to explain something about myself," Rebecca said, turning to face the morose Adrianna. "Since I was a child, I have experienced . . . I suppose you would call them waking dreams . . . My subconscious processes information, problems, and puzzles in my sleep and then—well, the results appear to me in my dreams."

"So now you're saying you have visions?" snickered Adrianna.

"No," Rebecca said. "I'm saying that I have a brain that doesn't quit when it gets hold of problems. Even when I sleep, it worries over them. It's a well-documented condition."

Jim could feel the tension beginning to rise between the two women.

Horatio must have felt it too because he cleared his throat dramatically before asking, "So just what did your dream reveal to you, Rebecca? Apart from the fact that I should never play against you in a game of baseball."

Rebecca either missed the large man's joke or chose to ignore it because, instead of replying, she stood up and walked to the head of the table. "We've been looking at solving the problem of the residual T-fallout all wrong," she said. Adrianna began to object, but Rebecca cut her short. "It's a simple mistake, understandable under the circumstances, I suppose. We have been treating the signal as if it was indisputably the same one that left the future when the Slip occurred, searching for anything that would have caused the disruption and for differences between the original signal and the one we have been receiving and analyzing. Instead, we should have been looking more closely at the signal itself."

Rebecca paused as if to give her next statement more dramatic effect, and a sudden smile flickered across her face. "Actually, we should stop referring to it as a signal and instead start referring to it in the plural."

"Signals?" asked Lorentz questioningly.

"Signals," repeated Rebecca.

Jim would not have been surprised to see Adrianna slap herself on her forehead, such was the suddenness of the realization that crossed her face. It would have been comical if the situation were not so incredibly important.

"Of course," she said. "How could I have been so stupid? It's a harmonic, isn't it?"

Rebecca's smile widened as realization swept across the faces of those seated around the table. All except for Horatio Mabry, who continued looking perplexed at his colleague's revelation. "Am I the only one here who doesn't understand what the hell you're all getting excited about?"

"A harmonic," said Adrianna, "is a component frequency of a harmonic motion. It's an integral multiple of the fundamental frequency, yet separate and distinct from the overall waveform."

"There's more than one frequency in the tachyon wave that was sent?" said Mabry.

"I think," Rebecca continued, "that there are probably far more than one or two extra frequencies in this harmonic."

"So you're saying the original team sent more than one transmission?" Mabry asked.

"No," Adrianna said. "We sent only one transmission."

"So where did these extra frequencies come from? If you didn't send them via the original transmission, then who did?" Mabry directed his question to Prof. Lorentz, who had remained silent after the revelation, his fingers steepled in front of his lips, head slightly bowed as he listened to his protégés talk. Now all heads turned in his direction.

"Perhaps it's an echo," Lorentz offered. "A bounce from some event in the past—"

"Or future," interjected Mabry.

"—that has caused the signal to amplify and distort. My honest answer is that I do not know." Lorentz seemed suddenly to shrug off the melancholia and exhaustion that had dogged him for the past few weeks and a wave of enthusiasm overtook him. "There's only one way to find out. Adrianna, can you refocus your attention to Rebecca's discovery?"

"Yes. I can put what I'm doing on the back burner."

"I've run some preliminary calculations," added Rebecca as she pushed a paper printout across the table to Adrianna. "They are all uploaded onto the central server for anybody who wants to take a look at them."

"You've managed to isolate five streams already?" Adrianna asked.

"Yes. But that's really just a cursory initial run-through of the data."

Adrianna began scribbling notes and figures on the printout before finally looking up. "This first figure—how sure are you of its accuracy?"

A cloud passed over Rebecca's face. "As sure as I can be under the circumstances. Why?"

"Because if your calculations are correct, then we have a bigger problem than we first thought."

"Please, Adrianna, do elucidate," said Lorentz.

"Here." She handed the printout to Lorentz, her own calculations written in her childish scrawl alongside Rebecca's.

Lorentz flipped the sheets open as if he were reading a newspaper. All signs of his earlier hopeful mood evaporated into thin air as his face drained of color.

"My God," he said, the words falling from suddenly dry lips.

"What is it?" Jim asked.

"It seems," said Lorentz, his voice barely controlled, "that our initial estimation severely underestimated the amount of time we have left before the second Slip occurs. Prof. Drake's figures appear to indicate we no longer have years to stop this problem."

"How long?" said Mabry.

"Two months," said Adrianna, and then she added, "If we are lucky."

A silence fell across the room as Jim's gaze moved to the face of each of his colleagues gathered around the table. They looked as though they had been handed a death sentence.

"You're telling me that we can expect another occurrence of the Slip in just two months?" he asked.

The question was directed to the room of people, but it was Lorentz who answered.

"If Adrianna's figures are correct—and I have no reason to believe otherwise—then yes. We have just weeks before we will find ourselves back where we were on that fateful day again."

Jim's mind began to comprehend the impending disaster: the destruction of all their work to date, everything reset to where they were when the Slip first occurred. All progress lost. The thought made him want to throw up. Plans would need to be made for when the second Slip occurred. They would have to arrange a meeting place for the group so they could ensure that they began work immediately. There would have to be—

A terrible realization became suddenly and horrifyingly apparent to Jim.

"Lorentz, if this new event is going to occur twenty-odd years earlier than we estimated, how is that going to affect where we get deposited back down the time stream?" Jim asked.

Adrianna pulled the printout from Lorentz and quickly jotted down more figures. A minute later she stopped writing and stared impassively at the paper. A single tear appeared in the girl's eye, flowed over her reddened cheek and across her quivering lip, before falling silently to the table. "Oh no," she whispered. "Someone tell me this isn't right."

Rebecca stood and walked around to the back of Adrianna's chair. She placed an encouraging hand on the girl's shoulder and stared down at the printout. Among the jumble of calculations, she saw a single figure in the professor's childlike hand, underlined with three thick, slashing strokes from her pen.

The figure read "1989."

Rebecca felt the room begin to spin. She threw her hand out and grabbed the back of Adrianna's chair for support until her vision stopped swimming.

"Christ, Rebecca, you look like someone just walked over your grave." Horatio Mabry was halfway out of his chair, the look of concern on his face quickly followed by one of embarrassment as he caught his poor choice of words to the resurrected woman.

"I'm . . . okay," Rebecca responded, making her way, on leaden feet, back to her chair.

"So, are you going to give the rest of us the good news?" Mabry asked solemnly.

Rebecca took a deep breath before answering. "According to Adrianna's preliminary calculations, the second Slip is going to push us back the same amount of time as the first one."

"Back to 2017," said Mabry. "Right?"

Rebecca's eyes met Jim's as she regarded him deeply for a moment before answering in a barely audible voice. "No. Because the second Slip is going to occur so much earlier than we expected, it's going to drop us somewhere in *1989*, and that means most of us will either be infants or . . . unborn. Either way there won't be anyone left to figure out how to stop this thing."

TWENTY-EIGHT

*Excerpt from "Discourse of a Believer—an Interview with Father
Edward Pike, Founder of the Church of Second Redemption."*
Time Magazine, *October 2018*

. . . you see, the Catholic Church is faulty. It is so
entrenched in the doctrine of "faith above all else" that
should God himself come to us and tell us that a certain
belief or practice the church had mandated is incorrect, he
would be unable to persuade those who govern the faithful
of his veracity. If he sat across from you in this very chair
and said, "I am the one and only true God," the aver-
age Catholic would reply, "Get thee behind me, Satan."
Everyone seems so very sure God has no desire to talk
directly to *them*. The very tenet binding us to the church
denies us true contact and understanding of God. People
had forgotten, myself included, that God speaks *through*
the church and that the church is not God—that is a dis-
tinction which must be remembered at all cost.

There is a modern parable I am particularly fond of
that illustrates my point: A man is caught in a flood, and

as the water begins to rise, he climbs up onto the roof of his house and awaits rescue. As the hours pass and the water rises, no help comes, so he begins to pray: "Dear Lord, in your divine mercy, please save me from the rising floodwater."

Suddenly a helicopter appears and lowers a rope down to the stranded man. "Take the rope," says the pilot. "No, thanks," replies the stranded man, "I'm waiting for God to rescue me." Three more times the pilot of the helicopter tries to convince the stranded man to climb up the rope, and three more times he refuses: "I'm waiting for God."

All the while the water is rising and rising, until finally the house is swept away, the man with it, his last words being "God, why have you forsaken me?"

So you see, when God announces his presence, he always makes it obvious to humanity. How much more obvious than the events of the last few years does he need to make it before *you* will believe?

TWENTY-NINE

"Look at this," said Adrianna, gesturing to figures on her computer screen. "I've been working on this for the last few days. Check this out." She punched a key on the computer keyboard, and row upon row of numbers began to scroll down the screen.

The team, gathered around her computer, regarded the rapidly scrolling figures with confusion.

"What are they?" asked Jim.

"Those," said Adrianna as the numbers continued to scroll, "are the frequencies of the tachyons contained within the harmonic."

"My God! How many are there?" asked Lorentz.

"I managed to isolate over seven hundred." Adrianna swung around in her chair to face the others. "Most are close to being immeasurable. They barely registered on the scanner—it was a bastard to have to go in and extrapolate them individually—but that's not the best of it. Take a look at this." She pressed another key, and an animated graphic replaced the figures.

"See?" she said, her voice a hushed tone of awe.

"Very pretty," said Jim, "but what the hell is it?"

"It looks like a string of DNA," Mitchell guessed, but as he leaned closer to the screen he reappraised his observation. "Or more precisely, it looks very much like a DNA double helix."

On the computer screen, slowly rotating around its axis, a blue strand wove its way helically up the screen. Attached at varying points along the strand were small, glowing spheres of phosphorescent light, most bunched in groups of three, but the farther away from the center of the strand, the less the spheres were bunched.

"So what does DNA have to do with the harmonic?" asked Mabry, his bushy eyebrows arched questioningly.

"It's not a DNA strand," replied Adrianna. "It's a graphical representation of the frequencies I pulled out of the harmonic."

"What's that?" asked Rebecca, pointing at the center of the strand, where a single red globe, bordered on either side by two green spheres of glowing light, pulsed gently.

"That represents the frequency of our original signal, the one that initiated the Slip. I've isolated it and confirmed its characteristics; it is definitely the original signal. It's also the strongest.

"The two spheres on either side of it"—Adrianna used the index and middle finger of her right hand to point at the screen—"are frequencies that were just below and above it. There's barely a difference of just a few megahertz really." She moved her tiny fingers to the top and bottom of the strand.

"You see here and here, the clustering of frequencies drops off. The farther away you get from our central frequency, the weaker the signals become. I have a feeling that if we could amplify the signal significantly enough and maybe clean out some more of the noise, we would find the missing frequencies to these clusters. Hell! For all I know, the stuff my equipment is reading as noise could be more frequencies, too faint for me to extract. Without more sensitive equipment I will never be able to tell."

"Amazing," Lorentz said quietly.

"Yes, definitely amazing," said Jim. "But what does it *mean*?"

Adrianna swung slowly around in her chair until she faced the group of scientists standing behind her. "I have absolutely no idea," she said candidly. "We really don't know enough about it to be able to speculate with any degree of accuracy. It could be echoes, a naturally occurring event that we have never been able to monitor before, maybe even similar experiments in other countries."

"Well," said Lorentz, "keep running the tests. Let's see what else you can pull out of it."

***

The music filled Jim's apartment: Rachmaninov's *Rhapsody on a Theme of Paganini*, the seventeenth variation flowing seamlessly into the first few gentle piano notes of the eighteenth.

The lights were turned down low. A glass of red wine (a welcome gift from Horatio, who was apparently quite the connoisseur) rested in Jim's hand as he relaxed on the sofa, allowing the swell of the music to flow over him. No matter how many times he heard those opening notes, he always found himself falling under the sway of the music. It was the sonic equivalent of a relaxing massage, unwinding his muscles and his mind while allowing him to mentally escape the confines of the facility that had become his home over the past few weeks. He might not be able to leave the compound, but he could travel on the passion of the symphony.

Because the scientists were forbidden from leaving the base, Lorentz had asked if he wanted anything brought in from the outside world beyond the complex's security and razor-wired perimeter. Jim knew that without his music he would go mad. He needed to maintain a connection with normality, something to remind him he had a life . . . once upon a time, at least. There wasn't even a radio in the apartment, for God's sake. If he was going to have to work here for any length of time, that would need to be rectified.

The following morning he poked his head around Lorentz's office door. "Knock, knock," he said.

Lorentz was busy at his desk running over figures, his eyes were red and puffy, and Jim could read the relief in the scientist's face at the excuse to break away from the computer screen.

"Come on in. What can I do for you?"

Jim had outlined his request to Lorentz, who in turn called on Mina. She relayed Jim's request to the appropriate security staff, and less than twenty-four hours later Jim awoke from a late-afternoon nap to a heavy-handed knocking at his door.

Standing in the corridor, two burly-looking men in overalls and crew cuts waited next to a couple of carts stacked with brown boxes.

"Dr. Baston, we have your requisition," said the bigger of the two men matter-of-factly. "Where do you want 'em?"

"Just drop them in the middle of the living room there, please."

The two men wheeled the carts into the room and quickly unloaded the packages.

"Thanks, guys," Jim said as he closed the door behind them.

He ripped through the packing tape with a knife grabbed from the kitchen and pulled each of the separate components out of their respective boxes. By the time he opened all but one of the boxes, he had a set of seven components neatly laid out on the apartment floor: an amplifier, CD player, a tuner, and four speakers, each with their own stand.

Fitting all the pieces together, he moved to the final unopened box, quickly cut through the packaging tape, and rummaged through its contents until he found the exact thing he wanted. Jim pulled the silver disc from its case and slipped it into the tray of his newly assembled music system, turned the volume shuttle to an acceptable level, and pressed the "Play" button.

Instantly the room was filled with the synthesized tones of a Wurlitzer, and as Ali Campbell began to sing about the magic of Kingston Town, Jim—fingers snapping to the offbeat accent of the tune—reggae-danced back to the box containing his music collection from the cabin at Shadow Lake and began to search through the CDs.

There were many years of memories tied up in this collection. The CD had been replaced years ago by digital downloads. But even in the distant future, Jim had maintained his collection on disc just as those who had grown up with the vinyl album swore CDs just didn't have the same kind of sound quality that their LPs had.

The album he was playing now had been a gift from his dad when Jim had been a kid, his very first music CD. He still remembered opening the tiny gift-wrapped package on his—when was it? His eighth or ninth birthday? He also remembered with a smile the look of conspiratorial smugness in his mom's and dad's eyes when he had said to them, "Thanks, but you need a CD player to play a CD." His mom had suggested that maybe he should go take a look in his bedroom. He'd grabbed the UB40 CD and sprinted upstairs. Bursting into his bedroom, he saw a large wrapped box sitting on his bed, a big red bow tied around it, and a note written in his mother's elegant hand that simply said, "Happy birthday. We love you, son."

He was surprised the CD was still playable; he had listened to it so many times when he was younger, it was a wonder it hadn't simply worn out.

Jim let out a sigh as bittersweet memories came rolling back.

His dad had died in 2012 from lung cancer. A lifetime of smoking had first taken his left lung, then twenty-five percent of his right, and finally, on a rain-swept evening in September, his life. His mom, always a rock he could hold on to no matter what the problem, had simply fallen apart. Over the span of three years, he watched her collapse inward, until one day he received a call from his mother's neighbor telling him he should maybe come on home, that something terrible had happened.

His mom had locked herself in the old Chevy Blazer, run a hose from the exhaust system into the interior, and turned on the engine. She left a note to him that said, "I love you and I know you will understand." The real sadness was he *did* understand. His mother and father had been inseparable, two halves of a single soul that could not bear to be apart for any longer than they already had.

Now, as he sat in the electronic glow of the amplifier and graphic equalizer display, he allowed his mind to drift back to his childhood, to better days.

Jim had never been a fan of convention. He had found the stodgy, methodical teaching of most of his lecturers to be boring and unenthused, too slow for his desire to explore everything. His teachers were forever berating him for wanting to move on to the next experiment before they believed he was ready: *You have to learn to walk before you can run, James* was a cliché he had heard more times than he cared to remember. They failed to understand his natural ability to instinctively comprehend the processes involved in every experiment or project he worked on, mistaking his enthusiasm to move on for sloppy procedure.

That was all before he met Mr. Davies.

Jim knew that here was a teacher who was unlike any other he would ever meet when he witnessed the new teacher pull up for his first day at school in a grungy, weatherworn leather jacket and sitting astride a huge Harley-Davidson. The bike had roared and growled into the reserved area of the teacher's parking lot like some tiger clawing at the gates of academia.

It was Mr. Davies who had shown him for the first time what it was to be a true scientist: you had to be thrilled by the wonder of it all, and you had to allow your imagination to run rampant if you ever wanted to push back any of the boundaries facing science.

Yes, he owed Mr. Davies a great deal.

Jim remembered the first day he had met him. Davies had wandered into Jim's seventh-grade class, and immediately the children had fallen into silence. Looking more like a pirate than a teacher with his thick ginger beard and massive build, he had stared at the students for a moment, his eye finally falling on Jim. "You!" he had said, pointing at Jim. "Come on up here and give me a hand, would you?"

Obediently, Jim did as he was asked. "Take this," the new teacher said, handing Jim one of a pair of speakers, while holding its twin in his other hand. "Now hold it directly over your head." The pirate opened his leather jacket, unclipped a portable CD player from his belt, then connected it to the speakers. He pressed the silver "Play" button. Instantly the sound of some rock group Jim did not recognize began pounding out from the speakers. Jim could feel the speaker reverberating in his hands with each drumbeat. "For those of you who don't know," said the pirate to the rapt class of kids, "that's a group called the Beatles. Now watch this."

Slowly, he brought his own speaker parallel with Jim's and began moving it closer. When the teacher's speaker was about six inches from Jim's, the music had suddenly and inexplicably stopped. Jim could still feel the drumbeat reverberating through his hands and down his arms to his shoulders, but no sound came out. The teacher moved his speaker back an inch, and the music magically began spilling into the classroom again. Forward an inch, it stopped. Back an inch, it could be heard.

The pirate's face had suddenly been split by a massive grin, and his eyes lit up with childlike excitement. "Cool, eh?" he said to the class, and it was at that point Jim knew his life was about to change.

That day had stuck with Jim. When he needed reminding of the force that drove him, or when he found himself slowed by the whys rather than whats, he would drift back and remember that display of physics.

So many times he had . . . Jim stopped midthought. He picked up the remote control and switched off the music, walked over to the wall, and flipped on the lights. Grabbing a pen and pad of paper off the table, he quickly jotted down some formulas before dropping his hands to his hips.

"Well, shit!" he said, tearing the page of figures from the pad before heading out the door.

THIRTY

Rebecca was midway through getting ready for bed when a knock at her door stopped her.

"Rebecca. It's Jim. Do you have a couple of minutes?"

She quickly threw on the baggy gray sweatshirt she had just tossed onto the comforter, buttoning up her jeans as she made her way to the door.

"I'm sorry to disturb you so late," Jim said as Rebecca ushered him into her apartment. "I just needed you to verify some figures for me if that's all right."

"Sure," came her reply. "It's not a problem."

Jim looked at her peculiarly, his head tilted just a little, and his lips turned up in a lopsided smile. "Are you sure I'm not disturbing you?" He reached out and pointed to her neckline.

Glancing down, she saw that in her rush to throw her sweatshirt back on she had somehow managed to put it on not only inside out but also back to front. The tag was protruding pertly out from the sweatshirt's neckline like the tongue of some mischievous kid.

Rebecca felt her face flush with embarrassment. "Umm! Could you excuse me for just one moment," she said, and tried to walk with as much dignity as she could muster back to her bedroom, leaving Jim in the living room attempting to suppress his laughter as best as he could.

When next she emerged, she was wearing a white blouse, and she could not help but notice the appraising look from Jim before he averted his eyes.

"It needed washing anyway," Rebecca said, pointing a thumb back to her bedroom.

"Take a look at these," Jim said, placing the sheet of paper he had torn from his pad on her coffee table. "Tell me if I've made a mistake."

Rebecca sat on the sofa, picked up the piece of paper, and scanned Jim's scribbled figures. Jim took the seat next to her, his hip brushing against hers; she caught a faint trace of his cologne and her heart skipped a beat. She was surprised he could not hear it thudding behind her ribs, it was so loud in her own ears. She swallowed hard and tried to concentrate on the numbers in front of her.

"It all seems to work," she said a minute or so later. "Why? What is it?"

"Great," he exclaimed, grabbing her hand and pulling her in the direction of the door. "Come on. We need to wake some people up."

***

"You really have to stop doing this to me," said a haggard-looking Horatio Mabry as he flopped his huge bulk down into a chair in the conference room.

"There, there," chided Adrianna, patting his hand with her own, her face a picture of mock sympathy and understanding.

Jim passed Horatio a cup of coffee and addressed the assembled scientists. "When I was a kid, I had this teacher. A great guy who helped me understand a lot of things. First time I met him, he showed me an experiment that stuck with me."

Briefly, Jim outlined the experiment involving the two speakers.

Lorentz said, "It's called cophasing. It's just simple waveform canceling—oh! My goodness."

Jim smiled at Lorentz as he saw realization dawn on the scientist's face. "Exactly! The action of one waveform canceling out another, like the electronics in noise-canceling headphones."

"Exactly," Jim said, snapping his fingers.

"How is that going to help us?" asked Adrianna.

"It's really kind of simple. If we can set up and transmit a second tachyon stream equal and opposite to the one that's heading toward us, it should have the same canceling effect as the sound waves from the speakers."

"In theory," said Lorentz.

"Will it stop the Slip?" asked Mabry.

"Dead in its tracks," answered Jim, and then he echoed Lorentz: "In theory."

***

It was stupendous, magnificent news.

Lorentz pushed open the door to his office and sat down in the plush leather chair. Finally, there was hope. The burden of responsibility had weighed so very terribly on his mind, and Jim's news was like a glimmer of light to a man trapped deep beneath the earth. It represented freedom from his personal prison, the chance to redeem himself for his own miserable failure. But most of all it symbolized hope for the billions of men, women, and children who would never know just how close the human race had come to being finally run.

Lorentz picked up the phone from his desk, then quickly punched in a set of numbers and waited for the person to answer.

"Hello," he said, the call answered after just two rings. "I have wonderful news."

THIRTY-ONE

A large mahogany desk occupied the center of the office, its surface bare except for a telephone and an empty in/out tray. Seated in his black leather executive chair, Homeland Security Deputy Director John Humphreys replaced the telephone receiver into its cradle, his ample belly straining the fabric of the white button-down shirt he wore beneath his three-piece suit. The aged leather of the chair creaked as he leaned back, his fingers steepled in front of his face while he stared distantly at the corner of his office.

He could not have hoped for better news; the president would be very pleased. Humphreys had begun to have some misgivings about the gap between the scientist's intelligence and his actual capabilities. He was concerned Lorentz could not handle the stress his position created and had come very close to removing him from his post. That was all behind them now, and for the first time there was hope.

Reaching a pudgy hand to his desk, he pressed a button on the telephone. "Ms. Brahms, would you come in, please."

No sooner had his finger left the machine than the door to the office swung open and a ramrod-straight woman, gray hair tightly tied behind her head, accentuating her sharp, bony features, entered the room, electronic notebook in hand.

In her early sixties, Ms. Brahms exuded a sense of perfect secretarial efficiency. Everything about her confirmed this was a woman of competence, from the stride of her walk and aloof jut of her chin, to the way she immediately took the seat on the opposite side of the bureaucrat's desk and flipped open the screen of her notebook, her fingers paused over the keys ready to begin transcribing her boss's words.

Humphreys did not acknowledge her presence, taking not even a moment to thank her for staying so late at the office; instead, he continued staring through the triangle of his fingers before finally, with a sharp intake of breath that made the jowls of his sallow face jiggle, he began: "Mr. President . . ."

***

Ursula Brahms was shaking as she left Deputy Director Humphreys's office; she was trembling all the way to her very core. She had worked for many powerful people in her lifetime—from CEOs of Fortune 500 companies, to senators and the odd captain of industry—but never before had any position placed such a great burden of responsibility on her as she now felt.

She had been chosen. She could feel God's gaze focused on her like a spotlight, almost hear his words in her mind: *Your time has come, Ursula.* The ecstasy of his love welled up within her heart.

Her last job had been for the director of the FBI at the J. Edgar Hoover Building, but that had come to an abrupt end in 2027 when, stepping out of the shower one spring morning, she slipped on a wet patch of tile and crashed to the floor of her bathroom, smashing her head against the porcelain sink unit.

Ursula had never married, never felt the need, and with no close friends to call on her, she lay on the floor of her apartment's bathroom, unable to move, while an ever-greater pool of blood spread around her head.

She prayed for someone to come and find her.

No one came.

Almost thirteen hours after her accident—by that time she was falling in and out of consciousness—Ursula died.

The next thing she knew, Ursula had found herself walking to her car, keys in one hand and her clutch bag in the other, on her way to some suddenly forgotten destination. The cold floor of the bathroom was replaced by the warm rays of the early-morning sun, and the pain in her head was gone. She felt young and energized. She felt . . . *alive.*

Ursula had always been a firm believer in God. A regular attendee of her local Presbyterian church every Sunday, she was convinced she was one of the chosen. When she had died alone on the cold, tiled floor, there had been no real fear in her heart because she had known she would be going to heaven. So as the days after the Slip had passed by and, as much as she tried, she could summon no memory of her ever having been to heaven, Ursula began to worry. She had begun to worry that maybe she was not in God's favor. She had worried that her life spent in piety and denial—denial of both her own desires and of the few men whose interest in her had allowed them to see past her frozen exterior—had not met with the approval of the Almighty. She worried that maybe—just maybe—there was no afterlife, that the preachers and priests had all been wrong, and the atheists had been right all along. It had been too terrible a thought to contemplate—what a terrible waste of her life if the unbelievers had been right all along.

Ursula had thrust the thoughts from her mind. But gradually as the days ticked by, despair began to overtake her. A despair so dark and depressing it enfolded her like a funeral shroud, dragging her down into an abyss she knew she could never escape.

Deeper. Deeper. Deeper.

Until one warm spring afternoon, as she sat staring at her TV screen with the curtains of her room closed against the sunshine of the day, Ursula saw an angel of the Lord. Admittedly, to all outward appearances he was just a man, but as she listened to him talk so eloquently and knowingly, she knew he was an angel sent to save her, that the sign from God she had been waiting for had finally arrived.

The angel stared out of the TV screen; his eyes seemed to fix on hers, and his words seemed meant for her ears only. The message of redemption he passed to her was the spiritual lifeline Ursula had been waiting for, and it showed her there was still a chance of redemption.

The Lord had not forgotten her. She was not abandoned.

Immediately following the interview, Ursula had called the number displayed at the bottom of the screen and spoken to a woman who told her the address of the nearest branch of the angel's church. She had thrown on her overcoat and left the apartment, not even bothering to turn off her TV set, such was her enthusiasm and excitement.

The man-angel's name was Father Edward Pike, leader of the Church of Second Redemption.

Now, as Ursula slumped at her desk, her head still reeling from the information she had just learned from her boss, she quickly tapped in the number of her local church representative and arranged a meeting for that very afternoon to pass on the terrible news.

THIRTY-TWO

*Think not that I am come to send peace on
earth: I came not to send peace, but a sword.*

—Matthew 10:34

"Are you aware that the instant you die, your body loses twenty-one grams of weight?" The questioning voice of Father Edward Pike wafted pleasingly through the stark room like a cool breeze on a warm day. "That's the weight of a hummingbird." The priest's voice took on a tone of childlike awe as he continued: "Amazing, isn't it, the wonder of God's creation? Truly amazing."

The spiritual leader of the Church of Second Redemption regarded the only other person in the room with a serene smile. Seated across the simple wooden table, the other man was almost invisible, shrouded in shadow.

The room's only source of illumination, a small window high up on one wall, allowed a single shaft of light to penetrate the room. The light fell directly on Pike, revealing the paleness of his skin and the contrasting dark bags hanging loosely beneath his eyes.

Dust motes floated gently from darkness into light and back again to darkness. The room seemed more a cell than the office of the leader of what was quickly becoming one of the most powerful religious organizations on earth.

"Are scientists able to explain this?" Pike's fist banged suddenly down onto the table, the explosion of noise echoing off the bare concrete walls.

"No! Of course they cannot. What do they offer instead? Empty theories, ideas, and possibilities. Anything but accept the simplest truth. The scientists promise us a technological paradise, but instead they open the doors to hell."

The priest's hands came together above his heart and then apart in an imitation of a bird taking flight. "Twenty-one grams—the weight of the soul as it escapes the confines of our body."

The other man in the room was used to these outpourings. As time had gone by since they first met, the priest's frequent soliloquies had become more and more extravagant as his growing delusions began to manifest, his mood swings becoming more extreme with each passing day. As the priest continued his erratic tirade, the companion detected a hint of contempt—just a smidgen of venom—creeping into the priest's voice as he spat, "Scientists! They are as worthless as lawyers. They both take the truth and twist it to match their own warped perceptions."

The other said nothing. He continued to watch impassively while the priest raised himself to his feet, leaned across the table until he was just a few inches away, and whispered, "It appears the devil has finally awoken and shown his face." Tears ran down the priest's cheeks as he spoke, collecting in a glistening pool on the top of the table as his mood swung toward ecstasy.

"We have been given a task," Pike whispered. "God has asked much of us before, but now he has sent us his final test, and we *will* prove our worthiness."

THIRTY-THREE

"Have you seen this?" demanded Mitchell Lorentz as he tossed a copy of the morning edition of the *Washington Times* onto the table next to Jim.

"And a very good morning to you too, Prof. Lorentz," said Jim, glancing up from his breakfast plate. He licked toast crumbs from his fingers as he swiveled the paper around to read the newspaper's headline.

"Scientists Admit Their Involvement in the Slip," the headline screamed. Jim quickly scanned the lead article. It carried all their names and quoted an "unnamed source close to the project" as having admitted they were leading an investigation into the probability that Project Tach-Comm had been responsible for the Slip. Interestingly, though, there was no mention of the cascade effect, only that the team in Reno was now investigating the events leading up to the catastrophe following the initiation of the experiment.

"Oh! That's not good," said Jim.

"My God. How do these things get out?" squawked Lorentz as he paced back and forth behind Jim's chair.

"Do you want me to call an emergency meeting?" asked Jim.

"No. No. I know it wasn't anybody here. Security is too tight, and none of us have left the building. This leak has come from outside of our team. Besides, we can't afford the time to launch an investigation."

Jim nodded his head in agreement, then asked, "Why no mention of the cascade effect? That's a little odd, don't you think?"

Lorentz pulled out a chair from under the table and sat down. "Who knows? Maybe they only heard some of a conversation or got hold of part of a memo. I've ordered the head of security to review all protocols and pull all the communication logs, but I don't think he will find anything."

"Can't we just deny it? Say we have no idea what they are talking about?"

"What's the point? Pretty soon every half-baked loony will be coming out of the woodwork, ready to tell their side of the story of how they destroyed the future. I half expect to be sued for copyright infringement by every eccentric within a hundred miles for stealing their ideas in a dream." Lorentz's head dropped slowly to the table, where he gently tapped his forehead repeatedly on the tabletop. "Why me?" he asked.

"The price of fame, my friend," said Jim, placing a reassuring hand against the scientist's shoulder.

Lorentz sat up. "Yes, I suppose so."

"So what are you going to do? Issue a rebuttal?"

"Nothing. I've been half expecting it to occur. It was always unlikely we could keep something of this magnitude under wraps. If your theory is right, then all of this"—he waved a dismissive hand at the crumpled newspaper—"will mean nothing, and if your theory is wrong . . . Well, none of us will have anything more to worry about ever again, anyway."

"I can't fault your logic," said Jim. "I don't like it, but I surely can't fault it."

THIRTY-FOUR

The first protestors showed up outside the security fence the morning after the article appeared in the *Washington Times*. They came in cars and minivans, on foot and on bike. At first there was just a trickle, but by the end of the day there were close to two hundred members of the Church of Second Redemption gathered around the entrance to the base.

The first the scientists knew of it was when Lorentz received a call on his office phone from the head of security.

"Sorry to disturb you, Prof. Lorentz," the voice of Sam Calhoun, head of security for the facility, announced. "I thought it best to let you know about a developing problem we have out here at the front gate." He went on to explain about the newly arrived protesters, who were in the process of setting up camp on the stretch of grass adjacent to the main entrance gate to the facility.

"Are they likely to be a problem?" Lorentz asked.

"Hard to say, sir. They're behaving themselves for the moment."

Lorentz trusted his head of security. He was a career officer who commanded his soldiers well and had gained their respect. His men called the big Irishman "the Chief," and Lorentz knew he could trust the man's assessment of the situation.

"Can't you just arrest them?"

"Well, the problem is they haven't broken any laws yet, sir. They're not trespassing, they've made no threats; there's been no stone throwing or bottle tossing. They appear to be a pretty well-behaved bunch. If that changes, you can bet we'll be on them like flies on shit—begging your pardon, sir."

"If there's any change, let me know."

"It's nothing serious. I'm sure we can handle a few whacked-out Jesus freaks. Besides, they're not doing anything other than build their tent city and stare at the building."

Lorentz hung up the phone and settled back in his chair. He had a bad feeling about this.

***

Over the next twenty-four hours, the number of Second Redemption followers collecting around the entrance to the base grew disturbingly. Buses began arriving, dropping off their passengers, then immediately departing for locations unknown only to return an hour or two later filled to capacity with more protestors.

The security chief didn't know whether to call them protestors or not. No demands had been made for the scientists to stop their work. No banners were being flown or placards painted demanding the complex be shut down or for the personnel to be handed over to the gathered crowd. They stayed far enough away from the gate to allow traffic in and out of the scientific complex. There was no misbehavior, no threats, nothing.

By the time the last bus deposited its final group of silent passengers, there were two thousand souls outside the gate and spread out along the north perimeter fence. The Chief knew because he had had his men count every damn last one of them.

They sat on the open grass verge on the opposite side of the road encircling the complex, talking quietly among themselves, or praying in huddled groups, or staring at the security guards as they walked their way around the perimeter fence, or reading quietly from their open Bibles.

That made the Chief *very* nervous.

***

One of the phones on Mitchell Lorentz's desk was ringing, demanding his attention. There were three phones, each one on a separate line. Two of them had to come through the front-desk operator and allowed either Lorentz, the receptionist, or Mina Belkov to filter out any unwanted callers. The third phone was a compact black box with a stub of plastic protruding from the top. It was a military-issue satellite phone that enabled him to stay in communication from anywhere in the world. The only person who knew the number to the phone was John Humphreys, his government contact at the Department of Homeland Security.

Lorentz kept a strict weekly routine of contact with Humphreys. Each Friday he would call him and apprise the department of how well the project was progressing. In the months since the project had begun, Lorentz had made only outgoing calls on the handset. The fact that the phone was now ringing insistently was doubly disturbing because he had made his report just two days earlier.

Lorentz picked up the sat-phone and pressed the "Receive" button.

"This is Prof. Lorentz," he said.

The familiar voice of his government handler spoke quickly and insistently into his ear. "Doctor, we have a problem."

***

The team of scientists gathered in the conference room, chatting quietly among themselves. Prof. Lorentz had summoned them all to the room half an hour earlier for an emergency meeting. Mina had delivered the message to each of them personally: "Drop everything and get yourself to the meeting room right now."

The chatter stopped as a red-faced Lorentz stormed into the room and slammed a folder of papers loudly down onto the conference table, spilling some onto the floor. Mina Belkov, who was following close behind her boss, started to pick up the spilled papers.

"For God's sake, leave them be," snapped Lorentz.

Belkov blanched at the sharp tone of voice, and Jim thought that this was probably the first time he had seen the little girl who hid deep beneath the frosty, efficient exterior of Lorentz's personal assistant.

The room became still. All faces were now regarding Lorentz, who seemed just about ready to explode.

The doctor took a deep breath and then exhaled slowly. "I must apologize for my anger," he said, laying a reassuring hand on his assistant's arm, a smile of contrition fixed to his face, "but I have just received some utterly incomprehensible news, which I will now share with you all."

His face took on a deeper shade of red, and the gathered scientists could see the control Lorentz was exerting to keep himself composed.

"The deputy director of Homeland Security, in all his wisdom, has just informed me that we will soon be receiving a delegation whose explicit responsibility it will be to document our procedure and monitor our efforts here."

"Doesn't sound so bad," said Jim. "These government crews are pretty respectful of our space and usually—"

"They are not government," interrupted Lorentz.

"Oh!" exclaimed Jim.

"No. They are representatives of Father Edward Pike and his *Church of Second Redemption*."

That news unleashed an immediate uproar of protest from the gathered team.

"They can't—"

"Who the hell do they think they are?"

"You have to be kidding!"

When the room finally quieted down, the tension and anger were as palpable as fog. Their miasma clung to them all.

"How the hell can they get away with this?" asked a shocked Adrianna Drake, her voice an even higher pitch than usual.

"They are the church. They can do as they damn well please, apparently," spat Mabry.

"It is really quite simple," said Lorentz. "The massed followers of the Church of Second Redemption now amount to approximately thirty-five percent of the voting population of this country. Pike has apparently informed President Roderick that if he wishes to continue to count on the votes of his parishioners, he will allow his team of monitors—Pike's name for them, not mine—complete access to our program. And with the death of President Sarandon and the upcoming election—well, you know the drill with politicians."

"Is there anything we can do?" asked Mabry.

"Of course I refused," Lorentz continued, "and I was told quite bluntly that if I wished to maintain my position as director of this project, the matter was closed and I *would* comply with the request, or else." Lorentz leaned on the table, his tone matter-of-fact. "We are too close to allow my personal ethics and pride to get in the way of our success."

There was a mutter of discontent from around the table.

"When can we expect our . . . guests to arrive?" asked Jim.

"Tomorrow. They'll be here tomorrow."

This drew more groans of discontent from the group.

"What does the church want with us?" Adrianna said. "I thought they were convinced the Slip was an act of God."

"Apparently, they want to be here if the experiment fails. So they can gloat, I suppose."

"But don't they understand that if the experiment fails, it's over? There won't be anybody left to gloat."

"These people are religious fanatics," continued Lorentz. "They are not driven by rational thought or empirical data—their faith is all they accept. It doesn't matter anyway. The decision has been made, and the church team will be here tomorrow, and that's that. We will all just have to do the best we can to make sure they do not get in our way."

It took another twenty minutes for the team to vent their feelings over the intrusion of the church into the project, until finally Lorentz stood and said, "Meeting adjourned. Let's all try and relax, shall we?"

As the rest of the team made their way back to their quarters, Lorentz beckoned to Jim.

"Could you hold on for just a minute. I'd like a word," Lorentz said as he took Jim by the elbow and led him to one side.

"What's up?"

When Mitchell Lorentz was uncomfortable about broaching a subject with one of the team, he would continuously tap the tip of a pen against his lips while he thought on how best to approach the matter; it was a personal tell that Jim had learned to recognize. He noticed him doing it now and smiled inwardly as he waited for his boss to find the right words while simultaneously bracing for what he was sure would be more bad news.

"James," Lorentz began, between beats of the pen, "there was a second demand—request—from the church."

"They want us all to convert?" Jim pondered.

"No. No," said Lorentz through a half smile. "They have insisted that you should be the liaison between our team here and the monitors when they arrive."

Jim looked perplexed. "What? Why me? I've never had anything to do with the Second Redeemers."

"They asked for you specifically. I was told you *must* be the liaison, and if you did not respond favorably to the request, that I should immediately suspend your position here and have you removed from the project."

Jim started to object, but Lorentz held up his hands. "Wait, wait. Before you say anything, Jim, just let me say that I will not put you in the position of being ordered to do this. I want you to know that if you decide not to accept their dictate, I will back you one hundred percent, even if it means my own resignation. It's a monstrous imposition for both of us to endure."

"Mitchell, it's not a problem, and I appreciate your candor. Of course I accept. We are too close to completion now. I just wonder, why me?"

"Well," said a smiling Lorentz, clapping Jim on his back, "maybe you ticked somebody off in a previous life."

THIRTY-FIVE

The monitoring team arrived as scheduled the following day.

Jim stood on the steps of the main building, shooing away the occasional fly that buzzed annoyingly past his head. The sun was high overhead, beating mercilessly down. Along the asphalt approach to the lab, a heat haze hung in the air just above the blacktop surface, distorting the image of the vehicle carrying the Second Redemption crew into crazy fun-house mirror shapes as it waited to clear security.

"Here they come," said Mina Belkov, her hand raised to shade her eyes from the glare.

The security gate slid back. The white nondescript minivan pulled forward and began heading toward the main building. Lorentz had loaned Mina to Jim as his assistant for the duration of the visit; she was to help him with anything he might not know or be able to handle, a situation neither was particularly comfortable with.

The van drove the quarter mile to the steps of the reception area and pulled to a halt in front of Jim and Mina with a screech of overheated brake pads.

Through the windshield of the van, Jim could just make out the driver. The other windows, blacked out with a reflective material, revealed nothing of who else was inside. The driver was stocky, with wide shoulders and big arms that bulged under his T-shirt. His large hands clasped the steering wheel of the vehicle. The man sported a full beard and mustache neatly trimmed to match his dark-brown, crew-cut hair. He regarded Jim with intense green eyes, a sardonic smile creasing his face.

Jim was fairly sure he didn't know the man, but it was hard to be certain with most of his face hidden behind the beard and mustache. And what the hell was he smiling at? He looked like the proverbial cat that had caught the canary.

The smiling man pulled himself out of the driver's seat and strode around to the steps where Jim and Mina waited. He was tall—six four, maybe six five, Jim estimated—with a very slight limp. The bearded man grasped Jim's hand in his own, and Jim felt as if he had placed his hand in a vise, so powerful was the man's grip.

"Tony Gallagher," the man said by way of introduction, his heavy Texas drawl turning the pronunciation of his Christian name into "Toe-Knee."

"Pleased to meet you, Mr. Gallagher," Jim started. "This is my associate Mina Belkov, and my name is—"

"I know who you are, Mr. Baston," Gallagher said with a smirk. "I've heard a lot about you, man. A *lot* about you."

Before Jim could question Gallagher about how he knew so much about him, the second newcomer stepped out of the back of the van and walked over to the reception committee.

He was the exact opposite of Gallagher: reed thin, in his early twenties, and clean shaven, his sandy-blond hair a carefully arranged masterpiece of physics. A sky-blue designer shirt, its look ruined by dark sweat stains under each armpit, clung to a body that probably weighed less than a hundred and twenty pounds when dripping wet.

"Justin Beaumont," the skinny man said, extending his own bony hand.

Beaumont's handshake was every bit as limp as Jim expected for such a birdlike physique, but the man's voice was deep and sonorous, and Jim had a problem matching it to the skinny young man he saw in front of him.

The third and final member of the church's monitoring team stepped around from the back of the van. Almost as tall as Gallagher, she wore a sleeveless summer dress that stopped just above her shapely knees and showed off her lithe calves and well-toned arms. Her abundant blond hair would have reached to the middle of her back had it not been tied back in a French bun, exposing her sleek, long throat and the beautiful curve of her jawline. High cheekbones accentuated her round, opalescent blue eyes and the strawberry red of her full lips.

"Hello, James," the woman said as she stepped up onto the curb next to the other new arrivals. "How have you been?"

There was no name for the gamut of emotions that seized Jim Baston at that moment. It was a strange cocktail of intense rage bordering on murderous fury and disbelief, two different strands of emotion woven together to form a rough cord of sorrow that tied up his soul. It felt as though every atom of his body was vibrating, and that at any moment he would simply shake himself into his constituent parts, leaving nothing but a bubbling pool on the steaming sidewalk. Jim's vision narrowed to the exclusion of all else but the beautiful perspiring woman standing in front of him.

The words tumbled from his mouth before he even knew he would speak them: "Is. She. Alive?" he spat.

Biting her lower lip, the woman glanced at Gallagher, who nodded once to her.

"Yes, she's alive," said Simone Baston. "Lark is fine."

THIRTY-SIX

"God damn it!" yelled Jim Baston. "Son of a goddamn bitch!"

Absolutely irate, he paced back and forth in the living room of his apartment, hands clasped firmly on top of his head as if to stop it flying off from the force of his rage. The knuckles on his right hand glowed red where he had punched the door to his apartment, leaving a fist-shaped dent in the wood.

He had been like this for five minutes now—since he had stormed away from the reception area, leaving a shocked Mina Belkov to deal with the new arrivals. *I had to*, he reasoned. *Otherwise, I might very well have strangled her right there on the steps.*

Tears of frustration threatened like storm clouds at the corner of Jim's eyes, but each time he felt the tears about to flow, the anger would surge through him again, overwhelming the sorrow, and he was ready to kill. Dear God, he was going to *explode*.

"Are you okay?"

The voice surprised Jim, and he stopped where he was, halfway between the bedroom and the kitchen, and slowly raised his head toward its source: Rebecca, standing in the open doorway, her face bright with empathy and concern.

"I don't know," he said, his anger falling away at the sight of her and exposing the raw pain that had left him wallowing in his own emotional vomit.

"My little girl, I killed her and now . . . now she's alive again." His voice fluctuated between sorrow and anger and disbelief as the words tumbled from him, the imminent tears finally welling up, soaking his cheeks with their warmth before he even knew he was crying. "My ex-wife . . . she . . . she's alive . . . and she has my baby girl," he stuttered. "She kept her from me for all this time. Why the hell would she do that? *Why?*"

Rebecca took a step toward him, and as Jim crumpled to his knees, she knelt down beside him, enfolding him in her arms. "Hush!" she said, her cheek pressed tightly against his forehead, her own tears dampening his hair. "It's all right," she whispered as she gently rocked him in her arms.

THIRTY-SEVEN

Later, Jim used his left hand to rap gently on Simone's door. His right hand was still swollen and sore.

With Rebecca's help, he had finally pulled himself together. She had left him to go find a first-aid kit from the women's communal lavatory. After checking nothing was broken, she slathered antiseptic cream onto his raw knuckles, quietly chastising him for being a big baby when he winced at the sting of the cream on his broken and bloodied skin. She wrapped a thick, padded bandage over his hand, which did nothing to alleviate the disinfectant smell from the cream, a smell he had never enjoyed, which brought back memories of scraped knees and cut elbows from when he was a kid.

Over a pot of coffee, he talked for almost three hours, recounting his whole history with Simone and Lark and how, after Lark's death, he had checked out of the human race and hidden away for almost a year. He told her he was lost, that he had been since the Slip had happened. The pain of losing his child and his ex-wife for a second time—it had eaten him up.

Then suddenly this: Simone had arrived out of nowhere, carrying the news that not only was *she* alive but Lark was too. All those months and months of worry and pain. How could she have done this to him? Why didn't she try to contact him? Christ! He'd lived at her parents' for a while, hoping against hope that they were alive. It seemed the logical place for her to contact. She could have called, sent a letter, e-mail, anything, just to let him know she was okay. And to top it all she was working for the *Church of Second Redemption*? It just didn't add up to the sum total of the woman he had once known. To the woman he had once loved.

Rebecca listened quietly, offering no opinion, no criticism of his actions. She had simply listened, holding his hand gently in her own, and when he was finished, she told him the only way he was going to get an answer to all those painful questions was to go and ask the one person who could answer them.

So that was why he was standing here now, waiting for Simone to come to the door, wishing there would be some good reason for all this confusion and deception, his anger at her still simmering just below the surface.

He rapped again and waited.

Simone answered the door in a white terry-cloth dressing gown, the lingering smell of her shampoo or bodywash filling his nostrils with the scent of gardenias and patchouli. Simone looked like a Bedouin princess, her perfect features framed by a towel wrapped in a twirl around her wet hair. A single strand of hair had escaped the towel's grasp, and Jim fought the urge to reach out and tuck it back under for her.

Simone was almost exactly as he remembered, her lips turned up in a halfhearted attempt at a smile, her unembellished beauty flawed now by worry lines that creased her forehead.

"Hello, James," she said quietly.

"Can I come in?" he asked, half expecting her to say no.

Her answer was slow in coming, but finally she stepped aside, opened the door wide, and said, "Sure. Come on in."

A set of green luggage sat unopened on the living room sofa. She grabbed the bags and carried them toward the bedroom. "Let me get rid of these. Have a seat," she said, nodding in the direction of the sofa.

When she returned to the living room, Jim was still standing nervously in the center of the room.

"Do you want a drink?"

"Please. Water would be fine," Jim replied, suddenly aware his throat was parched and rough as an emery stone.

Simone moved into the kitchen. "I guess we have a lot to talk about." Her voice filtered back to him like a long lost memory.

"I . . . I just need to know why," he said as Simone handed him the glass of water, which he immediately set down on the nearby coffee table, his hand shaking so much he thought he might drop it.

Simone's head tilted slightly as she bit down on her lower lip, an unconscious tell of nervousness Jim recognized from their years together. She was gathering her thoughts, zoning out for just a second while she organized what she was going to say. She sat down on the sofa and gazed up at Jim.

"I was at a conference in Baltimore. The station I was working for—did you know I was working as a producer again? Anyway, they wanted me to cover it for them. I'd never been to Baltimore before—always wanted to—so when the conference was over I decided to stay a couple of extra days to look around. I was heading back to Baltimore-Washington airport to catch the flight back home. I remember there was a backup from the off-ramp down to the access road, and I was sitting in the queue listening to the radio; it was an oldie. I'd just put the car's AI on auto so I could finish reading over my notes from the conference when . . . everything changed."

Jim had witnessed Simone's next reaction in virtually everybody he had met since the Slip. When the conversation inevitably turned to the question of "where were you when the Slip happened?" people got a certain look in their eyes, as though they were still trying to come to grips with that moment of change. Her blue eyes focused off into infinity as her brain reran the movie of the instantaneous jump from normality to this surreal version of reality.

A lopsided smile broke over Simone's face, and her voice took on a reverent quality as she continued. "And then I was leaning out the window of our old Chevy—the yellow one you hated so much. You called it the puke mobile, remember? I had a lunch box in my hand, and I was saying 'Don't forget your lunch.' I was talking to a little girl. Oh! God forgive me, but I didn't recognize her at first. She was running away from me toward a building. It was her kindergarten, there were other kids all around us, and there was the sound of children yelling and chattering and parents talking. Normal stuff. Normal human stuff. And . . . and . . . then everybody froze and there was a deathly silence."

Jim did not remember when he had sat down next to his ex-wife; he did not recall where the anger had gone, and he did not recollect when he had taken Simone's hand in his own.

There were tears in her eyes now. "And then she turned and looked at me. She said, 'Mommy?' with this look of surprise on her face. I just stared and stared at her. I thought I was dreaming. Then overhead this jet came screaming in low, almost at treetop level, and it disappeared behind me. I couldn't follow it—my eyes were fixed on Lark—but I saw the other kids turn their heads, and I heard the explosion, but I couldn't do anything but stare at my daughter because I knew that this had to be a dream. I'd fallen asleep at the wheel on the way to the airport and this was just a dream. So it wasn't a real plane that had just crashed behind us, and if I took my eyes off her for even a second, I just knew I would wake up and she would be gone.

"Then this stuff started falling from the sky—bits of metal and burning things. It started like a rainstorm, little pieces first just pattering on the pavement. It made everybody look up. Then it was raining chunks of metal, and the other kids started screaming and shouting. The parents just grabbed their own and started running. It was pandemonium."

Jim handed Simone a tissue from his pocket. She took it gratefully and patted away the dampness from her cheeks.

"Lark started crying, and I just reacted. I jumped out of the car and grabbed her. Threw her in the backseat and drove." Simone took a long swig from her own glass of water. "It was like a meteor storm, bits of debris smashing into the ground all around us, bouncing off the roof of the car. There were houses on either side that were already burning, and I was trying to drive and calm Lark because she kept repeating over and over 'Where's Benjamin? Where's Benjamin?' and I took my eyes off the road for one second to look back at her . . . just one second.

"When I turned back, there was an old man standing in the middle of the road. His mouth was wide open and he was staring into the sky, back toward where we had just come from. I tried to swerve past him, I really did—Christ, he was standing in the middle of the road and I had my dead daughter in the back and I . . ." The words were tumbling from her now, cascading out of her mouth. "And I hit him. I killed him."

"You don't know that for certain," said Jim quietly.

"I killed him," she repeated with certainty. "And God forgive me, I didn't stop."

"Well, there you go. You didn't stop, so you don't know for certain that—"

She looked across at him and stared directly into his eyes. "I was doing close to sixty and I hit him straight on. It took me an hour to wash the blood and . . . stuff off the car. I killed him." Simone stared at her feet, her elbows resting on her knees and her head bowed deeply.

"Who's Benjamin?" asked Jim, attempting to change the subject away from the morbid tale.

"Who? Oh! I don't know. Maybe one of her softies."

A "softy" was the name Lark had given to her stuffed toys. She had names for all her toys, so Benjamin was probably one of them, Jim reasoned.

"So where did you go? Why didn't you come to your parents'? I was waiting there for you."

"I started to head to the house, but there was so much confusion and the smoke and the fire from the crash. It was right there where our old house used to be in West Hills. I knew it wouldn't be any good trying to get home. Besides, I had a little girl in the back of my car that I thought was my dead daughter."

"What do you mean, you thought it was your daughter? Of course it was our daughter."

"For all I knew I was suffering some kind of psychotic episode, and I'd just kidnapped this child off the side of a street in Baltimore because she looked like Lark."

"But she called you Mommy."

"I know, I know, but I was confused and, even after all these years, I missed her so very much. I thought I was over her death, but all I had done was hidden it away in my mind somewhere where I wouldn't stumble over it very often."

"We were all confused. I think most of us still are," said Jim. The ghost of his first few hours back in this time still haunted him.

"I drove and I drove, and I made it out of the city. The freeways were all on fire and blocked, so I took the side streets. I can't even remember most of it, but I think I got out of LA on pure instinct."

"You could have come to me at any time, Simone."

"I wanted to, I really did. You were the first person I thought to get to. But then I thought that maybe you were like you used to be. And it scared me. You . . . changed, Jim. You became so morose, so very angry and . . . you left me—"

Jim started to interrupt, to say that he hadn't left her; how could she say such a thing?

"Don't say you didn't. You know goddamn well you did. You were barely home when Lark was alive, and then when she died you might as well have been living on Mars. You never spoke to me. You . . . withered away, and you took any chance for us with you."

He knew she was telling the truth, and he let her continue with the tirade because he also recognized he deserved it.

"I loved you *so* much," she said as hot tears streamed down her face, emotional nitroglycerin born of an explosive mixture of fury and sadness. "All I wanted was to be with you, to share your pain, carry some of it for you. We still had a chance back then, but you wouldn't let me in." Her voice dipped and rose as she fired the words at him, a lifetime of bottled resentment finally let loose. "Sometimes I wish it had been me who killed her, Jim, because then you would have had an excuse to hate me, and it all would have made sense."

"I don't hate you. I never did," Jim said softly.

"Then why did you leave me all alone?" she said between sobs.

"I had no choice, Simone." His own voice crackled with the emotion of the moment. "I killed our child. All because of a stupid argument—because I felt misunderstood and underappreciated. That was something I had to deal with, and it took me years. *Years!*"

Simone used the arm of her dressing gown to wipe the tears from her face, the sodden tissue too wet to be of any further use. "What's important now is that she is alive, and I intend to give her the best life she can get. She has a second chance, Jim . . . We all do."

"And you think she will get that from a mother who's a part of the Second Redemption?"

A subtle blur of emotion moved over Simone's face. It was there for only a second, barely discernible, but still Jim was surprised that even after all the time that had passed between them he was able to pick up the delicate emotional changes in this woman.

"I'm not a part of the church," she insisted. "I just work for them, that's all."

"Then why did you run to them instead of your family? We were all waiting for you. My God, your parents were worried sick about you."

She let out a slow sigh of exasperation. "How many ways can I tell you, Jim? I was confused. I'd just found myself standing next to a daughter who'd been dead for over eighteen years. I'd witnessed a plane crash and killed a man with my car. I doubted my own sanity, for God's sake."

"You could have contacted us, let us know."

She paused, assessing whether she was ready to tell him the next part. "I did."

Jim's look of confusion was saddening to see. "Well, I never got the—"

"I didn't try to contact *you*," she interrupted. "I contacted my parents. About five months after the Slip, once the phones were back up and running again and I knew that I was not imagining all of this."

"What?" Jim's voice took on a tone of indignation. "They didn't even mention it to me."

"They wanted to," said Simone, laying her hand on his now, "but I made them promise me they wouldn't."

"Jesus Christ, Simone," said Jim, leaping to his feet.

"I'm sorry, okay? They told me you'd changed and that you were looking for us, but I didn't want to be found. Lark and I both needed time to adjust. I needed to make sure she was . . ."—she searched for the right words—"still whole. The last time Lark had seen us, we were still married, we were a family. I had to ensure she wasn't damaged irrevocably by everything that was happening."

"We could have done that together. We could have been a family again," he cried.

"No, Jim, we couldn't. It's been over twenty-five years for you and me, but for Lark it never happened. I needed to make sure she was okay with that; I needed to let her down gently. I convinced Mom and Dad not to tell you, because I couldn't trust that you weren't just like you were when we split up. Dad was the hardest. He respects you so much, and he wanted to tell you we were okay, but I knew that if he did, you would find us. I had to make the right decision for her, not for you or for me. For Lark."

"Were you ever going to let me know?"

"Of course I was. I just needed time." Now it was Simone's turn to sound defensive.

"So where did you go? If you didn't come home and you didn't go to your parents'."

"For the first couple of days, we spent the night in the car." She saw the shocked look in his eyes at her statement. "Don't look so worried. I think it was probably the safest place for us both to be. We parked up in some big store's parking lot. You'd be surprised how many vehicles were just abandoned at these places."

"No, I wouldn't," he said, remembering his own experience on the first day back.

"So, anyway, once the chaos had subsided somewhat, I made for San Diego. I had a friend out there—no one you knew—who I knew would take us in and not ask too many questions. We stayed with her for a couple of months before moving back to LA."

"How did you end up a convert to the church?" Jim asked, unable to keep the sarcasm out of his voice.

"I'm not a convert," she replied pointedly. "I just work for them. One of their outreach programs helped us when we needed a place and they offered me a job. As the church began to grow, they needed somebody with a background in television to handle their ads and TV shows. They offered me the position and I accepted. The church has been very good to us."

"I'm sorry," he said. "It's just the shock. I'm still getting used to the fact that you are both still alive. I searched for you both for months. Now I don't know whether I should be angry or singing from the rooftops."

"I understand. Really I do. And I'm sorry it had to be this way, but I hope you can understand. That you can put yourself in my shoes and appreciate that I had no choice. Lark *had* to come first."

Jim nodded his understanding and then in a boyish voice he asked, "It's going to take a while, I know, but when this is all over maybe . . . I could—"

"Yes," she said with a gentle nod, "you can see Lark."

***

That night Jim sat with Rebecca and recounted his conversation with Simone. A single candle sat on the living room coffee table, the glow of its flame creating long, flickering shadows in the apartment. In its comforting glow, Jim relaxed for what felt like the first time in his life.

In his cramped little kitchen, they cooked a meal together from what items they could scrounge from the cafeteria staff: spaghetti carbonara with a bottle of Bergerac Jim had cajoled out of Horatio Mabry's dwindling private wine stash.

They danced their first slow dance together, shared their first kiss, and finally, with the wine buzzing gently through their heads, Becky stood, took Jim by the hand, and led him into the bedroom.

The next morning Jim awoke to the smell of fried bacon wafting into the bedroom. He searched for his boxers, found them hanging over the back of a chair by the door, and pulled them quickly on.

In the kitchen he slipped his arms around Rebecca's waist as she stood at the stove. A frying pan held bacon and a couple of eggs. He gently caressed the back of her neck with his lips.

"Hope you don't mind, but I borrowed your shirt," she said nonchalantly. "How do you like your eggs?"

"Over easy," Jim whispered into her ear.

He took the empty coffeepot to the sink and filled it from the faucet. "How'd you sleep?" he asked.

"Well," she answered, before adding, "Is this going to change any-thing?" her voice suddenly serious and, Jim thought, very vulnerable.

"Yes," he replied honestly, placing the coffeepot back on the counter. His hands found the young woman's shoulders, and he gently turned her to face him. He stared into her eyes and ran his hands through her hair before pulling her close and kissing her gently on the lips. "This changes everything."

THIRTY-EIGHT

Simone's crew set their camera up in the corner of the conference room. Jim shot her a quick look as he walked to his seat, but she was all business now. Only the cold eye of the camera met his glance as it swung around to track him entering the room.

Pulling out his chair, Jim looked at the rest of his own team. He could tell they were all nervous; there was not the usual lighthearted banter flowing between them. Of course, it was hard to concentrate and relax when you had a troupe of strangers pointing a camera at you.

The camera crew was, to give them credit, trying their best to remain anonymous but it was impossible to ignore them. They were dressed in muted colors in an attempt to blend into the surroundings, Jim guessed, and not appear too conspicuous. But it was the sheer incongruity of the three of them that was impossible to disguise: Simone, radiant and elegant, every movement part of a graceful dance; Beaumont, skinny and gawky, his body an explosion of angles and bones; and finally Gallagher, his hulking body dwarfing both his colleagues and the digital video camera he had fixed to a tripod stand.

Jim could smell the coffee over the other side of the room, but he decided it wouldn't be too cool to stand up and walk over to grab a cup while the camera was rolling. *Amazing how the simple act of focusing a lens on an individual immediately changes their behavior,* he thought.

Once Jim seemed comfortable, Lorentz began the meeting.

"I must apologize," he began, "for the intrusion, but as you know my hands are tied as to their presence within this compound." Lorentz looked straight into the camera as he continued. "I will point out right now, however, for the benefit of all here and the establishing of ground rules that my team is under no obligation to answer any questions other than those relating to their role within the project." Now his gaze fell on each of his people sitting around the table. "If at any time you feel our visitors are being too obtrusive or just getting in your way, call security."

Jim thought he heard a snicker of laughter emanating from behind the camera, but he couldn't be sure.

Lorentz picked up a sheaf of papers, the meeting's itinerary and battle plan for the day. "Now," he said as he gazed at the first item on the list, his voice returning to its normal joviality, "let's get this show on the road, shall we?"

***

Jim found it hard to concentrate on Lorentz's briefing. All he could think of was Rebecca, the feel of her hair in his hands, the scent of her as she had slept silently beside him, curved into the concavity of his body. The taste of her skin beneath his lips.

It was hackneyed, he knew, clichéd even, but for the first time in his life he finally felt complete.

"Jim, are you with us?"

"What? Oh! Sorry." Lorentz's voice broke him from his reverie, and he realized the entire team gathered around the conference table was staring at him, smiles creasing their faces. He glanced at Becky and saw her face flush with embarrassment.

They had decided not to tell anybody that they were an item yet. Hell, he didn't even know if they were an item. They would wait until the experiment was over and then they could announce it. Until then they would be forced to sneak around like a couple of teenagers. But judging by the knowing smirks on the rest of the team's faces, it looked like their secret was already out.

He turned his face to a smiling Lorentz and said, "I'm sorry, Mitchell. What were you saying?"

"I was talking about the preparations for tonight's action, Jim," said Lorentz, returning to seriousness. "How is the purity of the power supply?"

"I had a couple of problems with interference yesterday, but I managed to isolate it to the guards' radio system. Horatio was kind enough to install a low-band filter in line with the generator, and that's done the trick. Purity of ninety-nine point seven percent now."

"Excellent. Excellent," said Lorentz, ticking the item off his list.

"Now, Mr. Mabry, how are your final preparations coming along?"

THIRTY-NINE

It was 2330 hours and just half an hour remained until the project's midnight deadline. The already-cramped confines of the transmitter room had become even more claustrophobic with the presence of the church's camera operator, sound technician, and, of course, Simone.

Lorentz was growing more frustrated by the moment; Jim could see it in the rosy flush that was beginning to creep into his cheeks. The church crew shadowed Lorentz as he moved through the room, running diagnostics on the seemingly antiquated solid-state computer systems they were forced to use. No Nano-Comps this time; they wouldn't be invented for another fifteen years or so.

Lorentz stopped at a terminal and peered closely at the screen. The action was an old habit, one Jim had seen repeated numerous times by the majority of people who had found themselves returned to their younger selves. When you had spent the best part of what were supposed to be the last years of your life having to adjust to poor eyesight, it was hard to escape the habit of leaning in to get a better view of what you were trying to look at. Jim saw Lorentz catch himself and withdraw to a better focal point.

The tension in the room was palpable. As the clock ticked away the minutes to the experiment's start, the weight of responsibility and the inevitable destruction of humankind if the experiment failed were now finally coming to bear squarely on the team's shoulders. Tempers were short, excitement was high, and Simone's team was definitely not helping matters.

Dressed in a two-piece tweed suit, Simone looked the epitome of nouveau gentry—elegant and stylish, yet conservative enough to appeal to the church's true believers. She was blindingly beautiful, and Jim watched her graceful movements as she placed herself behind Lorentz's back and began talking in a quiet voice to the camera, explaining to her viewers exactly what was occurring.

Earlier in the afternoon she had met with each of the Tach-Comm team members to personally interview them, extracting information about their role within the team and precisely how the experiment would be conducted. When it had come to Jim's turn, she had been the consummate professional, almost cold in her interview technique, with no hint that there was any kind of a past between them. He had found himself becoming angry at her lack of warmth, answering her questions with equal iciness. But her final question had caught him completely off guard.

Leaning back in her chair, Simone had bluntly asked him, "Do you believe in God, Mr. Baston?"

Jim had blinked reflexively at the question. In all the years they had been married, he could not recall a single discussion between them on the subject of religion. He had assumed she was as much of an unbeliever as he was.

The whir of the camera lens focusing tightly on his face drew his eyes from Simone's to the machine's own single cold eye. Behind the camera lens the rest of humanity, current and future, watched, and they would hold him accountable for all eternity by his words and actions.

He stared directly into the lens for a long moment and then said with a deliberate tone of nonchalance, "No. I do not."

Simone had smiled at Jim, thanked him for his time, and left, along with her crew. Now here she was, explaining to her viewers the process of the experiment and its setup. Her voice was hushed and concerned as she spoke directly to the camera, her back to Lorentz. The microphone, suspended from the limb of the mic boom held by the cadaverous Beaumont, hung over her head as she spoke.

Lorentz was concentrating on calibrating the equipment; Jim could see his eyes scanning over the figures displayed on his VDU, his fingers flying over the keyboard as he entered data into the system. With a final stab at the "Enter" key, he swung around and collided with Simone's back, sending her staggering forward. The cameraman threw out a free arm and caught the stumbling woman before she could fall.

"Good God Almighty," bellowed Lorentz. "Must you follow me everywhere? I have a job to do here. Do you people not realize what's at stake? Do you think your God is going to wave a finger and stop what's about to take place from happening? Do you? Well, do you?" Spittle flew from his mouth as his rage and frustration began to manifest.

Simone stood up and adjusted her crumpled suit, turned to Gallagher, and said something to him that Jim did not catch. He immediately brought the camera to bear on Lorentz, and Jim watched the color in the doctor's face go from pink to nuclear red.

"You have been quoted as having accepted the blame for the Slip, Prof. Lorentz. Father Pike has also been quoted as saying that he believes that is just scientific ego attempting to claim responsibility for God's great work. How do you feel about that?" Simone finished her question with a slight inquisitive tilt of her head, awaiting the professor's reply.

Lorentz, seemingly on the verge of exploding, raised his finger and pointed it directly at the camera. No words came from his mouth, such was his rage; they were trapped behind his teeth, battling to be first out, first to make the cutting blow that would reduce this bunch of interlopers to so much chopped liver. A pale Mina Belkov stepped up to Lorentz and took his elbow in her hand, but the scientist shook her off.

Unarmored and unarmed, Jim jumped into the fray. "Why don't I show you the rest of the facility?" he said softly to Simone as he stepped between the camera and the glowering Lorentz. "Follow me," he continued, his tone of voice making his words a command rather than a request.

Simone gazed at Jim before saying, "Sure, but we will need to be back here for the final experiment. Come on, let's go."

"I need a bathroom break anyway," said Gallagher as he laid his camera equipment on a table near the doorway. "The damn food here is playing havoc with my system." As if to emphasize the point, he let loose a loud belch. "I'll catch up with you in the other room."

Jim escorted the group out into the corridor and pointed in the direction of the men's bathroom. "The men's room is down there," he said to the cameraman. Looking back into the room as the door closed behind them, he caught sight of a fuming, visibly shaking Prof. Lorentz speaking angrily to Mina.

When will this day be over? he wondered.

FORTY

Something was happening with the crowd outside the security fence.

From his position within the security booth at the complex's front gate, Corporal Robert Parsons heard the murmur of a thousand voices whispering as one. It sounded like the distant rumble of half-heard thunder.

Glancing at his watch, the young guard saw it was nearing twenty-five minutes to midnight. Outside his warm booth, the overhead security lights illuminated the darkness to only midway across the perimeter road. It was too dark for him to make out the massed church demonstrators who had set up camp on the opposite side of it. They remained hidden from him in the darkness of a starless night.

Parsons opened the door of his security booth and stepped out into the cool night air. The noise from across the road was louder outside of the soundproofed glass booth, but it was still little more than an unintelligible murmur to him, like a conversation heard through the plasterboard wall of a cheap motel.

But the young soldier could sense something was going on, and it set the hairs on the back of his crew-cut head tingling. For a moment

Corporal Parsons felt a creeping unease claw its way up his back, but then his training kicked in and he took a step closer to the closed security gate.

The twenty-acre lot housing the Project Tach-Comm team and its precious experiment remained secure on all sides thanks to the deadly high-voltage electrified fencing surrounding the complex's perimeter. If anybody was stupid enough to try to gain access to the facility through the fence—well, they would be in for the shock of their lives: literally.

The gate the young soldier guarded was the only entrance into the complex, so if there was going to be any trouble it would be focused here. He was confident he could call up sufficient reinforcements to hold the gate from any kind of assault if the need arose. Within a few minutes he could have thirty-plus heavily armed soldiers at his side. All it would take was a simple radio call from him.

Suddenly, the rhythmic sound of the chanting voices ceased, replaced by a silence broken only by the chirruping background hum of a thousand cicadas. Corporal Parsons took another tentative step closer to the gate. There was something moving out there, he was sure of it; out there deep in the shadows beyond the security lights. His eyes strained to see into the umbra beyond the high-intensity floodlighting, but he could not make out any discernible shapes.

When they finally stepped into the light, the startled soldier let out a sharp gasp of shock. A thousand men, women, and children were walking purposefully from the darkness across the road toward him, their arms interlocked with their neighbors' in a line that stretched off in both directions along the road. The night was suddenly alive with their collective voices singing as one, praising the glory of God on high as they marched in unison across the road toward the security fence.

Shaking off the shock of what he was witnessing, Parsons sprinted back to the security booth, grabbed the red emergency phone, and quickly dialed in a four-digit number.

"Sir!" he shouted into the phone, trying to make himself heard over the rising surge of voices outside. "We have a serious problem out here." Parsons quickly relayed what he was witnessing to the person at the other end of the line, who in turn told him exactly what he should do. "Yes, sir," he replied, and slammed down the phone.

Parsons grabbed his M16 from the rack. He rammed home a magazine of live ammo, then hit the large red button fixed to the wall near the door of the booth. Immediately the *waaaa-waaaa* drone of the emergency klaxon began ululating through the still night air of the base. Parsons knew that right now all off-shift security personnel would be frantically throwing on their uniforms, grabbing their weapons, and making their way to his location. It was a reassuring thought for the young man. He could see the glare of the lights from the mobile security patrol's electric carts already heading his way.

Glancing at the front gate and the approaching horde of protestors beyond it, he chambered a round into his weapon and stepped out to face them.

FORTY-ONE

"What exactly are you trying to do?" Jim tersely asked Simone as he escorted both her and the soundman, Beaumont, toward the project's receiving room. The receiving equipment was housed in a smaller lab near the restrooms at the opposite end of the same long corridor to where the project's transmission equipment was being set up.

"I'm just trying to do my job," Simone shot back.

"You do realize what's at stake, don't you? Nothing less than the future of humanity. For all we know, the future of the damn universe is in the balance here tonight. If we don't get this right, that's it . . . It's all over."

"Well, perhaps if you hadn't seen fit to meddle in the first place we wouldn't be in this situation, would we? Have you thought about that little gem?"

He wanted to fire back some pointed comment, but instead Jim fell silent. He had forgotten how infuriatingly spot-on his ex-wife could be sometimes. But she was right of course: science was responsible for the Slip, and now they were frantically scrambling not just to try to repair the mess they had made but to also try to stop the disaster from becoming even worse. It was hard to be a hero when you were also the villain of the piece, he realized.

Rather than replying, Jim fixed his gaze straight ahead and continued on his way to the receiver room. Rebecca and Adrianna were busy setting up the receiver and the recording equipment they would use to monitor the effect of the transmission when Jim popped his head around the door. The room was even more cramped than the transmitter room. If everything went according to plan, they would receive the message here a second or so before it was even sent.

"Stupid question, but are you busy?" he said, smiling at the two women.

Rebecca looked at her watch. "With less than twenty minutes to go before we begin the experiment that will determine whether we save the world or help plunge us back into nonexistence, you ask, 'Am I busy?' Come on in," she said, matching his smile with one of her own.

Jim walked into the room, closely followed by Simone and Beaumont. He was sure he felt the temperature of the room drop as they entered.

"You've met Simone and her crew?" he asked.

"Yes, we met earlier today when she interviewed us. Nice to see you again, Simone," said Rebecca.

Simone smiled perfunctorily back at the younger woman and then turned her attention to the equipment scattered across the table.

Adrianna did not bother to fake any esteem for the church team. Instead, she regarded the interlopers with a patent disdain that bordered on open hostility. Mumbling something under her breath, she climbed back onto the specially made raised dais that allowed her to reach the workbench and its equipment.

"So tell me," said Simone. "What is the purpose of this equipment?"

"It's the sister unit to the transmitter you saw in the other room," explained Rebecca. "When the signal is sent at midnight, we will pick it up here and be able to confirm its success. This other equipment"—she pointed at a bank of electronics near the far wall—"will record the data for us for later analysis."

"Assuming it works, of course," said the soundman.

"It will work," Adrianna said, turning to give the skinny man her very best cold, hard stare.

Beaumont returned it with equal ferocity. "Well, for all our sakes, let's hope it does."

Once again Jim found himself caught in the middle of a potential conflict, and once again he found himself defusing the obvious dislike that was perilously close to escalating into full-blown conflict between the stick-thin Beaumont and the diminutive Adrianna Drake.

"Mr. Gallagher has been a while," Jim said finally, hoping to distract them both. "Mr. Beaumont. Maybe we should go and make sure he's not lost."

Beaumont didn't argue, and with a final smirk at the red-faced Adrianna, he left the room through the door held open by a waiting Jim Baston.

"Kids today," said Beaumont sarcastically as the two men made their way along the corridor leading back to the transmission room.

"You check in there," said Jim as they reached the door, "and I'll go see if he's still in the men's room."

Beaumont nodded and pushed through the door into the bustling transmission room. Jim caught a glimpse of Lorentz still busily checking the equipment and heard a snatch of his voice reading off some figures before the heavy door closed, sealing the room. He continued down the corridor until he arrived at two doors marked with the universal symbols for male and female bathrooms. Jim pushed open the door to the men's room and stepped inside.

Immediately, the astringent smell of disinfectant and stale urine filled his nostrils, reminding him of long-ago hospital visits. The automatic overhead lights were already on, which only added to the antiseptic feel of the bathroom as they illuminated the white-tiled floors and walls. The lights were motion activated and set on a timer of a few minutes before they switched off, so either Gallagher had recently left or he was still here in one of the stalls.

"Mr. Gallagher, are you in here?" Jim called out, his voice echoing off the tile floor. There was no answer for a few seconds, and then he heard a quiet cough, and Gallagher's voice issued from one of the nearby stalls.

"Yeah, I'm in here," said Gallagher. "Won't be too long."

"Well, you're cutting it pretty close," replied Jim, glancing at his watch. "You think you will be okay?"

"Sure thing. I'm about done. You go on ahead, and I'll meet you in the transmission room."

The sound of the toilet flushing emphasized the sentiment behind the statement.

He was a strange one, that Gallagher, thought Jim. He still wasn't sure what it was about the man that made him uneasy whenever he was around. Maybe it was the shit-eating grin he always seemed to have plastered on his face. Kind of like he knew something you didn't. Or maybe it was the way he watched the women. Whenever they were near, his eyes would always be following them, even though his mouth was still talking to you. Whatever it was, this time tomorrow Gallagher and the rest of the church-appointed team would be out of his hair and no longer his problem.

Thank God for small mercies, Jim thought as he exited the bathroom and walked slowly back toward the transmission room.

FORTY-TWO

Tony Gallagher listened until he was sure Baston had left. He ducked outside the toilet stall and double-checked the bathroom. When he was sure he was alone, he slipped back into the stall and closed the swing door, locking it behind him just in case. He dropped the seat cover on the toilet, sat down, crossed his legs, and leaned back against the tank. He would have to give that guy Baston a minute to get back to the transmission room before he made his move.

From the breast pocket of his shirt, Gallagher pulled a small non-descript calculator and caressed it with his big hands like it was some priceless jewel. And in a way it was. This tiny solar-powered calculator was the key to everything. It worked just like a regular calculator, but if he typed in a specific string of numbers and then hit the "%" button, it would send a radio signal to the passive receiver unit hidden in the video camera he had left sitting on a table in the transmission room. The signal would detonate the explosives lining the inner walls of the camera unit, and it would be game over.

He—and the church, of course—would win.

The wonderful thing about General-Munitions Haywire Gel was that it was so malleable, which meant it could be easily disguised or hidden just about anywhere. Easily molded into virtually any shape or size desired, it made the perfect explosive for smuggling into a complex such as this. It was also impossible to detonate the explosive by dropping it, stomping on it, or throwing it. Its shock resistance made it the ideal tool for this kind of covert job.

The only way to detonate the explosive was to trigger it with a smaller blast from another explosive; in this case it was a tiny amount of black powder hooked up to the receiver of the low-frequency detonator. He had wired the detonator directly into the battery of the camera, so it needed no telltale secondary power source for the security scanners to pick up—as long as the camera's battery remained charged, the bomb was ready to rock and roll.

Gallagher deftly tapped in the sequence of code numbers that would prime the detonator: 1-9-5-3. The bomb was now activated and armed; all it would take was for him to hit the "%" key and it would be done. His index finger hovered above the key as he sat on the closed lid of the commode and waited for Baston to get back to the transmission room. A thrilling sense of expectation pounded through his veins at the thought of the lives he now held in his hand.

They were all going to die; it was just such a shame it would be over so quickly.

**

Lorentz glanced up as the door to the transmission room opened and the skinny soundman stepped inside. Through the opening, he caught a glimpse of Jim, still in the corridor, saying something to Beaumont before the door swung shut again. The soundman scanned the room as if he was looking for something before noticing Lorentz watching him. Their eyes linked for a brief second, and then Beaumont broke the connection, his face flushing with embarrassment at the contempt so obvious in the doctor's eyes.

"Mina," Lorentz said, "would you look after our guest? Make sure he doesn't touch anything, would you, please?"

Mina nodded and walked over to where the soundman stood shuffling his feet.

Harry Mabry sidled—as much as anybody of his enormous size could ever hope to sidle—over to join Lorentz at his computer station.

"All ready at my end, Doc," he said.

"Good. Good. We can start running the diagnostics as soon as James returns."

The soundman was still looking about as comfortable as a nun at a whore's convention. He was attempting to hide his obvious nervousness by pretending to adjust his sound equipment.

Good, thought Lorentz. *Keep the bastard off balance.* They had no right to be here anyway. Things were tense enough without their intrusive presence.

Over the radio link the sound of Adrianna's voice crackled. "Prof. Lorentz, we are all set here in the receiver room."

Lorentz picked up the small handheld radio from the desk next to him and pressed the "Send" button. "Very good, Dr. Drake. Please stand by to begin running the final diagnostics."

"Will do." Then a long pause and "Good luck."

Lorentz smiled before replying, "We don't need luck, Dr. Drake . . . we have *science*."

***

The swing door of the men's room had closed behind Jim as he made his way back to the transmission room. With less than twenty minutes left until go time, he was running late, and he needed to get to the lab for the final diagnostics check to make sure his end of the experiment went smoothly. If he had not been playing nursemaid to the church crew, he would be there already.

As Jim made his way along the corridor, he thought he caught the faint wail of an alarm sounding somewhere off in the distance. The main lab building was so well insulated it was hard to make out any sound from the outside. It was probably nothing, and he dismissed the thought.

Jim placed the palm of his hand on the door to the transmission room and paused for a second. Took in a deep breath and exhaled slowly. *Thank God this is almost over*, he thought to himself, and began to push the door open. Inside, he saw Lorentz talking into his handheld radio. Towering over him was Horatio Mabry, a look of concentration fixed on his face as he stared at the screen over Lorentz's shoulder.

"Ah! James. Finally!" said Lorentz at the sound of the door opening.

***

In the stall of the men's room, Gallagher stared at the plastic calculator he held in his hand. *Such a tiny thing*, he thought, but at this moment it hung like the Sword of Damocles over the heads of everyone in this building; the power of life and death was in his hands once again. It was a physical manifestation of the chaos theory these scientists were always getting so excited about—a butterfly flaps its wings in Brazil, and a storm is unleashed on the other side of the world.

Well, let's see how well that theory plays out in the real world.

He pressed the "%" key.

FORTY-THREE

The line of protestors stopped just short of the perimeter security fence. They continued singing as they formed a chain of bodies that stretched for almost three hundred feet in either direction of the main gate.

Security Chief Calhoun had pulled most of his men to this location—nearly thirty in all, a small number by comparison to the thousands they faced, but the added muscle made Corporal Parsons a lot less nervous. The Chief had assessed the situation immediately upon arriving on scene. He relocated all but a handful of his men to this one choke point. If the crowd decided to try something stupid, he would ensure they would meet the full force available to him. He had already called central command and apprised them of the situation. As of five minutes ago, three Black Hawks containing a shitload of backup had taken off and were making their way to his location.

In twenty minutes he would have enough firepower at his disposal to repel a small army.

The Chief was not a violent man by nature; if he could resolve this situation peacefully without putting his men or the protestors in harm's way, then he would do his utmost to ensure that nobody on either side of the security fence got hurt. He had already grabbed a bullhorn from the security booth and walked purposefully up and down the innermost security fence, attempting to talk some kind of sense into those on the other side.

"This is a secure area," he announced. "You are trespassing on government property. For your own safety, please disperse and move away from the fence."

His amplified voice was barely audible to the armed soldiers assigned to escort him as he strode up and down the fence line. He was being drowned out by the sound of over two thousand voices singing some hymn he vaguely recognized. The volume of the protestors' voices was doubled by those who had remained in the makeshift encampment on the far side of the road. With one unified voice, the massive crowd cried out for deliverance.

"Please," the Chief pleaded with them. "Move away from the fence."

A wave of movement passed through the crowd as they simultaneously began unlocking their arms.

"Thank God," the soldier to the Chief's right said. "Finally, they're listening."

The hymn reached its final crescendo, and as if on some unspoken cue the mass of protestors threw themselves as one against the high-voltage security fence. Interlacing their fingers with the chain-link, the protestors embraced the current of deadly electricity as it arced through their bodies, scorching their hair, and blistering their skin as bright-blue sparks exploded into the air around them like flares. Mouths leapt open in silent screams as thousands of volts contorted their muscles into uncontrollable spasms.

No song leaped from their lips now, just curls of gray smoke that floated into the increasingly cold night air, suddenly redolent with the stink of burning flesh.

FORTY-FOUR

The explosive was a quarter-inch thick and covered the entire inside of the casing of the video camera. Safe in its airtight container, it had easily evaded the fluoroscope scan and the trace-scent "sniffer" employed by the security personnel at the compound's security checkpoint. The airborne nitrogen-compound vapor was contained safely within the airtight camera casing, concealing the characteristic nitrogen signature, which would have betrayed the fact that the camera was actually a cleverly disguised bomb, capable of destroying everything within a thirty-foot blast radius.

When the black powder initiator detonated, it created a shock wave that traveled through the Haywire explosive gel at approximately the speed of sound, breaking down the plastic explosive into its constituent molecular parts. The fuel and oxidizer that until a millisecond earlier had been chemically bonded into an inert material were set free and instantly recombined to form a gas. The gas rapidly expanded within the enclosed space of the camera housing until finally it exploded outward in a massive burst of heat and light, sending millions of shards of metal and plastic into the air, ripping through everything in their path.

***

The dull crump of the explosion in the laboratory wing was inaudible over the screams of those sacrificing themselves against the electrified fence and the yelling of the horrified security personnel as they shouted for the remaining protestors to get back.

In the unattended security booth, a red light suddenly glowed brightly and began flashing insistently on the fire alarm monitoring board, complemented by the trilling of an audible alarm.

It was all lost to the commotion outside.

FORTY-FIVE

Jim could not remember how he ended up flat on his back in the corridor. The tiled floor was cold against his cheek, and he could smell the piney odor of the cleanser the janitor used to clean it.

His head hurt. There was a deafening ringing in his ears, and he could taste the metallic tang of blood in his mouth.

Had he fallen?

His last memory was of heading back to the transmitter room. His hand had been on the handle of the door and then . . . here he was.

Maybe if he opened his eyes . . .

The door he had been about to open now lay on its side, blown from all but one of its hinges. It looked like a broken tooth dangling from a crooked mouth. No, wait. It looked like a broken tooth dangling from the mouth of a dragon, because an acrid white smoke was pouring through the open doorway.

The pallid-white fingers of smoke crept toward him from the open gash of the doorway. Alarm bells rang somewhere too. They became louder as the noise in his head subsided.

Jim's senses and memory suddenly came flooding back. He felt himself abruptly become aware of what was happening, almost like the reverse action of a drain, where the dirty water of his memory and senses rushed back *up* the pipe to fill his mind instead of emptying away.

"Oh Christ!" he said as he tried to stand.

The corridor twisted and contorted as he struggled to his feet, and he threw out a steadying hand to the wall, falling against it while he gathered himself, waiting for his dazed senses to stabilize. Something wet ran down over his forehead and dripped into his left eye; he felt its warmth as it trickled down his shock-numbed cheek. Jim wiped it away with his forearm and saw that the shirt that had been crisp and white when he threw it on that morning was now torn and ripped. A brown singe mark extended up the full extent of the shirt's right arm, turning the polyester into brittle brown strands. Bits of melted polyester crumbled under his fingers as he ran his hands over the damaged material. There was a fair amount of blood splattered down the front of his shirt too, but he knew most of it wasn't his. He was quite sure the blood belonged to whoever had originally owned the severed arm that lay in a congealing pool of gore next to where he had fallen.

He stared at the limb. It was thin and pale. It looked almost feminine in its delicacy, but the tufts of hair on the upper arm and the large metallic watch denoted it as having once been attached to a man.

Jim staggered away from the wall and took two tentative, stumbling steps toward the opposite one before edging his way to the ruined doorway. The door was broken off and smashed, and long splinters of wood jutted out from the frame, exposing the yellowish-white wood beneath the paint. Jim was careful to avoid impaling himself on any of them as he propped himself in the doorway and tried to see into the smoke-filled room that had until moments earlier contained the sole hope for the future of humanity.

It was a charnel house now. An abattoir.

A naked body lay crumpled against the wall just inside the room. Jim thought it was probably once a man, but now it was just a pile of broken bones held together by a bloodied sack of charred skin. The right arm was missing just below the shoulder, and a rag of flesh hung limply against a sharp piece of fractured bone jutting out from the body's collarbone.

"Is there anybody in here?" Jim called out. His voice was husky from the smoke he was inhaling with every breath. His throat felt like someone had taken an electric sander to it, and his breathing had an odd whistle each time he inhaled. He gently probed his mouth with his fingers and felt gaps where two of his front teeth should have been.

There was no reply from the room. He took a tentative step inside, careful not to let go of the doorjamb. The room was so full of smoke he could barely make out anything.

He called out again. "Anybody in here?" His voice was quickly overcome by a fit of coughing that racked his badly damaged body with pain, doubling Jim over as nausea washed over him.

There was a second body lying a few feet farther into the room, its outline blackened by a halo of debris and torn clothing. Its size and bulk meant it could only have been one person: Horatio Mabry. The big man's face was completely gone, now nothing more than a bloody sea of exposed muscle and gristle. His lips had been torn from his face in the explosion, exposing his remaining teeth in a lurid grin.

Everybody was dead in here. He could sense it . . . he could *smell* it; that odd burned-chicken smell cops and firefighters would sometimes talk about after a particularly bad fire. Jim backed his way out of the room until his spine hit the farthest wall of the corridor.

It was over.

Whoever had committed this atrocity had destroyed humanity's only chance at a future. Jim's eyes clouded over, and a tear made its way over his cinder-encrusted cheek. His legs folded beneath him, and he slid down the wall and into unconsciousness.

FORTY-SIX

A shelf of books crashed to the ground as the three startled occupants of the receiver room steadied themselves against the table that held the Tach-Comm equipment.

"What *was* that?" Simone demanded, staring wide-eyed at Rebecca. "An earthquake?"

Rebecca ignored the question. She glanced at Adrianna, her own fear reflecting back at her from the girl's eyes.

"Stay here," she said, clasping the woman-child's hand. "I'll go check."

Rebecca cautiously eased open the door of the receiver room and stepped out into the corridor. It looked normal, but up ahead, where the hallway she stood in bisected the corridor leading to the transmission room, a milky cloud of dust was swirling and falling in the light of the overhead fluorescents. Alarms were clamoring, and the emergency exit direction signs were glowing red as she made her way to the intersection and turned to face the source of the smoke floating toward her.

She could see the door to the transmission lab hanging from its hinges. Debris lay strewn across the opening, and smoke billowed out from it. The opposite wall was black and singed; the paint was covered in blisters and flaking from the wall. As Rebecca stood silent and stunned at the devastation, she saw an indistinct figure emerge wraith-like from the smoke, stagger across the corridor, and collapse against the far wall.

She was running then, covering the fifty feet separating them in seconds that felt like minutes. The man had collapsed to the floor, and as she drew near, she knew who it was.

"Jim," she cried, eating up the remaining ground, her lungs burning as she sucked in huge gulps of the smoke-filled air.

He was curled into a tight ball when she reached him, his arms crossed tightly against his chest and his legs drawn almost to his wrists. His shirt was black and dirt encrusted, his trousers torn and shredded. An ugly three-inch gash ran from his forehead through singed hair toward the top of his skull, and a steady stream of blood trickled down the left side of his face, gathering in a pool on the floor next to his unconscious body.

"Oh no," she breathed, falling to her knees beside him. Rebecca grabbed Jim by his shoulders and shook him gently, pleading with him to look at her. "Jim! Please."

Jim turned a smoke-blackened face toward her, streaks of white skin visible only from the tracks left by the tears spilling down his face. She saw his eyes were terribly bloodshot as they focused on her. He was badly injured, but at least he was alive.

"Dead," he said through cracked, blood-caked lips. "They are all dead."

Glancing into the room that was now completely filled with smoke, she saw the orange flicker of flames dancing like fire imps, and she knew Jim was right. They were all dead in there.

Mitchell, Belkov, Horatio—all gone.

"Stand up, Jim," Rebecca ordered as she slipped his arm over her shoulder and her own arm around his back. "We need to get you out of here."

Grunting with the effort, she stood up. Holding Jim as firmly as she could, she staggered with him down the corridor.

Security would surely be here any time now, but she had to get him out of reach of the choking smoke that was billowing from the burning room and filling the corridor. She half dragged, half lifted Jim in the direction of the corridor leading to the receiver room, away from the smoke. Perspiration popped on her forehead and began to drip down her face, stinging her already smoke-reddened eyes.

Jim lapsed back into unconsciousness, and his body suddenly became deadweight. Rebecca collapsed to the ground with him, wincing as his head thudded dully against the cold floor. Willing herself to stand, she wiped the perspiration from her eyes, grabbed Jim's wrist with both of her hands, and began pulling him the final few yards to the junction of the corridors. Once around the corner she let go of his wrist and dropped to her knees while she gathered herself, chugging in deep breaths of the cleaner air.

The gash on Jim's head was open again, and the blood was flowing freely down his face in thick rivulets. His right eye was badly swollen, and a bruise the size of her hand was beginning to form down the left side of his face. Worse, his chest was rising and falling shallowly. She had to do something until the emergency crews got to them, had to stop the bleeding. She looked around frantically for something to staunch the flow.

Of course, she thought to herself as she pushed herself up to a standing position. Rebecca began running back in the direction of the transmission room, throwing a hand over her mouth and nose as she picked her way through the rapidly expanding smoke. Clear of the smoke, she sprinted the last few yards to a place where she knew there would be a first-aid kit.

Rebecca rushed headlong into the women's bathroom. She headed to the cabinet at the end of the room. Throwing open the doors, she saw an empty space where the first-aid kit should have been.

"Damn it!" she yelled. Then she remembered. She had used the kit to fix Jim's hand the day of the church team's arrival. She must have left it in his room. No time to run back and get it now. Besides, she knew where there was another one.

She ran from the women's bathroom to the next door down, pushed it open, and rushed into the men's room.

FORTY-SEVEN

He heard the explosion as a hollow boom that shook the floor, rattling dust from the overhead acoustic ceiling panels and sending it falling gently to the floor like snow.

Tony Gallagher rose from his perch in the men's room stall, a satisfied smile spreading across his face. He opened the door with a creak of dry hinges and stepped out into the glare of the overhead lights.

Making his way past the porcelain urinals, he took the brown overnight bag from under his arm and set it down on the sink, leaned against the unit with both arms extended, and stared deeply into the mirror that ran the entire length of the wall.

He was tired of this disguise. It was time for a change. Unzipping the travel bag, he pulled out a straight razor and set it on the countertop, followed by a tin of unscented shaving cream and a face towel.

In Europe they called straight razors "cutthroat razors," an apt name for this particular instrument: a rigid steel blade hinged to its case by a small steel stud. The blade folded out of the black pearl case, which formed the handle when the razor was open for use. One slip with this thing could slice open an artery and leave you bleeding to death on your bathroom floor. No wonder they were no longer in use, replaced years ago by the safety razor and then by the electric razor and finally by Insta-Shave cream. He had found it at a flea market antique stall in Kansas; its rugged build and ability to turn something as mundane as shaving into a skill immediately appealed to him.

Gallagher pushed the plastic plug into the sink's drain. He activated the faucet and watched as it rapidly filled the sink with warm water, steam rising ponderously into the air. He splashed the water onto his face, squirted a large glob of shaving cream from the can, and smoothed it over his beard. Then with one final look into the rapidly misting mirror, he picked up the straight razor and began to hack off his facial hair.

FORTY-EIGHT

Rebecca flew into the men's room, slamming the door back on its hinges.

Fixed to the farthest wall, past the stalls and urinals, was the glass cabinet containing the first-aid kit and medical supplies she was looking for. The sinks were obscured by the toilet stalls, and as they came into sight, she was amazed to see the broad back of a man bent over the sink, his head dipped down toward the basin, his lower face mostly obscured by white foam.

"Thank God," she yelled to the man's back as she rushed to the cabinet. "There's been an accident. People are hurt. I need all the help I can get."

The man reached for the green towel resting on the counter and began mopping away at the residual shaving cream covering his face. She could make out his blue eyes as his reflection stared at her from the mirror, the rest of his face obscured by the towel.

She opened the glass door and grabbed the med kit.

"Didn't you hear the explosion?" she asked as he finished wiping away the foam from his face, those intense eyes still fixed attentively on her. Reaching out, she touched the man's arm and said with as much patience as she could muster, "You're with the crew from the church, aren't you? Are you hurt?"

He let the towel drop to the floor, revealing his newly shaved, grinning face in the mirror.

"Hello, Rebecca," he said, his voice holding back a barely restrained chuckle. "Remember me?"

***

At first the man's appearance made little impression on Rebecca. There was a sense of someone from her past, an inkling of recognition. His voice sounded familiar. His pink, freshly shaved face regarded her with an almost-benevolent smile.

And then the mask dropped away from him, and everything flooded back to her.

He was her nightmare. It was *him*. He was her killer.

A mewling whimper slipped from Rebecca's lips as she took a stumbling step backward. Her eyes widened in shock, and in what seemed to be time distilled down to its finest component, she began to turn and run. The very air around her had suddenly become molasses, her movement reduced to a slow-motion movie.

Somewhere in the back of her mind, pushed there by some primeval survival instinct, she watched herself as if from afar. She saw her body from above and watched as it twisted—slowly, ever so slowly— and began to lean forward. *Come on. Run*, her mind screamed. *For God's sake, run.* She placed first one foot and then the other in front of it, her heartbeat maddeningly slow in her ears, its sound drawn out to a long, low beat.

Thrummmmmp! One step away.

From the safety of her mind's vantage point, somewhere near the ceiling of the bathroom, she saw the man begin to move too. She watched as he used the sink unit to launch himself after her, his massive arms propelling him in a fluid movement away from the sink. She screamed down at herself to run faster. *Move faster.*

Thrummmmmp! Another step.

The door. She had to make it out into the corridor. If he caught her in here, she was doomed. Security would be too concerned with fighting the fire raging in the transmission room and dealing with the victims. No one would think to look in here for her, and no one would hear her screams over the wailing of the fire alarm.

Thrummmmmp! Her mind screamed, *Keep on moving.*

With a startling suddenness, she was back in her body. Seeing through her own eyes. Feeling the rhythmic thump-thump-thump of her heart pounding in her breast. Sucking in air through gritted teeth, she felt the dampness of perspiration underneath her arms and across her face as she accelerated toward the exit, her senses heightened now to the point that she could feel the hairs on the back of her neck tingling as the hot breath of her pursuer, so close behind her, spilled over her.

Concentrate on the door. Get to the door.

She was almost there. Her hand reached out; she was going to steam right through it and out into the corridor to safety.

She felt the punch just as her hand touched the aluminum finger-plate of the bathroom's swing door. It was like a hammer blow between her shoulder blades, knocking her forward. Her feet tangled, and she felt herself tipping over. *No! No! No!* her mind screamed, but it was too late. Her forward momentum was already carrying her toward the door and the floor at the same time. Instinctively, she drew her hand to her chest, trying to regain her balance and check her fall but instead allowing her head to strike the door with such force her vision doubled and her teeth snapped painfully together. She tasted blood, bitter and metallic, in her mouth.

Rebecca hit the floor on her back.

Her head still ringing from the impact, she realized she was lying half in and half out of the bathroom. Looking up, she saw the killer's huge body coming for her, a look of supreme triumph tattooed across his face.

Twisting her body away from him, Rebecca flipped onto her stomach and began a frantic hand-over-hand scramble out into the corridor in a last desperate attempt to flee. But the polished tiles just made her hands squeak as her sweaty skin slid uselessly over its frictionless surface.

The floor suddenly flew away from her, and she felt herself lifted bodily by the scruff of her clothing into the air, dragged away from the rapidly receding safety of the corridor and back into the bathroom.

"I get to kill you twice," Byron Portia whispered to her. "How cool is that?"

Rebecca clawed helplessly at the air, and when finally she was able to draw sufficient oxygen into her lungs, she knew it was already too late. Her scream of terror was cut short as the door swung closed behind her.

FORTY-NINE

"You know, I recognized you as soon as I saw you. It's just so amazing!" Byron Portia, until recently known as Tony Gallagher, shook his head in amusement at the irony. "What do you think the chances are? A billion to one? A trillion? Or maybe it was not chance at all. Hmm? Bet you haven't given that any thought at all, have you? No, of course you haven't. You have other things on your mind right now, don't you, sweetie?" His hand tightened around Rebecca's throat, squeezing off more air, so only a rasping gurgle escaped from between her lips.

He reached out to the sink counter with his free hand and picked up the straight razor, exposing the wet blade with a flick of his wrist. Becky's eyes widened and her body stiffened as he ran its cold edge lightly along her throat.

"Want to see something interesting?" he asked her. "Sure you do. Sure you do."

He closed the blade into the handle and deftly inverted the razor with his thick fingers. A silver stud near the end of the handle looked just like the other three that apparently kept the two pieces of black pearl together, but when Portia fingered it, a second blade snapped out from its hiding place. Five inches of glistening steel and, unlike the shaving blade, this was a double-sided dagger: flat and insanely sharp on both sides, the glinting blade tapered down to a lethal point. It was small but deadly enough if the user knew what they were doing, and Rebecca's oxygen-starved mind knew through terrible personal knowledge that this man had a lot of experience with it.

"Clever, eh? A gentleman can't be too careful on the road, you know. Lot of undesirables out there these days. A *lot* of undesirables. Not my instrument of choice, as I'm sure you realize, but needs must when the devil drives, right?" He grinned at the choking woman, revealing his tombstone teeth, white against his tanned skin. "I think I would have raised a few eyebrows if I had tried to get my tool of choice past security. You remember that, don't you, sweetie?"

Rebecca dragged the memories of her final moments from the crypt within her mind where she had kept them locked away; the memory of the untarnished blade of this man's hunting knife played back and forth before her eyes before he . . . before—

Rebecca's eyes rolled back up into their sockets; her skin was beginning to take on a slight blue tinge as hypoxia took hold of her. Her earlier frantic attempts to beat the big man's hand from her throat now became little more than autonomic twitches as her vision and cognition faded away from her.

Portia watched her suffering with fascinated attention, his head tipped slightly to his shoulder. With expert judgment he timed her slide toward death until, at the final moment, before he sensed her escape into unconsciousness, he released his grip from around her throat.

Instinctively, Rebecca drew in a long, labored gasp of air and, her oxygen-deprived muscles unable to hold her up, sank down the wall of the bathroom into a gasping puddle of folded limbs. Her eyes fluttered open as her chest heaved and strained to drag more of the precious air into her system. Vaguely aware she was still alive, she looked up into the face of the man who had killed her once already and who was, she was sure, preparing to end her life once again.

"Oh boy," he said. "Are we having fun now or what?"

A bead of blood trickled over Rebecca's chin. She felt its warm stickiness as it flowed down the arc of her throat before being absorbed into the material of her torn blouse.

"I really wish I had the time to spend with you that I feel this situation deserves. Unfortunately, I have to get out of here. So, regrettably I'm going to have to make this quick."

Rebecca screamed as Portia grabbed a handful of her hair. He viciously snapped her head backward, exposing her neck; then she felt the sharp kiss of the blade as he placed it against her throat.

"What a shame I can't spend more time with you." He sounded truly upset.

The smell of smoke became abruptly stronger in her nostrils, and she felt the pressure of the knife against her skin disappear as Portia suddenly released her from his grip.

"Well! Well! Well! Looks like we have an audience," Portia said, laughing.

Rebecca's head dropped to the floor, the muscles of her body so weak she could barely move let alone lift her head to look at what had suddenly grabbed her captor's attention. A white haze of sparkling fog filled her peripheral vision, but as she strained her head on objecting muscles, the haze began to seep away, clearing her vision sufficiently for Rebecca to make out who the man with the knife was talking to.

Adrianna Drake stood in the doorway, her hands braced against the jamb, a mixture of confusion, surprise, and horror painted across her little-girl face. Adrianna's mouth was moving, but Rebecca could not make out what she was saying, because the buzzing that filled her head like static from a mistuned radio station overwhelmed all other sound. She watched the girl's lips move, her eyes questioning what she was seeing.

"What . . . ?" she started to say, but before the professor could finish, Rebecca screamed at her. "Get out! For God's sake, run!"

For a second she thought Adrianna was going to ignore her or maybe she hadn't heard her; she could barely make out the sound of her own voice over the insect buzzing in her head. But she realized Adrianna must have understood, because her look of confusion was replaced now by one of anger and a glint of defiant understanding in those cool-blue child's eyes. Adrianna's body language changed subtly, and for an instant she seemed to solidify into some armored warrior-child. Rebecca thought the girl might stand her ground against this terrible man. She didn't understand what she was facing, of course. How could she?

"Get out . . . *now!*" Rebecca screamed again with all her remaining energy. Her head sagged for a second with the exertion of her scream, but when she managed to drag her eyes back to the door once more, the little girl was gone.

***

Byron Portia pulled Rebecca along behind him like a kid dragging a school bag through the dirt, his powerful hand enmeshed in her hair, lifting her head and upper torso a foot off the polished floor as he strode down the corridor after the fleeing Adrianna.

Rebecca's right eye was swollen shut, and from an inch-long gash across the soft skin of her cheek a slim stream of blood trickled, the result of her collision with the men's room door. Still she kicked and screamed, shouting the occasional obscenity at him through choking gasps of anger and fear, the pain held back for now by the pumping of her heart and the steady flow of adrenaline through her veins. Her own hands grasped the killer's thick wrist to try to alleviate the pain; she had already seen a large clump of her hair left behind, torn from her scalp by this man. Her shoes had fallen off almost immediately, and now her stocking feet refused to allow her any kind of grip on the highly polished floor, causing her to bump and slide along behind her captor.

Portia released her outside the door to the receiver room, dumping her unceremoniously into a heap on the floor. Squatting down beside her, he cupped Rebecca's chin in his rough-skinned hand and pulled her face close to his.

"Sweetie? I need you to focus for a moment, okay? Come on." He snapped the fingers of his free hand in front of her eyes.

Rebecca flinched uncontrollably and let out a quiet whimper, but it had the desired effect: she met his gaze.

"Focus! That's it, good girl. Now tell me, is there anybody else I need to know about besides that little bitch? Any other surprises I should be worrying over?"

Rebecca shook her head.

"You wouldn't tell me anyway, would you? Hmm?" Portia let out a bellowing laugh, grabbed his hostage by the arm, kicked open the door to the receiver room, and dragged the weeping woman inside.

FIFTY

"Well, doesn't this just go to show you can't trust anybody these days?" Portia directed his sarcasm at Rebecca.

She lay in a crumpled heap where he had thrown her in the center of the floor, but his eyes had fixed on the other occupant of the transmission room.

Simone had frozen where she stood when the killer kicked open the door to the room, separated from Portia and Rebecca by the midriff-high cupboard holding the now-useless experimental receiver.

Portia scanned the room, sniffing the air like a cat checking out a newly installed appliance, suspicious and wary of a trap.

"So where's that little bitch I chased in here?" he asked, his lips drawn back in a distrustful half smile.

"Don't tell—" Rebecca began to say from the floor, but her sentence was cut short with a swift kick to the stomach from Portia.

"Was I talking to you? No," he screamed at her writhing form. Then more quietly, "Now, Simone, where is Dr. Drake?"

A vein of anxiety pulsed just beneath the surface of Simone's voice when she answered. "I don't know. She left to go check on Rebecca and hasn't come back yet. Please, I don't understand what's going on. Why are you doing this?"

"Well, it's a long story, sweetie, and unfortunately I don't have the time to explain it to you, so why don't I just show you?" said Portia.

He stepped astride Rebecca's prone body, bent down, grabbed a fistful of her hair, and pulled her head back, exposing the white curve of her throat.

"Actions speak louder than words. That's what my daddy always used to say," he continued as he sank to his knees, straddling Rebecca's body. He drew the knifepoint down her throat and across her breastbone, until he reached the first button of her stained blouse.

"Please, no," Rebecca whimpered. "Not again."

Snick! Her first button disappeared with a flick of his wrist, bouncing off under a table.

"Oh my God, no. What are you doing? Get away from her." Simone took a step around the cupboard toward them.

"Stay right where you are, bitch," bellowed Portia, "or I swear I will pop her eyeballs right out of her head." He moved the point of the knife to Rebecca's bruised eye to illustrate his intention. Portia's grin widened, and his breathing began to increase as he saw the fear turn to terror in Simone's eyes.

"Please," Rebecca begged.

Snick! Her second button was gone.

"Too late for you, baby," he said through a maniac grin as he worked the knife between the cotton of her shirt and the final button. A subtle flick of his wrist sent it rolling away into a corner. Using the tip of his knife, he pushed each side of her shirt aside. Sweat glistened on his forehead, and his breathing picked up.

"Mmm!" he whistled appreciatively. "I'd forgotten just how sweet you were." He ran the blade back up over her breastbone until the tip rested just below her chin.

"Leave her alone, you son of a bitch," Simone cried, fighting back tears of anger and frustration.

Portia turned his head to face her, grinning at the distraught woman. "Don't worry, sweetie. You'll get your turn."

In the cupboard to his left, something rattled.

Portia's attention flicked instantly toward the sound. "Well, what do you know? Looks like you have rats," he said, his eyes narrowing to slits of suspicion. "Stay right where you are, sweetie. I'll be right back." He glanced at Simone. "If you move, I'll split her open," he warned.

The noise from the cupboard came again, this time louder, the sound of something shifting its weight.

Portia climbed off Simone, shuffling on his knees the few feet to the cupboard door. With the butt of the knife, he knocked twice, hard and loud. "Hello, little mousy. Come on out."

No reply. A cloud of anger crossed his face, and he drew back his arm for a more vicious swing at the closed door.

"I said," he bellowed, "come on—"

Before he could finish, the cupboard door exploded outward as, with a banshee scream, Adrianna Drake sprang from her hiding place. She ducked under Portia's guard and locked her hands onto the killer's head. Portia let out a scream of pain and surprise as the diminutive professor of physics sank her teeth into his nose and shook her head back and forth like a deranged chimpanzee, tearing away a chunk the size of her thumb. Blood splattered her face as she spat the lump of flesh over his shoulder, where it landed with a wet plop beside a stunned Simone.

Portia's hand instinctively flew toward his ruptured nose, forming a fist that smashed into the little girl's face, and sent her sprawling onto her back on the lab floor.

"You little . . ." he began, but he stopped midsentence as his peripheral vision caught the movement of Rebecca's now-free hand flashing upward, palm up, toward his knife hand. Her upturned hand caught the butt of the knife and forced it point first into Portia's exposed throat.

The blade sank deep into the fleshy tissue just above his Adam's apple. He immediately fell sideways, his hands clasping at the hilt of the dagger and the remaining two inches of blade protruding from his neck, a look of stunned amazement in his eyes. Blood began to pour from the wound. Portia's eyes widened with shock, his mouth worked spastically, and a sound that could have been an expletive but instead turned into a wet *ughmpph* rasped from between his lips as blood filled his mouth, spilling out in a thick red ribbon over his chin.

Rebecca rose uneasily to her feet.

"Bish," her killer rasped, *"You lishle bish."* His voice was now nothing more than a weak, blood-soaked gurgle.

Rebecca stood over the prostrate form of Byron Portia for a moment. Then, without a word, she raised her knee to chest height and stomped her foot down on the protruding butt of the knife, driving the remaining few inches of the blade deeper into his throat until it could go no farther.

With a look of utter astonishment in his eyes, Byron Portia, until that moment the world's most successful and luckiest serial killer, choked to death on his own blood in under a minute.

FIFTY-ONE

Rebecca continued to stare at the body of Byron Portia long after Simone had taken her hand in her own and led the shocked woman over to a chair. Adrenaline was still coursing through her body, and Rebecca's palms were wet and sticky in the older woman's hands as Simone knelt in front of her, blocking the grisly image of Portia's body from her sight.

Adrianna picked herself up from where she had fallen when the killer hit her. She fingered her face gingerly, feeling around for damage. Her upper lip was swollen and bloody, and she spat a glob of blood onto the floor as she made her way over to the other two women.

"Bastard," Adrianna whispered, staring at the corpse. "Hope you rot in hell."

As she passed the body of Portia, she gave him a vicious kick to the head.

Rebecca knew Simone was talking to her. Jim's ex-wife was kneeling in front of her, and she could see the woman's lips moving. There was a look of abject concern on her face, an odd counterpoint to the fear that still flitted across her eyes every few seconds as the woman glanced suspiciously over her shoulder at the dead man lying behind her. Simone's voice seemed to fade into Rebecca's frame of reference, much as someone waking slowly from sleep becomes aware of the sounds in their bedroom: the ticking of a clock or the whir of an overhead fan or the rush of a car passing by on the street outside their window.

Her voice faded in and filled the silent void of terror that the death of this man had left. She could feel the softness of Simone's hand as she gently stroked her hair, the woman's voice calming as she reassured her. "Okay. It's all okay now. He's gone. He's gone. He can't hurt anyone now."

Over Simone's shoulder, Rebecca could see the clock up on the opposite wall. As she stared dumbly at it, the display turned from –0015 to –0016.

Without another word, Rebecca began to weep.

PART FOUR

A NEW DAY

FIFTY-TWO

Brethren! We have a message from
another world, unknown and remote.
It reads: "One . . . two . . . three."

—Nikola Tesla

On a cold and windy morning, they gathered between the gray head-stones on the side of the hill, silently waiting for Mitchell Lorentz's coffin to descend into the ground.

There were few tears from the small group of mourners collected around the open grave. They had already been shed in the two weeks since the attack on the laboratory. And, of course, it was hard to wonder about the fate of someone's immortal soul when it was already proven beyond a shadow of a doubt that the dead did not always necessarily remain dead.

Jim's free hand absently wandered to the stitches lacing his scalp. A burr of fresh hair now roughened the cool flesh where the surgeons had shaved the site clean to get to his wound.

He had come to in an ambulance on the way to the hospital. The first thing he had seen was Rebecca's concerned face staring at him from the bench on the opposite side of the ambulance as paramedics worked on his injuries. She was holding his hand lightly in hers, and he felt her tenderly squeeze it when his eyelids fluttered open. A smile of relief crossed her lips as she said something to him, but he heard nothing over the wailing *wah-woo* of the ambulance's two-tone siren and the rattling of the gurney to which he was strapped. He managed a weak smile in return and was halfway through asking if she was all right when consciousness slipped away from him once more.

Jim's next memory was of a pounding in his head that was ameliorated only by the strange, distant feeling of separation he had from his own body. He was lying in a bed, soft cotton sheets cool against his skin; a medical drip was suspended from a hook next to him. The clear plastic bag contained a bluish fluid that ran down a tube to a catheter embedded in his hand. The only sound in the room was the electronic beep of a heart monitor, like a metronome synchronized to the rise and fall of his chest. Rebecca was gone, and in her place was a little girl whose feet barely reached halfway to the ground from the lip of the chair she was perched on. Her blond hair stretched down to her shoulders, and she wore blue leather buckle-down shoes on feet that swung back and forth to some personal tune only she could hear. She was watching him, and as Jim's eyes had cleared enough that he could finally focus on her, the beat of his heart monitor suddenly leapt to a bossa nova rhythm.

Seeing he was awake, the child scooted off the chair in three swift shimmies and ran to the door, before disappearing into the hospital corridor beyond. Jim was too weak to do anything more than croak a plaintive "Don't go." But it was too late; she was out the door before the words left him. His heart sank. He was sure she was just an illusion, a wish fulfilled by the blue liquid being fed into his arm by the doctors, and he sank back in the bed and allowed the darkness to claim him once again.

When he next awoke, the little girl was back.

His daughter.

Lark, he whispered.

Her name drifted on the air like a ghost.

Slowly, the fog began to lift and the room swam into full view. Lark was not alone. Her mother was with her; their daughter perched comfortably on Simone's lap.

Simone looked tired. Her eyes were red and puffy, and her hair had lost some of its luster, as though it had not been washed in a couple of days. Her skin was pale, and there was no hint of any kind of makeup.

"There you go," said an unfamiliar voice from the other side of the bed. "That should make things more comfortable for you."

Jim tilted his head to the right. A doctor in a white coat stood fiddling with the feed to his drip.

"The pain might seem a little more pronounced," he said, "as I've reduced the amount of painkiller, but it should make you a little sharper." The man smiled, showing a set of ivory-white teeth. "I'll leave you alone," he continued, making his way to the door of the hospital room. "I'm sure you have much to talk about."

When the door closed quietly behind the doctor, Jim returned his attention to his ex-wife and child sitting next to his bed.

"Hello, Lark," he said. His voice was still little more than a weak croak.

The little girl looked up expectantly at her mother. Simone smiled and nodded a silent okay to her daughter's unspoken request. Lark hopped off her lap and trotted to the bedside cabinet, filled a paper cup from a pitcher of water, and took it to her father, careful not to spill a drop.

"Hello, Daddy," Lark said as she raised the cup of water to his lips. "I missed you very much."

***

An autumn mist shrouded the ground, and a light breeze whistled between the headstones. It whipped up a flurry of dust and leaves that rustled and tumbled through the grass before blowing into the black hole that was to be Mitchell Lorentz's final resting place.

The priest, his white robes fluttering, spoke his final words as the deceased scientist's casket, its gold handles glinting in the sunlight, lowered slowly into the waiting ground. The sibilant hiss of the pneumatic lowering device was barely audible over the priest's voice.

Lark stood with Simone across the divide of the grave, her fingers interlaced tightly with those of her mother. His little girl gave him a lopsided smile as she caught him staring at her. Jim felt pressure on his own hand, and he turned sideways to look at Rebecca. She looked so beautiful in the early-morning light, but tears glistened at the corners of her eyes, and he was unsure whether it was the sad task of laying their friend in the ground or the chill breeze that whipped through the graveyard that put them there.

This was the third service they had attended in as many days. First was Horatio "Harry" Mabry, the big man's remains incongruously fitted into an urn until his cremated ashes could be sprinkled off the California coast as per his final wish. Mina Belkov lay in her grave less than fifty feet away from the man she had dedicated her life to, the man whose body rested in the slowly descending casket before them.

Edward Pike had reclaimed the remains of Justin Beaumont, the soundman with the church's team, soon after the explosion, despite protests by the coroner. The church had cited religious grounds and insisted his body be released without an autopsy being conducted. Pressure had been brought to bear by the government, and the charred remains of the unfortunate young man had been moved back to the Church of Second Redemption's headquarters in California for burial.

Within hours of news of the explosion reaching the outside world, Father Pike issued a statement distancing himself and the church from the attack, blaming it on "elements within the organization who were bent on blemishing the name of the organization and advancing the goals of nonbelievers." The faithful were called together and asked to pray for the poor unfortunates who had lost their lives in the explosion and those who had sacrificed themselves against Project Tach-Comm's electrified fence.

Jim wasn't buying anything that Pike was selling. His excuses were too convenient and appeared on the networks only hours after the news of the explosion was announced, raising suspicion and causing widespread debate as to just how deeply the organization had been involved. Father Pike had refused all interviews since the attack, which only fueled critics of the new religion's involvement.

The body of Byron Portia, linked posthumously to a rapidly growing number of previous and future murders, had not been claimed. His remains were cremated and his ashes dumped into the local landfill without any kind of ceremony.

But the true mystery that perplexed Jim and the remainder of the Tach-Comm team was just why the second Slip had not occurred. The explosion had stopped the vital signal from being broadcast; that was a certainty. The bomb carried in the assassin's camera had destroyed the transmission equipment and its operators minutes before the signal was supposed to be activated. It left only one obvious conclusion in Jim's mind: they had been wrong. Their calculations had been off in some way, or they had missed some subtle aspect of the event.

That observation led to an even more disturbing question among the remaining scientists: Were they free of the possibility of a second event occurring? Or should they expect at any moment to be plunged back to some point on the timeline where they all would cease to exist?

It's enough to make you paranoid, Jim thought morosely.

The sound of earth hitting the lid of Lorentz's coffin broke Jim from his thoughts. He knelt and took a handful of the damp soil, tossed it down into the open grave, and said a silent farewell to the man who had changed the lives of so many people.

The service over, mourners began walking slowly back to their waiting cars. Jim and Becky made their way over to the concrete path running beneath a copse of trees. Simone stood with Lark, waiting patiently beneath the trees' leafless branches.

"Hello, Daddy," said Lark as she ran full force into his legs, throwing her arms around his knees.

Picking the little girl up, Jim planted a kiss on her forehead. "Hey there, baby girl."

"Mommy said that I could come stay with you," she blurted out excitedly. "Can we go to the lake, Daddy? Can we?"

Jim's heart skipped a beat as his little girl let slip the answer to a question he had asked his ex-wife while still in the hospital. The chance to spend time with his child would be a gift that he could never repay.

"Can we go this weekend, Daddy? Please?" pleaded Lark as Jim set his child back down onto the ground.

Jim looked up at Simone, who smiled back before saying, "If that's okay with your father—"

"Yes, of course. Definitely. This weekend would be fine," said Jim, the words racing from his mouth as if he was afraid the offer would be retracted.

That elicited a whooping cry of delight from the child as she launched herself at her father's legs again.

"I have your cell number," Jim said. "I'll give you a call with a time I'll be able to pick her up."

Simone looked tired. She had endured much in the time since the explosion. Her involvement with the church had immediately drawn suspicion from government sources. Questioned about her involvement with Gallagher and his plot to sabotage the experiment, she had pleaded her ignorance of any involvement. And when finally the identity of Gallagher and his link to the murders of so many women had been revealed, Simone had been released.

Jim thought the government's part in allowing the killer access to the Tach-Comm project may have contributed to her halfhearted interrogation and quick release.

Leaning in close, Jim kissed his ex-wife gently on the cheek and whispered, "Thank you." Then, with a final hug for his kid and a "See you this weekend, sweetheart," he took Becky's hand in his own and started down the concrete path toward the parking lot.

FIFTY-THREE

A black Lincoln sedan with government plates was idling next to Jim's car in the parking lot of the cemetery. Jim recognized Colonel Geoffrey DeWitt leaning against the hood of the vehicle, blowing gray clouds of cigarette smoke into the air.

At the sight of Jim and Becky walking toward him, he tossed the cigarette to the ground and crushed it into the gravel with a quick twist of his booted foot. DeWitt walked around to the rear of the Lincoln and opened the passenger door, spoke to the occupant, and then stepped aside.

"Hello, you two," squeaked Adrianna Drake as she stepped from the car, looking somber in a black coat that reached to just below her knees, a white rose pinned to her breast. Not waiting for a reply from either of her friends, she positioned herself between them and took a hand from both in her own. "Come with me," she said. "We have lots to talk about." Turning her head to speak to the colonel, she said with a smile, "If I'm not back in half an hour, send out the search party."

A smile and a nod in return from the soldier acknowledged the remark. "Will do, Dr. Drake."

"He's cute, don't you think?" said Adrianna with a knowing wink to Rebecca as they strolled across the parking lot, gravel crunching beneath their feet.

"A little old for you," said Jim, summoning his most fatherly tone of voice.

"I'll grow into him," replied Adrianna with a mischievous glint in her eye.

***

Annexed between the parking lot and the entrance to the cemetery was a garden of remembrance, a two-acre field of green cordoned off by English yew trees that stretched like sentinels into the sky, standing eternal watch over the dead. A concrete path meandered among flowerless rose beds and pools of koi, past poetry-inscribed copper plaques and the occasional park bench strategically placed to overlook the most peaceful scenery the location offered.

The three friends strolled slowly down the path until Adrianna stopped them at a pond. With a cacophony of quacks, a flurry of ducks swam lazily toward them from their island sanctuary at the pool's center.

"Wish I had some bread," said Adrianna as she watched the fearless birds gliding their way.

"I don't think you brought us here to feed the fowl," Jim said.

"No. No, I didn't," she said, smiling. "I didn't get a chance to sit and talk with you both with all the commotion after the attack and you being in the hospital and all. I thought I needed to explain what happened."

Becky interrupted her. "It's okay," she said, laying a reassuring hand on her small shoulder. "I understand why you—"

"No, you don't understand," insisted Adrianna. "I'm not talking about what happened at the lab. I'm talking about what happened after you left me to go check the explosion."

"What do you mean, after I left?"

Adrianna raised her hands out in front and spun slowly around. "All this: the ducks, the park, you, me, everything . . . It's still here. And it shouldn't be."

"We made a mistake in the calculations or we misinterpreted the signal—that's the only possible answer. Otherwise, we wouldn't be here having this conversation," Jim said.

Adrianna shook her head. "No."

"No?"

"I mean that's not the explanation. There's another explanation. There's a reason we are all still here."

Adrianna led her two friends over to a wrought-iron bench overlooking the pond. She motioned for Rebecca and Jim to join her.

"After you left to go check out the explosion, I was waiting next to the receiver," she said as the three of them sat. "And at exactly midnight I heard a voice coming over the receiver: it was Lorentz's." Jim started to object, but Adrianna stopped him dead. "I know what I heard, Jim. It was definitely Lorentz's voice."

Jim looked askance at her. "But he was already dead. The transmitter was destroyed in the explosion, as well as the generator. There was no way he could have broadcast any kind of a signal, even if he had survived the explosion."

"It *was* him, Jim," she insisted.

The soul and memories contained in this child's body were those of a much older woman, Jim remembered, but right now the emotional response to Jim's disbelief was that of a little girl. Adrianna stared down at her feet as though chastised.

Jim placed a reassuring arm around her shoulders. "It's okay," he said, and then after a moment, before they both felt too awkward he added, "So what did he say?"

"Who? . . . Oh! Lorentz."

For a little while she turned her attention back to the ducks as they swam away back to their island nest, tired of waiting for food from the human interlopers to their world.

Finally, she said, "'One. Two. Three.' He said, 'One, two, three.'"

***

The cold of the metal park bench began to seep through Jim's clothes, chilling the skin of his back and legs, but he didn't really notice. He was too intent on listening to Adrianna as she explained her theory of why the second Slip had failed to occur, even though the team had also failed to send the preventative tachyon signal. Equally as strange was her insistence that she had heard Lorentz's voice emanating from the project receiver. The owner of that voice had already been dead for close to ten minutes by Jim's estimation, destroyed, along with the transmitting equipment, in the bomb's explosion and the fire that followed.

"You remember a few days before the experiment was due to commence I showed you the data I had pulled from the harmonic. Do you remember the graphic I used to display the data?"

"Of course," said Rebecca. "It looked like a DNA helix."

"Exactly! And the more I worked on it, the more frequencies I extracted from the harmonic, the more it looked like DNA."

Jim gave a little chuckle. "You mean you've detected the DNA of the universe?"

Adrianna didn't laugh. "Well, I wouldn't go so far as to jump to any conclusions . . . yet. But I would say there seems to be a strong similarity between the genetic makeup of life and the equivalent genetic structure of the universe."

Jim and Rebecca glanced at each other.

"But that's ridiculous," said Jim. "There must be a thousand reasons why the information could be interpreted that way."

"Of course there are. And I've gone over them all, and none of them work. *None . . . of . . . them . . .*" Adrianna paused as if considering whether she felt them worthy of sharing in some secret knowledge. Apparently satisfied that they were, she added dramatically, "Except for one."

"Well, come on then," said Rebecca. "What's the answer?"

Again there was a long pause before the girl-scientist spoke. This time her voice was filled with a reverent awe at what she had discovered. "You remember what a DNA helix looks like?"

Jim and Rebecca both nodded.

Adrianna took a deep breath before she continued. "Now, imagine each of the nucleotides that make up the double helix is an alternate reality or alternate universe clustered together in groups with similar but unique alternate universes, all of them fixed around the main strand of a shared timeline."

She let the idea sink in for a moment, and just as Jim seemed about to object she continued with her explanation.

"Now, each of those clusters of alternate universes, similar in most respects to its neighbors, is touching others within its cluster—overlapping, if you like—and it's through these overlaps that the other tachyon signals we were picking up at the lab managed to escape. They filtered through into our universe through the overlaps, but they don't belong in our universe. I called them 'vagrant particles' because they wander from one universe to another. Remember how they were so similar to the signals that we sent? Except there were some minor distinctions in variance and frequency."

"But that would mean tachyons have qualities we haven't been able to measure, that we didn't even suspect existed," Rebecca said.

"Yes. That's right. They would have to be able to not only move backward through time but also across time too. I've tentatively labeled it the Drake Bridge theory."

It was crazy. Mad. Insane. Ludicrous. It undermined everything the entire scientific community knew. But . . . it had a ring of truth to it that Jim could not deny. Hell! If you had asked him prior to the Slip whether he thought time travel was even a possibility, he would have laughed in your face. Look at what happened to that theory. Jim balked at admitting it, but experience had proven the scientific community a fool once already this century. So what if Adrianna was right? The possibilities were fantastic.

"But how does any of this apply to us? To the experiment? Assuming your theory is correct."

"Oh, I know I'm right," said Adrianna, her voice assuming an air of incontrovertibility.

"How?" insisted Rebecca.

"Because I have proof. The voice I heard coming over the receiver," said Adrianna as she stared out across the pond, "was not the voice of Mitchell Lorentz—at least, not the voice of our Mitchell Lorentz."

Now it was Jim's turn to gaze into the distance. He listened to the breeze as it winnowed the naked branches of the trees, the dry rustle like whispers from a far-off time or, he thought ponderously, maybe from another universe.

"It was an alternate Lorentz, wasn't it?" Jim said quietly. "A Lorentz from one of these other cluster universes."

She nodded her head, confirming Jim's statement. "Of course it's going to take a while for me to fully confirm my findings, but the hard data I'm getting back seems quite compelling."

"You've already begun your investigations?"

"The government seemed very happy to supply me with what I needed once I managed to convince the president's scientific advisers of the potential, should I be right. Thank God the government is so paranoid about itself these days; they gave me a lab and a small staff as well as a research grant. Besides, they don't want me wandering the streets, where I might let slip exactly what happened, right?"

Jim laughed sadly. He had noticed his own shadowy government tail following him a couple of days after getting out of the hospital, an obvious warning that they were watching him and his family. He was sure monitoring devices had been placed on his phones and that if he made any kind of approach to the news media, he would be stopped before he could get anywhere near them. That suited him just fine. All he wanted to do now was put everything behind him and get on with his second chance at life.

"I'm sorry," said Rebecca. "I hate to interrupt you two physicists at play, but this lowly mathematician is a little lost here. I still don't understand how any of this stopped the second Slip from happening."

"Of course," said Jim, firing a quick smile in her direction. "If I understand Adrianna correctly, we were saved by the fact that in one of the alternate universes in our cluster on the space-time helix, the experiment was a success. Our alternate selves were a success."

Rebecca still didn't look convinced, so Jim continued, filling in the gaps as he saw them.

"Well, in this theoretical alternate reality, the experiment went ahead as planned. The tachyon wave was activated, and it stopped the Slip from occurring in their reality."

"Okay, but how did *that* affect us?"

"You remember the signals we received, how each was just a little bit different from what we were expecting?"

Rebecca gave a nod of understanding.

"The tachyons we were picking up were Adrianna's vagrant particles; they strayed into our section of the time stream in our universe. They must have come from a reality so close to us that the signal was still strong enough to neutralize our own impending Slip, as well as their own."

"How did they get here, though?"

"Through one of the many locations where our universe bleeds over into the alternates," interjected Adrianna. "Theoretically, there are plenty of them scattered throughout the universe, points in space and time that overlap both our universe and at least one other alternate reality, so similar at that particular point that all matter in that location is essentially shared by multiple universes. It's the universal equivalent of cloud computing: it saves space and energy. In fact there doesn't even need to be any of these overlaps in existence right now, so long as they do exist somewhere in the future and past of our timeline. Given that they will exist and that the primary trait of tachyons is they move backward in time . . . Well, you see?"

"Yes. Yes. Of course, the alternate tachyon beam could have passed through one of these overlaps and moved down the timeline until it reached our particular spot on the timeline, right? . . . Amazing!"

Adrianna's cheeks flushed at the praise. "Well. You know, it was right there in front of us, waiting for us to discover it. It's still just a theory, of course."

The breeze picked up and became a cold steel wind that made all three of them pull their coats tighter. The rustling branches now echoed with a mournful howl, punctuating the silence that had seeped into their conversation like an early-morning fog.

"So, what's next for you, Adrianna?" asked Jim, sensing all three were ready to move on.

An impish smile crossed her angelic face. "Well, now we know these alternate universes probably exist, I think it's high time we had a little chat with each other, don't you?"

EPILOGUE

Philosophy will clip an Angel's wings,
Conquer all mysteries by rule and line,
Empty the haunted air, and gnomed mine

—John Keats

Her toes made tiny waves that rippled out from the wooden dock toward the setting sun. The early-evening light flickered and glinted off the water as bats wove spectral blurs over the lake's surface, chasing their supper. From the far bank the musical trill of a bird hidden deep in the green of a summer lilac floated ghostlike across the water, carried by a cool breeze that rustled through the crisp fall leaves.

Daddy said the bird was called a shore lark and when Mommy and he had first found out that they were pregnant with her, they had sat on the old wooden dock and dangled their feet in the water just like she was doing now. Daddy said Mommy loved the sound of the bird's song, and they had decided that was what they would name their baby girl. Good thing Mommy didn't like hedgehogs, her daddy had teased.

Daddy cried when he talked about her and Mommy. He had told her lots of things that first night as he tucked her into bed in the cabin at Shadow Lake. He told her how sorry he was he had hurt her with his car, how he never meant to do it. He said he had been angry, that he and Mommy were having a fight, and that he had been mad, but not at her—never at her. He told her how very much he had missed her.

Her daddy's face had been damp with tears, so she had sat up in her bed, thrown her arms around his neck, and told him it was okay. After a little while she told Daddy about the warm place. She explained about the time after the accident, before she found herself standing on the street with Mommy. Lark told him about the pretty man who had found her in the darkness and who had scooped her up in his arms and carried her to the place with the shining people. The place where a single stream ran through a green field that stretched far up into distant mountains, and where butterflies and birds chased each other through a cobalt-blue sky, and the clouds spoke to her as though they had known her forever.

Her daddy had said nothing to her. He had listened with an odd look on his face. But when she was finished explaining, he had paused for a moment, then kissed her lightly on her head. "I love you, little bird," he said as he left the room.

Her memories of that other place were further away now, and the more Lark tried to hunt them down, the more elusive they became.

But she did remember one thing: the pretty man's name was Benjamin, and he could fly.

From the cabin, Lark heard the voice of Rebecca calling for her to come on in for dinner, and she released the thought, allowing it to float away from her like a leaf caught on a gentle summer breeze.